Open Case File

(Book 1)

Joy Jenkins

Girl Power Galaxy

The characters and events portrayed in this book are fictitious. Any similarity to real persons, living or dead, is coincidental and not intended by the author.

ISBN: 978-1-7361896-3-4
Cover design by: Benjamin Dehart
Printed in the United States of America

To you
Because you love Carter so much that it
inspired me to keep writing more.
This is all for you.

From: Joy Jenkins <joyjenkins@gmail.com>
To: Agents Keller and Owens <AgentKeller@FBI.com
AgentOwens@FBI.com>
Date: Tuesday, November 3 8:18:00 AM
Subject: **Request Of Files**

Agents Owens and Keller,

I want to start off this email by expressing my gratitude for allowing me to publish the story of how you met. I understand Agent Owens that you were reluctant at first, so thank you for agreeing.

I'm reaching out to you know because after hearing your story, I want to know more.

Donovan, I would love to hear more of your backstory and how you were hired to protect Link. Carter, I'm interested in learning about your impactful first year of high school.

As well I would love to know more about your lives now. I know you're married and I want to hear about how that came about. What is married life like for you two? Can you share any missions you've been on? What about some rough situations you've gone through?

Thank you for your consideration,
Joy Jenkins
Author

From: Agents Owens <AgentOwens@FBI.com>
To: Joy Jenkins <joyjenkins@gmail.com>
Date: Tuesday, November 3   9:00:00 AM
Subject: **Regarding Your Request Of Files**

Joy,

No.

Carter Owens
Special Agent
Federal Bureau of Investigation

From: Joy Jenkins <joyjenkins@gmail.com>
To: Agents Keller <AgentKeller@FBI.com >
Date: Tuesday, November 3   11:20:00 AM
Subject: **A Second Appeal**

Agent Keller,

As you are the more understanding of the Owens-Keller partnership, I want to ask that you reconsider letting me view the form mentioned files.

Thank you,
Joy Jenkins
Author

From: Agents Owens <AgentOwens@FBI.com>
To: Joy Jenkins <joyjenkins@gmail.com>
Date: Tuesday, November 3   1:32:00 PM
Subject: **No**

Joy,

Do not email my husband. The answer is still no. Those files are classified.

Carter Owens
Special Agent
Federal Bureau of Investigation

From: Agents Keller<AgentKeller@FBI.com>
To: Joy Jenkins <joyjenkins@gmail.com>
Date: Tuesday, November 3 1:34:00 PM
Subject: RE: **A Second Appeal**

Joy,

I would like to apologize for my wife, as you are aware she doesn't like letting others in or knowing more about her than she lets on.

With that said, I stand by her answer. These files are private and will remain that way.

Thank you for your interest,
Donovan Keller
Special Agent
Federal Bureau of Investigation

From: Becca Hooper <angelgirl04@gmail.com>
To: Agents Keller and Owens <AgentKeller@FBI.com AgentOwens@FBI.com>
Date: Wednesday, November 4   2:15:00 PM
Subject: **School Project**

Dear Agents Owens and Keller,

My name is Becca and for one of my classes, I have to research the lives of people who have made an impact on my life. I thought of you! After reading your story it inspired me and so I wanted to ask if I could know more about your lives, maybe some history of how you grew up. I have a list of questions ready if that would be easier. Please let me know.

Sincerely,
Becca

From: Agents Owens <AgentOwens@FBI.com>
To: Joy Jenkins <joyjenkins@gmail.com>
Date: Wednesday, November 4   2:30:00 PM
Subject: **Nice Try**

Joy,

You are aware that as agents of the FBI we have access to a lot of information, correct? That includes knowing the IP address of a computer from where an email was sent.

Creating a new email address with a false name isn't going to work, dear Becca. Drop the idea. Our privacy is too important.

Carter Owens
Special Agent
Federal Bureau of Investigation

From: Joy Jenkins <joyjenkins@gmail.com>
To: Mason Douglas <MasonDouglas@FBI.com>
Date: Monday, November 9   10:46:00 AM
Subject: **Help me out.**

Mason,

I know you are a tech analysis with the FBI. I also know that you love pissing off Carter, that's why I'm reaching out. I want all the dirt on our dynamic couple including: backstory, wedding, missions, impactful times.

Can you help me out?

Big fan of yours,
Joy Jenkins
Author

From: Mason Douglas <MasonDouglas@FBI.com>
To: Joy Jenkins <joyjenkins@gmail.com>
Date: Monday, November 9   11:07:00 AM
Subject: **Let me hook you up.**

Joy,

I'm happy to know that my goal at being the thorn in Carter's side has not gone unnoticed. Also I'm always happy to help out a fan. I'm sending over every file that I think you would want. Including some that features yours truly.

I will warn you, I know you wrote of their time in high school. Compared to that these files are intense and in my own opinion ridiculous. The things they go through seem completely dramatic, which fits them, they are over the top and honestly it makes me gag at times. So prepare yourself for some crazy and extreme situations.

I have to admit, some of the things in here I think they faked, no one gets shot at this many times.

P.S. Don't publish any of this.

Your dashing source of information,
Mason Douglas
Tech analysis
Federal Bureau of Investigation
The Guy in the Chair
First Son
Future Savior of America
Wonder Boy

From: Joy Jenkins <joyjenkins@gmail.com>
To: Mason Douglas <MasonDouglas@FBI.com>
Date: Monday, November 9 12:29:00 PM
Subject: **My Hero!**

Mason,

I don't know if America would call you its savior but you are mine at this moment. Thank you for the files. I glanced at them and you're right, some of these situations are so insane they don't even seem real, but hey they make for great reading. Thank you.

P.S. What if I cut you in for 5% of profits?

Joy Jenkins
Author

From: Mason Douglas <MasonDouglas@FBI.com>
To: Joy Jenkins <joyjenkins@gmail.com>
Date: Monday, November 9   2:52:00 PM
Subject: **I know I am**.

Joy,

Make it 10% and you have a deal.

Happy reading.

Your one and only analysis,
Mason Douglas
Tech analysis
Federal Bureau of Investigation
The Guy in the Chair
First Son
Future Savior of America
Wonder Boy

Early Years

Carter's Life

Carter And The Boy

The school was a flurry of motion and chatter that Carter paid no attention to. She stood before a row of lockers, arms crossed, staring at the ceiling and chewing gum. Only one thing sat on her mind today: Tyler Hayes. A trio of girls rushed up to her side, all wearing matching eager expressions.

"So are you going to do it?" Eva asked, her wild brown curls framing her dark face.

"I don't think you can," Courtney said, leaning against the locker near Carter, playing with the edge of her honey-blonde braid. "I mean this is Tyler Hayes after all! The guy doesn't speak to anyone! He's the hottest recluse there is."

"Carter said she could get Tyler to talk to her," Jaya said, caramel eyes alight with confidence. "So I believe she can get him to talk to her." She leaned in. "What's the plan?"

Carter pulled out a pocket mirror, pressed the chewing gum to the back of it, and pressed it against the locker.

"I know his class schedule, the book he's currently reading, and what subjects he's best in. Knowing that I'll use it to my advantage."

Eva eyed her friend. "Do we even want to know how you got that information?"

Carter threw them a mischievous grin. "You can't call it stalking if it's all posted on social media."

"He doesn't have any accounts," Courtney said.

Smiling with pride, Carter stepped out the view of the mirror so she could see the hallway behind without having to look back.

"No, he doesn't but do you know how many people in this school post constantly? I knew his first period, it just took time scrolling through other people's accounts to see where I caught glimpses of him in other students' photos and put it all together. Only a few hours of work."

To her delight, her friends stared at her like she knew the answer to life.

"So the next step?" Jaya asked, excitedly.

Carter peered at the mirror and grinned as a glasses-wearing, cute boy walking and reading a book appeared in flashes among the thinning crowd of students.

"Now," she said. "You watch and learn."

Carter collected a mass of textbooks, notebooks, papers, and books. She crossed the hallway and leaned against the wall, staring at her mirror situated high enough she could see over the heads of her fellow peers to down the hall to her left.

As Tyler hit the halfway mark on the hallway, Carter bounced up and down getting her breathing ramped up, her actions causing her friends to stifle laughter. When Tyler was a few feet away from the end of the hall, Carter sprinted around the corner and collided with him.

In a perfectly orchestrated act, Carter lost hold of her belongings and they went crashing to the floor along with the book Tyler had had. The pair stumbled away from each other.

Carter sighed, staring down at the mess around her feet.

"This is delightful."

Without saying anything, Tyler pushed up his glasses and squinted at the carnage, searching. Spotting his book, he moved. Knowing his intent, Carter acted, bending down at the same time, aligning their paths. Even knowing that it was going to happen, it hurt when their heads knocked together. Carter staggered back, clutching her bruised forehead.

"Seriously Hayes how hard is your head?" she asked.

Tyler rubbed his forehead, frowning at her.

"I don't see how this is my fault, you're the one who is supposed to be graceful?"

She cocked her head at him. "I see, you're stereotyping me because I'm a girl."

Tyler held her gaze, unwavering.

"No, I'm saying that because everyone knows on the soccer field no one can touch you."

Carter crossed her arms. "Strange bit of information for a recluse to know."

"I don't talk to people, it doesn't mean I don't hear what they say."

"Why are you talking to me then?"

"'Cause you ran into me."

Carter pursed her lips in thought. "I feel like that is a poor excuse. You kind of suck at this recluse thing."

The edge of Tyler's mouth twitched at a smile as he ducked his head. Knowing she had won the first round, Carter twisted away from him, gathering up her stuff. After a moment, Tyler followed suit, stacking notebooks and papers together. As Carter reached down to grab Tyler's fallen book, she stepped on her copy of Pride and Prejudice and nudged it further down the hallway behind her. When she straightened, she held out Tyler's book, A Novel Thought.

"Sorry I made you lose your spot," she said.

He exchanged her items for his novel. "It's fine. It's the second time I'm reading it."

Carter nodded. "Well, I feel like you don't see the nuance of the final scene until the third read but that's just my opinion."

Tyler paused, looking from the book then to her. "You've read it?"

"Four times. My dad is a Beck Daniels fan and that is one of his favorites. He used to read it to me. So when he's gone and I'm missing him I find I pick it up."

Tyler tilted his head, studying her. Before he could voice any thoughts, Carter retreated a step.

"Thanks for the help picking everything up." She touched the side of her head. "For future reference, try to do a better job at being a recluse, I'm not sure my head can take any more hits."

Without waiting for a reply, she walked away, turning down the nearest hallway. Concealed by the corner, she stopped and waited. The first bell rang, but still, Carter didn't move. When she heard the sound of approaching footsteps, she hurried back around the corner and nearly collided with Tyler again, but this time managed to jerk back in time.

"Seriously Hayes, you're a terrible recluse."

This time Tyler gave her a full smile. "Sorry, but you forgot this."

He handed her the copy of Pride and Prejudice. She scowled at it then finally accepted it.

"Wish you would have trashed it, would have given me a good excuse to not do the essay."

"You have Pierce?" he asked, shoving his hands into his pockets.

"Yup, fourth period. For some reason, I can argue someone to death but when it comes to putting those arguments on paper I'm useless." She saluted to him with the book. "Thanks all the same."

She spun away but Tyler's voice stopped her in her tracks.

"I could help you."

A spark of glee filled Carter but she kept it from showing as she slowly rotated back to him. "What?"

As if realizing what he had just offered, Tyler fidgeted and looked away. When he brought his gaze back to Carter she was regarding him with blatant disbelief and curiosity.

"Are you serious?" she asked, taking a hesitant step towards him.

He nodded once then stared at the floor in an intense consideration of the tile.

"I'm good at writing essays for English. I could help you."

"Wow." He lifted his head to find Carter grinning. "You do suck at this recluse thing."

His smile appeared quicker than before. "We can always do it in the stacks, so no one sees us."

Carter smirked. "So you can keep your reputation?"

He grinned.

"I can't have people know I talk, right?"

Carter laughed. "True."

"Do you want my help?"

At the earnestness behind the question, Carter felt a knot of guilt tighten in her stomach.

"Why help me?" she asked.

Tyler shrugged and scuffed his shoe. "Maybe I want someone to discuss my book with."

"Ah, so purely selfish reasons?"

"Completely."

At his teasing grin, she found she didn't want to say yes. The plan she had so perfectly laid out felt rotten in light of his easy, open manner. And she felt like something found in a dumpster. But when he smiled, she couldn't stop herself from smiling back.

"Since you are a recluse and might regret your offer later, I will say no. But if I happen to bump into you," she paused, accenting the joke, "in the library at lunch then we shall see what happens."

Tyler laughed and nodded. "Fair enough."

Carter spun away and walked down the hallway, hearing as Tyler retreated in the opposite direction. A second later she heard the patter of feet as Eva, Courtney, and Jaya sprinted down the hall to her.

"Oh my gosh!" Courtney said, shaking Carter excitedly. "You actually did it! I seriously can't believe it! He doesn't talk to anyone!"

"I knew she could do it," Jaya said, sounding proud like Carter's accomplishment were her's as well.

"I am impressed, Carter," Eva said. "I might have had my doubts."

Carter shoved Eva's shoulder. "Some friend you are."

They all laughed as the second bell rang, ushering them into their classroom. With the thought of getting to see Tyler again, she sank into her seat, trying not to smile. Her phone buzzed and she slipped it out of her pocket, giving it a quick glance. The message she read burst her giddy balloon.

Captain: *Sarge, great news, I heard back from Hamilton Prep, you got in! You can transfer within the next two weeks.*

It Happened One Night

Carter stomped her feet, trying to banish the cold that was diving into her bones. The noise of the school had diminished as kids were picked up and others drove away. The wind wrapped around her, the whisper of winter teasing her exposed nose. The girl beside Carter buried her face in the collar of her coat. A compact car pulled up to the curb and the girl raised her head, letting out a sigh of relief.

"Don't die in the cold, Carter. It would suck to die on a weekend and for me to lose my math partner," she said, racing down the steps to the waiting vehicle.

"I'll try not to," Carter said. "Cause who else would do your homework for you?"

The girl gave a dry laugh and slipped into the passenger seat. With a wave, she and the car drove off. Carter shoved her fists deeper into her pockets, urging her father to hurry up. When it felt like her toes were going to snap off, the black SUV appeared. Carter was already racing down the steps by the time it stopped. Yanking the door open, she hopped in.

A cocoon of warmth enveloped her. Dropping her gym bag onto the ground, she thrust her hands close to the heater, trying to regain feeling in the tips of them.

"I was almost a popsicle," she said, as the car melded back into traffic.

"Well, I'm glad you're still alive."

"No thanks to you. What took you so long?"

Feeling having returned, Carter shrugged off her backpack and sank back in the seat. D.C. was washed with a dull gray light, the blanket of clouds wrapping the world in winter. A few snowflakes were shaken free and swirled about in the wind.

"The President's meeting ran over. I'm sorry, Sarge. Did you call your mother?"

Carter nodded, rubbing her arms to get them working again.

"She didn't answer."

Carter didn't say what she was thinking, that even as she had made the call she had known it was pointless. Something had been pulling her mother away the last couple weeks and Carter was left in a void.

Her father nodded, his brow creasing with unsaid thoughts.

"Captain," Carter said.

At the hesitating tone in her voice, her father glanced over.

"If I married a Marine would you still love me?" she asked.

Her father burst out laughing. It was a sound that was as good as the car's warmth.

"What made you think I have any problem with Marines?" he asked.

"Well, I hear you and your Navy SEAL friends complain about them that I figure marrying one would be an act of treason."

Her father raised a curious eyebrow.

"Are you planning to marry a Marine?" he asked.

"I'm fourteen, I haven't even been on a date yet."

"Then why do you ask?"

"Cause I want to know if you would still love me even if I did?"

Her father chuckled and flicked on the windshield wipers, banishing the flecks of white.

"Of course I would still love you, Sarge."

Carter let out a breath. "Okay, then seeing how that could be the worst thing I could do and you would still love me...I have something to tell you."

Wearing a faint smile, her father's gaze cut to her again.

"Don't tell you met a Marine?" he said.

Carter shook her head and drew in a breath.

"Captain...I don't want to go to Hamilton Prep."

The words finally spoken, Carter gnawed on her lip, watching her father's reaction. He said nothing, his face controlled. Worried, Carter twisted in her seat, tucking one foot beneath her.

"I know what you're going to say, I know it's a really good school and it would actually challenge me and you worked really hard to make this all happen...but," she dropped her head and toyed with the edge of the seat. "I wouldn't have any friends. Especially since I would be transferring halfway through the year. Everyone would have already established their friend groups. I would be an outsider."

A slow breath came as a response. Carter lifted her face.

"I understand that, Sarge," her father said. "I know it will be different but you're a smart girl, you will make friends easily."

Carter rested back in the seat, lips twisted down in worry.

"How about this, we'll discuss it with your mom over dinner. Does that sound good?"

Sighing, Carter nodded. Minutes passed as the car cut away from D.C. and moved towards Georgetown. Seeing the familiar neighborhood, Carter perked up.

"Can we go to the deli that just opened up? I heard the sandwiches are really good. And we never eat sandwiches."

After a seconds pause, her father nodded. Carter beamed and stared out the window, watching the eddies of snow. When they pulled into a deli across from their street, Carter jumped out. Even from outside the aroma of toasted bread and melted cheese could be detected. The interior was swarming with families from about the neighborhood. The bright ring of chatter only added to the cheery feel of the place.

A woman in her early thirties with cinnamon skin and light brown hair stood behind the counter. As the pair walked up, she set aside the cloth she had been using and smiled at them. It was a smile that was so friendly it felt as if they had known her for years.

"Hi," she said. "What can I get for you?"

"We're not sure," Carter said. "Sandwiches aren't our thing. We live just across the street and decided to give this place a try."

The woman's smile widened, her eyes crinkling in the corners.

"Well, I appreciate the business," she said.

"You own this place?" Carter's father asked.

The woman nodded. "I do. My mother passed away a year ago and left me some money. It had always been a dream of hers to own a deli and now I get to make it real for her." She held out her hand. "I'm Maggie, by the way."

Carter's father shook her hand and smiled. "I'm Steve and this is my daughter, Carter."

"I'm happy to meet both of you. Now, since it's your first time I can make you some of my favorite sandwiches, how does that sound?"

Carter and her father exchanged a look.

"Sounds good," Steve said.

"But nothing with American cheese," Carter said, "my mom doesn't like that."

"No, American, Got it."

As Maggie worked, Carter studied the board displaying all the different types of sandwiches, including breakfast sandwiches.

"I didn't know there were breakfast sandwiches," Carter said.

Chuckling, Maggie came back to the front counter and placed three wrapped sandwiches down.

"I believe that there is a sandwich for every meal," she said.

Carter grinned at her father. "Look at that I actually learned something new today."

He ruffled her hair and she slapped his hand away. As Steve paid and Carter grabbed the sandwiches, she found Maggie smiling at them.

"I hope you both come back," she said.

They both nodded and waved goodbye. The cold was shocking after the heat of the deli. The swirls had picked up and snow was added to the mounds that had been built over the past months.

The lights in the apartment were glowing as Carter jogged up the stairs in front of her father. Like the deli, the place was warm and inviting. Photographs lined the walls. The early years of Carter's life were depicted with both parents holding her. As the years changed more of them held her father and her, though her mother was still always there.

"Mom, we have dinner," Carter called out.

Carter dropped her gym bag and backpack on the floor. When no response came, she walked to her parent's bedroom. Sitting in front of the desk with a computer in front of her, was Carter's mother. Her dyed blonde hair was pulled into a bun, exposing her neck and mocha skin.

"Mom, dinner," Carter said, holding onto the doorframe and leaning in.

Her mother didn't turn around.

"Okay," she said.

There was a strange note to her voice, but Carter shrugged and walked back to the dining table. One of the sandwiches papers were open and a bite had been taken out of the sandwich.

"Captain, you can't eat before us. It's rude."

He smirked. "Who is going to stop me?"

Carter darted forward and snatched the sandwich out of his hands. In retaliation, he tossed her over one shoulder. She let out a shriek of laughter.

"The sandwich is going to die," she said. "Put me down."

"You asked for it."

Carter was tossed and landed on the couch, the sandwich only half destroyed. Leaving the sandwich on the coffee table, Carter scrambled to her feet and launched herself at her father.

"Attack!" she cried.

Before she could manage any form of attack, she was scooped back up and turned upside down, hanging from her ankles, the floor brushing her head.

"How's that attack working for you, Sarge?" her father asked.

Carter twisted this way and that but couldn't find any leverage. Annoyed, she huffed and let her arms fall back to the floor.

"Did you say you had dinner?" Carter's mother asked, appearing.

Steve turned, taking Carter with him.

"Hey honey, look what I picked up for us?" he said, lifting Carter's ankles higher.

She let out a laugh, her face going red. Her mother offered up a weak form of a smile, her eyes never meeting Carter's. The flat response sucked the laughter from Carter's lungs. Steve set Carter down and she rolled onto her knees.

The playful energy gone, the trio all settled around the table. After the first half of the sandwiches had been consumed, Carter brought up the topic of Hamilton Prep and her lack of desire to attend. The discussion bounced between her and her father for the most part. When Carter asked her mother what she thought, her mother finally met her gaze.

"Go, Carter. It will help give you a better future," she said.

There was an intensity in her eyes that made Carter nod. But part of her feared being alone.

***

A shout startled Carter awake. She tensed, laying in utter darkness. Half asleep, she tried to remember what had woken her. As she was about to drift back asleep, the muffled sound of voices floated in through the closed room, the tones taut with discord. Another shout rang through the apartment. Carter shot up, her heart tightening with fear. She heard the sound of a heavy thud on the floor and another protest.

The cold air chilled her skin as she pushed the layers of blankets back. She tiptoed towards the door, barely making a sound. As she opened it, it squeaked but the noise was unnoticed. Words became clear as Carter crept along the hallway.

"Don't do this, Erica. We can work this out. Stay."

Her father's voice seized with fear, panic, desperation. The sound twisted Carter's insides, the voice and the emotions making no sense to her.

"Steve, I can't do this anymore. I need to go."

Blinking against the light, Carter paused. When the glare lessened, the first thing Carter saw from the hallway were bags by the front door.

They were at the feet of her mother.

Though late into the night, her mother was fully dressed in her coat and purse slung over her shoulder. The front door was like a gaping hole, letting in frigid air.

"Please, I need you," her father said. He gestured to Carter's room. "Your daughter needs you. There has to be something I can do."

Her father took a step forward, hands outstretched, the plea in every movement and breathe.

"She'll be better with someone who really cares for her. Goodbye, Steve."

As the meaning of the words settled on Carter, sweat begun to cling to her skin, her breathing shallow.

"Mom?" she asked, stepping out of the hallway.

Both parents started and looked at her. Despair etched its way onto the once loving features of her mother.

"Goodbye, Carter."

Her mother picked up her bags and left. Her father, the man of action, was frozen. Breaking from her shock, Carter bolted for the door. Cold air blasted her, ice burning the bottom of her feet.

"Mom!"

The dark figure was brightened for a moment in the light of the open taxi door before vanishing inside. The metal grating dug into Carter's feet as she rushed down the stairs. Snow soaked the bottom of her pajama pants. The red taillights melted into the distance. Breathing became unbearable.

She sunk to the ground, coldness gripping her as the snow melted against her. Reality was a tangled web of confusion and shock. Tears run down her face without any control. From behind her, she felt her father's strong arms wrap around her and lift her out of the snow. As she buried her face in the folds of his worn shirt, blackness settled around her.

***

With the morning, Carter jerked herself awake. The nightmare was so vivid she could still feel the cold of the wind biting into her skin. Because that was what it was, a nightmare. She swallowed, her throat raw. Her face felt puffy but she couldn't remember why. The brightness of the morning sun penetrated her curtains and lit her room. At the sound of her parent's bedroom door, she stumbled out of bed. When she yanked open her door, she saw her father.

It was the lost, red-eyed look of him that hit her in the chest.

It hadn't been a nightmare at all.

Her father's shoulders were rounded like an invisible burden had been placed there. He ran a hand through his short hair, the gesture heavy with loss and heartbreak. Carter felt the well of her pain flooding over. But as her father met her gaze, she could all at once see the overwhelming fear, grief, and pain that was eating away at him and so she trapped her own emotions down.

"Are you hungry?" her father asked.

She shook her head then nodded, aware of the gaping hole that was once where her stomach had been. For a second, neither of them moved. It was like everything that had once made sense in the world was gone. They had woken up to a reality that they didn't know how to navigate.

"Okay, come on," her father said.

Without bothering to change from their pajamas, the pair tugged on boots. Her father helped her into her jacket and he threw his on. The morning air was vicious as if it were trying to freeze the very breath in their lungs. At the bottom of the stairs, the pair stopped. The grooves of the taxi's tire tracks could be seen.

Her father held out his hand and Carter took it.

He squeezed it and Carter felt the same strength and determination in the grip as she always had. She clung to that familiarity, trying to fight the tears building in her eyes.

When they stepped into the deli, they found they were the only customers that early in the day. A service door swung open and Maggie backed out of it, a large box in her arms. Spotting them, she beamed.

"Back so soon," she said.

Really seeing them, the smile on her face faltered and fell away.

"Sit down," she said softly. "I'll get you something hot."

Without a word of acknowledgment, Carter and her father took the closest table. The silence between them pulsed with everything that was too fragile to say.

After an eternity, Carter spoke.

"I'm fine going to Hamilton Prep."

Carter and Mason Meet

Carter stared at her reflection. The new Hamilton Prep uniform fit her well enough and looked impressive, freshly pressed, and with its badge on the chest. But she didn't care. The girl in the mirror had lifeless eyes and a hollow look about her. The vibrant, determined girl of two weeks ago hadn't reappeared and Carter didn't think she ever would.

Her father stepped into the bathroom doorway and Carter met his eyes in the reflection. They watched each other, twin mirrors of pain.

"You ready to go?" he asked.

She lied when she nodded. She didn't want to leave the apartment. Most days she found it hard to climb out of bed. Grabbing her beat-up backpack, she followed her father out of the apartment.

The car held silence. The news played but went unheard. As the car passed the security check and pulled through the gates into Hamilton Prep, Carter couldn't muster anything at all.

Gray brick with vines climbing the outer walls, it looked like history and old money. A fraction of Carter still functioning knew that she did not belong here. But after everything her father had done to make it a possibility, she would say nothing. Besides, it meant she knew no one. That no one knew the old her. She liked it better this way.

As she followed her father up the front steps, she noticed the way other students wore their uniforms. Despite all appearing to wear the same navy blazer, oxford shirt, and khaki pants or skirt, they each held their own distinctive take on it, setting them apart from each other. For Carter that set her apart in a way that was all too apparent that she didn't have their type of money.

When Carter and her father walked into the main office, a man in a gray suit with graying hair approached them, a smile at the ready.

"You must be Mr. Owens," the man said. "I'm Principal Withers."

The two men shook hands and Principal Withers smiled in greeting at Carter.

"We're happy to have you here with us, Ms. Owens. Your test scores are unlike any we've seen before and we have no doubt you'll do well here." He gave a joking laugh. "As long as you stay out of trouble."

Carter's father laid a hand on Carter's shoulder and for a moment she wanted him to hug her. She wanted to feel like she wasn't drowning on dry land. He met her gaze and gave her a slight nod. She straightened, letting it be what she needed.

"Don't worry," her father said. "You'll have no trouble from Carter."

After the two men exchanged more information, Carter was handed a class schedule. The cheery-looking secretary guided her out of the office door and pointed down the hall.

"Your first class is just around the corner," she said.

Carter thanked her and looked to her father, who exited the office.

"Have a good day at school," he said.

"Okay."

As she turned away, he spoke again.

"I love you, Sarge," he said.

Carter felt her throat tighten in response.

"I love you too, Captain."

Forcing a smile for his benefit, she turned away, her face falling the second he couldn't see her. She needed to be strong for him. By the time Carter got to her classroom, the bell had already rung. She stepped inside and the room fell silent, eyes pinning her in the doorway.

"Hi," a sweet-faced teacher said. "You must be our new student, Carter Owens. I'm Ms. Woodson. Why don't you take a seat. There is one open in the back by Mason."

Before Carter could ask who Mason was, she heard a faint muttered curse and found a familiar blonde-haired boy. Mason Douglas looked exactly as he did in photos and on TV, except for the scowl he wore right then.

"Do I have to be paired with the new kid," Mason asked. "I actually want to get a good grade on this project."

A few kids around Mason chuckled and offered him sympathetic glances. A spark of annoyance flared in Carter but fizzled out quickly.

Ms. Woodson smiled at Mason, but there was steel in her eyes.

"Yes, Mason, you do. And I'm sure as someone who understands the importance of good relations, you'd be happy to lend her a hand."

Mason didn't reply, but Carter could see he hadn't at all changed his mind about wanting to be her partner. Not having any other choice, Carter took the seat beside him.

"At least tell me if you're stupid," Mason said. "That will make my decision on how much I ask you to help with this project."

Irritation flared again and this time Carter grabbed hold of it. For the first time in two weeks, she felt something other than numbness and didn't want to go back. Besides, something about this boy's arrogant attitude pissed her off. Instead of helping her adjust to a new school, he was going out of his way to make it difficult for her. If he didn't plan on playing nice, neither would she.

"I'm about the dumbest person you'll ever meet," she said. "Looks like you'll have to do the project all by yourself and simply tack my name onto it. If you left it out I'm sure Ms. Woodson would assume you did it out of spite."

Mason stared at Carter, eyes narrowed as if not sure if he should be annoyed or impressed with the way she handled the situation.

"A girl with a quick tongue, aren't you a little cliche?" he asked.

"A President's son who thinks he's above everyone else, aren't you a little cliche?"

The pair eyed each other for a long minute while Ms. Woodson continued explaining the guidelines of the in-class project. Blood rushed through Carter. It felt good to feel something again.

Free to get started on the project, Carter and Mason worked alongside each other. At one point Carter glanced at Mason's work and pointed out his mathematical mistake. She gave a dramatic sigh.

"Great," she said. "Because I'm the new kid they paired me with the idiot of the class."

"What happened at your last school, mouth off enough people that they kicked you out?"

"My brains got me into here. It makes me wonder how have you stayed here?" She tapped her chin in mock thoughtfulness. "That's right, your daddy is someone, so naturally they couldn't kick you out."

"If it means I have to spend another class with you, I hope he gets impeached."

"Wow, such loyalty. Do you plan to be President one day? Because so far it doesn't look like you have the qualities to make it. I've known you all of half an hour and I want you kicked out of office."

The bickering continued until the bell rang and they had to turn in their project. At the door, Carter saluted Mason with a patronizing smile.

"Good luck on your future campaign, Mr. President," she said.

As she strode off to find her locker, Carter realized she felt fully awake. Though that bit of pain that her mother's abandonment had left behind still hung around her, she didn't feel like she was drowning anymore. Savoring the reprieve from the grief, she stopped at her locker and worked her combination.

"You sat with the new girl, she's kinda hot. What was she like?" a male voice behind Carter said.

She froze and rolled her eyes as she heard a now familiar and irritating voice.

"Don't waste your time, Lucas," Mason said. "She is a complete pain in the a-"

"Are you talking about me?" Carter asked, spinning around. "Because the Future Savor of America would never use such language when describing a future voter."

The boy next to Mason grinned, eyeing Carter in a proprietary manner. She glared at him.

"Watch where your eyes go," she said. "You should know it's hard to see anything with two black eyes."

"Feisty, I like it," Lucas said, smiling wider. "I'm Lucas Benton."

Carter eyed him up and down. "What makes you think I would care? You find me attractive after I've just threatened you, that shows some serious psychological problems. I would never be interested in you."

Completely unfazed, Lucas winked at her as he headed away.

"We'll see."

Mason rolled his eyes and walked away, not bothering to glance at Carter again.

As each class passed, Carter slowly built up her armor to the students around her. Not partnered with anyone, she was left alone. It wasn't that they ignored her, it was that she didn't even warrant notice at all.

In her off-the-rack uniform and loose ponytail she clearly didn't come from money. And not recognizing any aspects of her face, she couldn't have been related to anyone of worth. Therefore she could have been a part of the scenery for all they cared.

When Carter stepped through the doorways to the cafeteria, she paused gazing around for a spot. The only empty table lay next to the trash cans in the back corner. Not daring to show uncertainty, she strode to the free table and claimed it for her own.

Instead of pulling out the sandwich Maggie had dropped off early in the morning, Carter surveyed her peers. Though she didn't have her father's skills, she had his voice in her head telling her to look at the details, read what was being said by how others responded. She threw herself into the analysis of her fellow students. It felt like a challenge, one that could make her forget for a time the gnawing pain of loss.

An older girl with auburn curls approached Carter, breaking Carter from her thoughts.

"Hi," the girl said. "I'm Liv."

Carter noted the tailored uniform, glossy hair, and flawless makeup. She wondered why this girl was talking to her.

"Look, I know you're new here," Liv said. "I figured I would give you a piece of advice."

Carter said nothing.

"Don't get on the wrong side of Mason. He's the golden boy of the school whether any of us like it or not. Piss him off and you might as well say goodbye to making any friends."

Though Carter felt the absence of company around her, she also knew she wasn't likely to be popular with many people. The lack of response to her presence already told her that people were reluctant to go out of their way to befriend her. In turn, she didn't feel like jumping through hoops to make others accept her. Better self chosen isolation than rejection.

"Thanks for letting me know," Carter said.

Since this girl had approached her, Carter almost asked her if she wanted to sit down, despite her resolution, but a handsome faced boy called out to Liv and she nodded to him.

"Well, good luck," she said, walking away.

Feeling a prick of disappointment, Carter searched for a distraction, finding it in a couple who were on the brink of an argument. Before she could see the eventual explosion, Mason crossed in front of her table.

"First day and already at the trash table," he said. "You must have mouthed off to someone important."

Carter blinked at him. With the lack of an instinct response, Mason frowned.

"Did you hear me?" he asked.

Carter shook her head as if shaking off a thought.

"Sorry," she said. "I was trying to remember what you actually said because whenever you open your mouth all I hear is 'blah blah blah I feel inferior and must assert my dominance by picking on someone else blah blah blah."

Mason reddened.

"Was that not what you said?" she asked.

"You should watch yourself, Owens. You won't like your life here if you cross me."

Carter grinned, an action that felt foreign after frowning for so long. "Oh, I think I'm going to like life a lot better here if I keep crossing you. Where else would I get the entertainment?"

Mason backed up a few steps, but the look in his eyes told Carter that this wasn't over. As he turned away, she saluted him.

"This," she thought, "is the start of a beautiful friendship."

Detention

Carter sat with her head on her desk and her arms draped over the sides. It was so quiet in the classroom she could hear the clock ticking over the whiteboard. She could hear the shuffling of papers as Ms. Woodson graded tests. She could hear the faint pulsing beat coming from her teacher's headphones. She could hear the breathing of the boy next to her.

"Could you be breathing any louder?" Carter said into the top of her desk.

"I'm breathing normally, Owens," Mason said.

Carter raised her head. "Really because it sounds like you have a lung problem you're so loud."

"Or maybe you're just attuned to my breathing because you want to know if I catch my breath when I look at you."

Propping her elbow on the desk, Carter rested her head in it, regarding Mason.

"I know that you've most likely seen hundreds of therapists, your father's attempts to understand the problem he calls a son, but have they deduced where these delusions stem from? Is there a cure or are you doomed to suffer from them for all your life?"

Mason scoffed. "You think I'm a problem? Owens, you've been at this school for three months and have yet to make a friend. That shows some serious issues."

Carter controlled her expression, keeping it blank, a tactic she'd quickly picked up at this school. She didn't need these self-important elites knowing how their taunts and judging glances got to her. She wouldn't let them get to her.

"Please," Carter mocked. "Do you even understand how obnoxious you all are with your 'I'm important because I simply happen to be related to someone important' act is? Seriously, it makes me so nauseous it's a wonder I manage to eat at all here."

"Ha ha, the girl who has no one important finds us all unimportant, wow never saw that one coming. You understand that's what therapists call a coping mechanism, right?"

"See I was right about the hundreds of therapists." She smiled encouragingly at him. "It's nice to know that some things can make an impact on you. Don't worry, I'm sure they will eventually help you solve your daddy issues."

Mason held her gaze but nothing in his face changed. Why would it, he was raised by a politician after all, hiding the truth was what they did best. But Carter knew this was a sore nerve, just like she knew calling him Mr. President pissed him off.

And it was why she did it whenever they crossed paths. Wasn't there a saying, fight fire with fire? Well, she was at Hamilton Prep now so she brought her flamethrower.

Mason turned his head away and Carter dropped her chin onto her crossed arms, grinning. At least she'd won that round.

"You know this is your fault that we're in detention," Mason said, clearly winding up for round two.

Carter straightened, mentally tugging on her boxing gloves.

"My fault? You were the one who wouldn't read the instructions on the project."

"I knew what I was doing."

"That makes sense, 'cause you were doing it all wrong!"

"No! I wasn't and if you had listened to me in the first place you would have seen that!"

"Who in their right mind would listen to you, you're an idiot!"

"I guess that would mean the school is full of idiots since they listen to me and not you."

"Yeah! It is!"

"HEY!"

Carter and Mason froze, not realizing when they'd stood up. Slowly, they looked to Ms. Woodson, she was staring at both of them.

"This," she said. "Is why you have detention. You constantly fight in my class and I'm tired of it. Now sit down and be quiet."

The stern voice coming from the soft-faced and smiley teacher made Carter and Mason sit without a word of protest or accusation. Carter sank down in her seat, laying her head on her arms and closing her eyes. As the clock ticked on and the tension gradually eased away, Carter's thoughts took a road she really didn't want to go down, needed not to go down. To avoid it, there was only one thing she could do: distract herself.

"Mason," she said, still keeping her eyes closed.

"What?"

"When's your appointment?"

There came a long pause and Carter fought her grin. In a world where she was at the bottom of the social ladder at least her mind elevated her above her peers. Finally, Mason broke.

"What appointment?" he asked, though she could tell by his tone he hated himself for asking.

"When's your lobotomy appointment? I want to mark it on my calendar as a day to celebrate."

Mason snorted. "I wouldn't call it a day to celebrate because it will be the same day everyone comes for you and demands you get one yourself. If I'm not here to match wits with you the world is doomed."

Carter grinned at him and he scowled as if trying to understand why his insult received this reaction.

"I believe there was a compliment in there."

"Only you would find a compliment where an insult was meant."

"What can I say," Carter said in a perky voice. "I'm an optimist."

"What you are is delusional."

"Takes one to know one."

Mason shook his head and slouched in his chair. Carter went back to pretending to sleep, happy with the outcome. Before either of them could find another way to verbally abuse the other, Ms. Woodson spoke.

"All right," she said. "The hour is up. I hope you've both come to realize how arguing never solves problems, only makes them. Come get your phones."

Neither of them spoke as they gathered their things, retrieved their phones, and left the classroom. The hallways were clear of students and Mason stopped at the classroom entrance to wait for Smith and avoid Carter. In turn, she quickened her steps to outstrip him. When the cold blast hit Carter, she swore and hugged her coat tighter around her. Snow whipped through the air, a late blizzard for the year.

Behind her, the doors opened and Mason walked out with Smith in tow. Mason eyed the stormy sky and shot Carter a smug grin.

"Enjoy your walk to the metro," he said.

Glaring, Carter hurried down the steps, needing to keep her blood warm with movement. Without the distraction of poking at Mason, Carter was left with the thoughts of her father and how he'd said he'd be home two days ago, but had been delayed. She jammed her fists into her coat pockets, trying not to feel the ache in her chest. But it was always there. When he left on a trip it grew until sometimes it felt like it would make her heart explode.

As Carter trudged down the sidewalk, a sleek Lincoln town car glided up alongside her. Carter didn't glance at it. She didn't want Mason to have the satisfaction of seeing her miserable. The back window rolled down.

"Owens, get in the car," Mason said.

"I'd rather freeze, thank you."

"See," Mason said. "I told you she didn't want a ride."

At this statement, Carter stopped and so did the car. The passenger side window lowered, showing Smith sitting there. His serious face was kind.

"Carter," he said. "Let us give you a ride home."

After a second's hesitation where flurries hit Carter in the face, she climbed into the back next to Mason. He eyed her like she was something they picked up off the side of the road. Which technically she was.

"Where to?" the driver asked.

"Georgetown," Carter said then rattled off the address.

The driver pulled back into traffic and Carter reveled in the warmth of the car's interior and the pine scent that filled it.

"It should be known I didn't approve of this plan," Mason said.

"I've never assumed you had a heart, Mason."

Carter delivered the comment but didn't deliver the mocking tone it should have been accompanied with. Once her mind had turned to her father it felt impossible not to think of him. Mason replied, but Carter didn't hear, her focus on the scenery outside, blurred by the snow.

"Is your dad going to be home tonight?" Carter asked.

"I don't know," Mason said. "It's not like it affects you and you don't have a heart either, so why should you care?"

Anger sparked in Carter and she swung around to face Mason.

"You understand that those people who are assigned to protect your father have families too, right? Or are you so self-centered that you didn't think about the fact that someone like Smith actually exists beyond the times you see him?"

"I'm not that self-absorbed, Owens. I just don't see why that would matter to..."

When Mason cut himself off, Carter turned her head away. Why she'd even asked was beyond her. A long silence expanded between them.

"Umm...your father?" Mason asked, hesitant.

Carter didn't answer but that was answer enough.

"My dad said he'd probably be home sometime today," Mason said.

Carter still didn't look at him. "Thanks."

"Yeah."

The rest of the drive was spent in uncertain silence. When they got close to Carter's house, she directed the driver to stop at the front of the lane, she could walk from there. As Carter opened the door, Mason spoke.

"This changes nothing between us," he said. "Just because I know what your dad does, doesn't mean I still don't loathe you."

Carter climbed out but poked her head back in. "Fine by me, I've planned to loathe you for the rest of my life."

"Works for me," Mason said. "So long, Owens. Make sure to slip on ice and break your neck for me."

"As long as you keep that lobotomy appointment then fine. I'll die knowing the world doesn't have to deal with your drivel any longer."

She shut the door and hurried off, but not too fast, it was icy. The apartment lay dark and empty when she stepped inside. The only positive was the fact that it was warm. Dumping her bag by the couch, Carter headed into her room. As she was changing from her uniform into sweats, the front door opened.

Carter froze, listening. When she heard the click of keys in the bowl, she yanked her hoodie down and raced from her room. Her father barely had time to register her presence before she threw her arms around his waist. He let out a warm chuckle, hugging her back.

"I take it you missed me," he said.

"What in the world would give you that impression, old man?"

Her father kissed the top of her head. "Did you stay out of trouble while I was gone, Sarge?"

Carter thought about Mason and detention and how without him there to keep her distracted from her fear and worry she might have done worse.

"Always, Captain."

School Project

Carter climbed the stairs to the second story of the library and strolled past the aisles. When she came to the final row, she stopped, resting her shoulder on the bookshelf.

At the end of the row, Mason Douglas was lip-locked with a girl. Carter glanced at the shelf she leaned on and swiped something off the ledge.

"You know," she said, rolling her eyes, her voice instantly breaking the couple apart. "Hundreds of years ago men would come to libraries like this seeking knowledge. It pains me how far humans have fallen."

The girl hurriedly tried to smooth out her hair as she flushed while Mason looked completely calm.

"Knowledge is everywhere, Owens," he said.

"Oh yeah? What's her middle name?" Mason frowned. "Clearly, you aren't a very good study. Come on, we have a project to do."

Having regained her control, the girl strode towards Carter. When her glance landed next to where Carter lounged, she paused. Carter raised her eyebrows, taunting.

"Looking for something?" she asked.

Mason came up beside the girl and she plastered on an unconcerned smile.

"Not at all," she said.

"Didn't think so," Carter said.

Throwing Carter an acid look, she swept away. Mason grinned at Carter.

"You sure you're here for the project, or were you looking for an alternative type of knowledge as well."

Carter pressed her hand to her mouth.

"So shocked I would offer," Mason said.

"No, I just threw up in my mouth."

Mason's expression fell flat and Carter headed away. When they got to the main level, she pointed to a table and a stack of books that sat before one chair.

"That is your stuff," she said, plopping into a seat opposite. "This is mine. Being at the same table I feel qualifies as 'working together'."

With a groan of annoyance, Mason sank into his chair.

"Eight months and you think our teachers would stop pairing us together."

Carter scowled at him like he was an idiot, which wasn't hard because she did think he was.

"How have you not put this together?" she said. "They pair us because then it's only one battle. Putting us with other students means there would be two battles since we seem to piss off our partners."

"Is that seriously true?"

Carter stared at him. "It also explains how you've managed to make it this far, my brain keeps saving you from failing. Oh." She pulled out a phone and slid it across the way. "Another thing I saved you from. Your French partner was recording you. Seems she wanted something worth selling."

Mason snatched up the phone and typed in the password. How he knew it was beyond her but she didn't ask. After a few seconds, the video was completely erased.

"It seems almost a crime to delete such a beautiful moment."

"I saw that moment, there was nothing beautiful about that. It looked like you were trying to maul her face. Real classy."

"Have you ever been kissed, Owens?"

"By a bear that's trying to eat me? Can't say I have."

Mason leaned forward, resting his arms on the table.

"I'll take that as a no."

It was but Carter didn't care. Not kissing someone didn't seem like a bad thing. Relationships were complications that ended in pain. She had enough pain, she wasn't dumb enough to go asking for more.

Instead of responding, Carter grabbed the first book in her stack and flipped it open. Mason smirked like he'd won something but he hadn't, Carter simply didn't care to play that game. They worked in silence for a while, which almost seemed like a miracle.

"Are you going to prom?" Mason asked.

Carter raised her head. "We're freshmen, we can't go to prom."

"We can if one of an upper class-man asks us."

Carter resumed her work of taking notes.

"Oh how my heart longs for such an occurrence," she deadpanned. "If no one shall ask me, truly I will die."

"No need to be dramatic about it, it's only prom."

Offended, Carter put her hand to her heart. "But don't you know that prom is all I've ever wanted, ever dreamed of!" She put her hand to her forehead. "Oh, what is life if some man shall not ask me."

"Go to prom with me, Owens," Mason said.

"Ew. Never mind, just let me die."

She pulled over another book and rifled through it.

"I'm going," Mason announced. "With Aubrey Lenex."

"You mean the girl that you weren't making out with half an hour ago." She pointed her pencil at him. "Thanks for proving my theory that politicians' offspring never breaking the untrustworthy mold is true."

Mason glared at her and she smirked. Always a sore point.

"Jealousy doesn't look good on you," he said.

Carter rolled her eyes. "Why of all days did our teacher have to burden me with you."

"What's important about today?" Mason asked, curious.

"Nothing, besides the fact it's ruined by your presence."

Checking her phone for the time, Carter closed the textbook. She gathered them all together and walked off to put them away. By the time she returned to the table, the school bell rang, ending her free period. She slipped her notebook into her bag and headed to the door, not bothering with a farewell to Mason.

"See you around, Owens," Mason called out. She didn't reply. "And happy birthday!"

She paused, her hand on the library door. Mason looked smug that he'd figured it out.

"I'm not as dumb as you think I am," he said.

Carter tapped her chin. "Nope, I'm pretty sure you still are."

She walked away as Mason laughed.

***

When Carter entered the deli, a loud pop rang out and confetti floated around her. She tried to scowl at Maggie for the dramatics, but couldn't quite manage it. Maggie beamed as she raced forward and wrapped Carter into a tight hug.

"Happy birthday, girly!" she said.

Despite how warm Maggie had been to Carter over the past half-year, it still took Carter a second before returning the hug.

It felt comforting and that scared Carter.

She'd lost a mother, someone who'd given birth to her. How easy would it be to lose someone who had no family ties to her?

Carter tried not to think about it and smiled at Maggie.

"Thanks," she said.

Maggie cupped Carter's face. "It's crazy how much you've grown up since I first met you."

"I know, now I can assemble a gun within a minute, huge improvement."

Maggie laughed and guided Carter to a booth.

"I have someone else filling in for me, so I'm here for you for the whole evening! But we can't go back to your apartment until Steve gives me the 'okay'."

This piqued Carter's curiosity.

"Why? What does he have planned?"

Maggie only grinned which made Carter spend the next hour guessing and trying to gauge from Maggie's reaction what was going on. Finally, Maggie received a text message and Carter practically shot out of the booth. Maggie tried to stop her, but that was not going to happen.

Carter dashed across the road and down the narrow lane. The stairs shuddered as she raced up to the front door. When she burst inside, Captain started laughing.

"Thirty seconds flat," he said. "That is impressive."

"Where is it? What did you get me?" she asked.

Her father's presents were the best because they were things Carter never expected like a book about reading body language. The most normal thing he'd ever gifted her was a MacBook.

"Aren't you going to let me give you a birthday hug, first?" her father asked.

"No, old man. I want to know."

Shaking his head, her father retrieved a box from behind the armchair and handed it to her. Maggie walked in as Carter tore away the wrapping. Inside was a set of boxing gloves. Carter raised her head but her father held up his hand.

"That's not all."

Placing his hands on her shoulders, he guided her to her own room. Inside, hanging in the corner was a brand new punching bag.

"No way!" Carter said.

She walked over and ran her hand over the smooth leather and touched the chain.

"When do we start?" she asked.

"Cake first!" Maggie said.

Carter made a face and her father laughed.

"You have years ahead of you to fight that thing. For now, we'll eat cake."

Carter kept the boxing gloves on her lap as she ate. She didn't understand how her father could know exactly what she needed. So many times a day she felt like she wanted to hit something or break down. Each time she held herself together it felt harder and harder. But this would be her release. A punching bag didn't cry or tell a teacher if she hit it.

Somehow her father knew that, knew her. Carter looked at him as he smiled at something Maggie said. She could still see his sadness, neither of their grief was going away anytime soon. But at least he was smiling again.

When he looked at Carter, she smiled at him.

Him and her. That's all she needed. All she trusted in.

Relationships were complicated and messy. But not them. She knew no matter what, they would be okay.

Half A Day

Mason glanced up from his phone as the car pulled through the White House side gates. Outside people dotted the sidewalk, all of them holding up their phones wanting to catch a glimpse of someone important.

Every morning heading to school was like this. He didn't understand why people waited. It seemed like a waste of time to him, with the blackout windows it was impossible to see inside. Still they waited. Idiots.

Mason focused back on his phone, the eager and expectant faces getting on his nerves more than usual that day. Maybe it was the exhausting three-hour photoshoot he'd had to bear through last night.

Nothing said family bonding time like having to force a smile for three hours straight. He stopped asking what the photos would be used for a long time ago. Besides it didn't matter, one of his friends would tell him.

At the school, Mason climbed out of the car and slung his backpack strap over his shoulder. He'd barely walked a foot before someone snagged the space beside him. Bradley nodded to Mason, all ease and friendliness. It pissed Mason off. He'd insulted this guy yesterday, yet here Bradley was smiling like Mason hadn't humiliated him. Wasn't he mad at all?

Of course he was. Mason had been vicious. But Mason was also Mason Douglas, First Son, it was better to be next to Mason than not. So Bradley probably cursed Mason in his mind while smiling in his face. It sickened Mason.

What annoyed Mason more was the fact that he nodded back to Bradley, mirroring his 'friend's' chill. After all, if Mason acted out too much the press would be all over it.

That meant as Mason walked through the school halls he wore his easy, All American Boy smile. Fours years had made the smile a natural reaction to anyone looking at him. He was pretty sure if he was strapped to a chair and tortured the stupid smile would still be on his face.

Bradley left Mason at his science classroom with a comment about seeing him later. It was ridiculous how people did everything for him because of who his father was. It's like they believed pissing him off was an act of treason.

As Mason headed to his table, he spotted Lucas leaning against the side of it, staring down at Carter.

"Lucas," Carter said. "You continue to stand there I'll be forced to neutralize you. And neutralize can mean a lot of things."

Her voice dropped and Mason couldn't see her but saw as Lucas flinched and could only imagine what Carter's implications meant. The girl was crazy.

Mason approached his seat and Carter cut her gaze to him, her permanent scowl in place.

"What's with that stupid smile?" she said.

His mask of a smile had been so reactionary he'd forgotten he still wore it. But Carter's words zapped it away. Here was one student who didn't seem charmed by it. The only student who would annoy him less if she was.

"Owens," Mason said. "Flirting with men above your social status again?"

Carter swiveled around. "Men? Men go here? Cause all I see are pathetic boys."

At that Lucas left. Mason didn't understand why he kept coming around. The girl clearly hated him, yet he returned time and time again. Never mind, Mason knew why. Lucas enjoyed a little challenge and no one was more challenging than Carter. Mason should know, they were lab partners.

"Aw, he's offended," Carter said. She eyed Mason. "Is it just me or do you reek of self-importance more today than usual?"

Mason couldn't believe the audacity of this girl. He was the First Son! Who was she to talk to him like he was nothing? It hit Mason like a freight train. She was talking like that to the First Son! And she didn't care. The whole world wanted to cater to him, but she'd rather stab him.

He looked at her like it was the first time he'd ever seen her. She wasn't the average type of pretty he'd grown up knowing, the flawless, always photo-ready type. But the combination of her light brown skin and dark blue eyes made her interesting. She was too thin for his taste but maybe it was just the ill-fitting uniform.

Carter cocked her head at Mason. "Mason, I have a question for you, when you became the First Son, Future Savior of America, All American Pain in The Butt did they give you a pre-packaged Personality, or were you always as bland as white bread?"

"At least my personality doesn't make people have daydreams of murdering me," Mason said.

The words flowed easily like they always did around her. The censor he'd been taught by his father, mother, and the entire White House staff, it seemed, disappeared with Carter. He could say whatever he wanted with her and she wouldn't even blink before throwing something back at him.

It was a relief. Especially in his world. He'd exploded on Bradley but that had been a rare occasion. He usually had more self-control, he had to. One blow-up would mean more attention from the world and not in a good way.

Since being paired with Carter it seemed he'd found a small space where he could breathe.

"Oh Mason," Carter said in a patronizing voice. "How sad not to know so many many people daydream the same thing about you. At least I'm not delusional."

Mason would have retorted back but class started. All through it, he was aware of Carter's presence in a way he hadn't been before. He noticed the little line between her brows as she concentrated. Noticed how she rolled her eyes when the teacher reviewed the same material she had moments before but in a slightly different way. Noticed how a strand of hair fell across her face. A strand she'd blew at but didn't take the time to tuck behind her ear.

By the time the bell rang, Mason was wrestling with a truth that made him lag behind everyone else. Was Carter Owens worth crushing on?

The question plagued him all through morning classes and into the cafeteria. His friends circled him like magnets. He knew they noticed how he didn't respond to anything they said and reacted because of it, trying to crack better jokes, trying to say anything that would win their King back.

Mason didn't care.

He sat down at his table and a minute later a girl slid his tray of food in front of him. She smiled and claimed the seat next to him. A spot that was only earned by getting his food for him. Mason didn't say anything. Instead, he stared across the cafeteria to where Carter sat at a lone table near the trash cans. She wasn't eating, even though a sandwich sat before her.

The scowl she always wore was gone, in its place was a scrutinizing expression. As Mason watched her, she surveyed the scene with a critical eye like she was dissecting everyone. She eventually looked over to him. Mason didn't look away. Carter scowled at him for a second then moved on.

Still, Mason watched her, watched the way her brows wrinkled as if solving a mystery. Watched how she completely ignored her food. He simply watched her.

When she met his gaze again, she didn't scowl, she watched him back. Something about her attention stirred Mason. Carter rose and walked towards him and Mason felt his heart give a weird jerk in his chest, whether it was anticipation or apprehension he wasn't totally sure.

Carter nudged two students aside and leaned on the table, pinning Mason to his seat with her eyes. All conversations stopped.

"Mason," Carter said. "If you don't stop staring at me, I will break five of your fingers."

Mason felt a tremor of fear go through him. Her tone hadn't been sassy, taunting, or angry. It had been completely even like she told him what sandwich she had. Carter nodded to Smith and walked away.

This girl was insane! What was Mason thinking?! Whatever thoughts he'd had about Carter he instantly banished. It must have been a really terrible night yesterday for him to think he liked Carter. He mentally shuddered at the thought. That girl was a walking nightmare. One that would come alive and kill him if she felt like it.

Needing to feel like himself again, Mason turned to the girl who'd gotten his food and smiled.

"Amber," he said. "You said something about a party this weekend, right?"

She perked up. "Yes, can you come?"

He winked at her. "Wouldn't miss it."

Playing Hooky

Make it to the library, that's all Carter had to do, she simply had to make it to the library and it would be okay. She cut through the sea of students, one more sophomore in the never-ending tide. She kept her steps confident but not fearful or hurried. She held firmly to her mask of indifference.

Nothing and no one around her mattered, she barely noticed them at all. She said that to herself over and over again, building up the wall around her that had crumbled a fraction.

Carter pushed through the library doors and managed a nod to Patty but kept moving. Patty often sent Carter soft and motherly expressions as if she knew the hardships Carter faced. But Carter didn't want that, she wanted the quiet of the second story corner where no one went.

Make it to the corner, all she needed to do was make it to the corner and she'd be fine. She quickened her steps as she reached the stairs and had to stop herself from bounding up them. Students still sat at the tables and would be able to hear her frantic steps and it would draw attention.

Almost there, she thought.

At the furthest back corner, she let out a breath and sank to the floor. She curled her legs in and dropped her head onto her knees.

Words it was only words, that was all it was. But those words were accompanied by laughter that still rang in Carter's ears. She could still see the smug smiles, the ones that said the girls knew they hit a mark even if Carter didn't react.

Carter clenched her fists, digging her short, rough nails into her palms. She pictured slamming her fists into her punching bag over and over again. She imagined the taut leather and heard the chain rattling. She imagined the release as she hit the bag again. She felt the strength in her arms, shoulders, down to her core.

She felt her body using every ounce of energy to punch the bag. All the energy she had meant she wouldn't use it to cry or fall apart. All she did was imagine that bag, her fists making contact.

Slowly, very slowly, one imagined punch after another, Carter felt her tension, anger, pain, and unshed tears retreating. She sucked in a deep breath and let it out slowly. Drained, but without a trace of crying, Carter raised her head and leaned it back against the bookshelf.

If she could, she would stay there all day. She'd wait for the final bell to ring, for the last light to be switched off and slip away, never having to walk with the pompous and self-important students again. Or at least for one day, tomorrow she'd be back, her face unrattled by their words, their looks, their smiles, their mere presence. She would be the Untouchable Girl.

But right then she wasn't, she knew it. She felt the weak parts of her curled into a ball behind her makeshift wall. She could feel how if put up against one more person that wall might crumble.

She couldn't let that happen. Maybe she would stay in the library, there were only two more classes left. But if she missed them would Captain hear about it? Would she have to tell him why she hid away? Was there a way she could keep it from him? Not likely, he saw everything.

"You can't be serious?"

Carter tensed at the voice but forced herself to relax and appear unconcerned.

"You promised me, you said that for this day we could do what I wanted. You said that, do you not remember?"

Carter continued to tell herself to remain completely unfazed as Mason walked into view at the other end of the aisle.

"You know what," Mason said, starting to pace. "This is my fault, I should have gotten it in writing. Maybe even had the Secretary of Defense sign it."

Mason glared at the ground and dragged his hand through his hair, ruining the perfectly styled blonde locks. Carter found herself relaxing more as she watched him. Someone else's life sucked, that was somehow reassuring.

"I can be as petulant as I want, it's my birthday and you promised we could have just a family dinner. Not a state dinner with five courses."

Mason stopped walking and straightened. In that action, Carter saw his resignation, hurt, anger, and sadness.

"Of course," Mason said, his tone no longer angry. "I'll be there, Mr. President. Was there anything else you required of me?" A pause. "Good."

Mason pulled his phone away and stabbed the screen. He stood there, clutching it and quietly seething. Carter watched him unabashedly but with little emotion.

Finally, Mason raised his gaze and spotted her. She didn't react and neither did he. For a long while, they remained frozen, staring at each other.

Mason strode down the aisle and sank to the ground beside Carter.

"I'm only sitting here because you look more pathetic than I feel and that's making me feel better," he said.

Carter shrugged and dropped her head back. "I'm okay with that since I only look half as pathetic as you actually are."

"I'm not pathetic."

Carter half smiled as she sensed Mason cringing at his own statement, knowing it made him sound pathetic. But her smile didn't last long before her own struggles stole it away.

"State Dinner on your birthday, huh?" Carter said.

"Your existence is only worth noting to be mocked, huh?"

"At least my father cares about me."

Mason winced and Carter grimaced.

"Sorry," she said.

"Don't apologize, Owens, it makes me think that you actually care about hurting my feelings and that annoys me."

"Fine."

They fell silent, neither of them looking at each other. The quiet felt strange as if they both had somehow found comfort in the other's presence and pain. Which Carter felt like was crossing a line they shouldn't cross. She didn't like Mason, he was annoying and self-absorbed.

Their teachers threw them together more often than not. It was the rare times that Carter hated that their intelligence was on equal footing. If only he could be as much as an idiot as she thought him to be then it would all be solved.

"Do you want to skip our last two classes and go somewhere?" Mason asked without preamble.

"Sure except you have a shadow that is six feet tall and two hundred and twenty pounds of pure muscle."

"Smith is guarding the library door, I told him I wanted to be alone."

"It's gratifying to think that you believe I could take Smith down from behind but I'm not delusional enough to believe that."

"I'm not delusional enough either, there's a backdoor in the library that not many know about."

"Your father will be pissed if you give Smith the slip."

Mason's grin was wicked and Carter understood, that was the point.

She didn't make any sign of planning to go with him. Sighing, Mason stood.

"Very well, I'll leave you to your mopping," Mason said.

He walked away and Carter watched him. A half a second after he disappeared around a bookcase, she jumped up and took off after him. She caught up to him and he smirked.

"Because of my father," Carter said. "I feel an obligation to go with you and make sure no one sees your arrogant face and has the urge to punch it."

"No, you're coming to spend time with me."

"Forget the random attacker, I might just punch your face."

Mason laughed and Carter hated that she felt her own mood lighten a bit.

Mason was right, there was a backdoor in the library and they slipped out of it. Despite knowing her father wouldn't approve, Carter didn't back down. She knew there was no way of convincing Mason to not slip away and figured going with him was the best option. Correction the best option would have been to tell Smith but Carter didn't do that.

Instead, she followed Mason around the school to the back entrance knowing that exactly seven different cameras would have caught their image and Smith would have no trouble figuring out how they slipped away once he realized Mason was gone.

Neither of them spoke as they walked to the closest Metro station and climbed onto a train. It was as if they had made a truce, they weren't friends but they weren't two bickering students either. They were using the other as an excuse to be brave enough to play hooky.

Eventually, they wound up at the Mall. It was late spring and the cherry blossoms were in full bloom which meant the entire world had come to see the event. Carter had to admit to herself that it was a perfect place to go unnoticed. To everyone, they were merely two students done with school. The trees were the main event, not the President's son.

"I'm getting ice cream," Mason announced. "If you're standing next to me when I pay for it you might be able to sneak your own ice cream."

"Whatever."

They headed towards the ice cream shop off the Mall and each got a scoop. Together they found a spot on the Lincoln Memorial steps and sat down. The Mall was packed with tourists all eagerly holding phones and snapping pictures. Some were even dancing before their phones and Carter watched them.

"Idiots," Mason said.

Carter nodded in agreement.

They continued to eat and observe the world with critical eyes. Eventually, they finished their ice cream but neither attempted to leave their spot.

"You know I don't pity you," Carter said.

"Good. I don't want your pity."

"As long as you know. I would hate for you to think because I've seen a deeper side of you I somehow have grown to have respect for you and your situation."

"You didn't see a deeper side of me."

"Because there is no deeper side to see."

"Exactly. And I don't feel any sort of gratitude towards you for coming with me. Just so that's clear. You're merely attracted to me and used this as an excuse to spend time with me."

"I'm here as your protection, nothing else."

"Funny."

They fell silent again.

"Can we really do this?" a hesitant voice said nearby.

Carter glanced over and spotted an odd pairing: a boy around her age with unkempt brown hair, glasses, and a rumpled appearance walking with a guy she could only think of as an attractive athlete. They both wore school uniforms though with the maroon blazers of Jefferson Prep than Hamilton's navy ones.

She watched them as the rumpled boy gazed around. Clearly, they were other students playing hooky, though Carter imagined it wasn't the hesitant boy's idea but his accomplice.

"It's fine," the athlete said. "You needed a break. It will be fine."

The rumpled boy nodded. As the pair walked off, the athlete gazed around and found Carter's gaze. She didn't react and he broke away first, his glance saying she barely warranted an impression. Carter continued to stare after them, marveling over the bizarre friendship. But then again she was sitting next to Mason and they would look like a strange match to any outsider.

Mason swore under his breath and Carter snapped out of her study of the two students. She searched and found what had caused Mason to swear. Striding towards them and making the crowd part was Smith. Along with Carter's father.

"Nice knowing you," Carter said.

"Was it?" Mason asked.

"Not really. But I did like the ice cream."

Mason snorted and stood, brushing off his blazer as if he were about to give a press conference.

"Hello, Smith," Mason said. "Just take me home. There's no point putting off the inevitable." He looked back at Carter and gave her a head nod. "Later, Owens."

Smith placed a hand on Mason's shoulder and steered him back through the crowd, leaving Carter to her father's furious glare.

"Let's go," he said.

"I'm pretty sure I'll be safer if I stay in a crowd," she said.

"Did you think it through?" he asked.

"Actually, I did. I figured Mason was leaving whether I went with him or not. Protection, even if it was just me was better than no protection at all."

"You could have told Smith."

"I would have lost Mason if I'd left him to tell Smith."

"You could have called me."

Carter opened her mouth and then shrugged. "Yes, I could have. But it's his birthday and he has to attend a state dinner instead of having a family dinner."

Her father sighed heavily and looked at where Smith and Mason had disappeared.

"You understand you're grounded for three weeks because of this, right?"

Carter nodded and walked down the steps. "Yeah, but somehow I feel like it is worth it."

Her father slung his arm around her shoulders. "Don't do it again."

"No worries there," Carter said. "I don't even like the guy."

Unwanted Attention

Carter sat back in her chair watching the stream of seniors enter the math class. One of the only two sophomores in the class, Carter warranted even less notice than usual. This didn't bother her, it was better than when anyone did pay her attention. Those times it didn't end well on either side.

A senior entered the room that Carter had never seen in that class before. He had perfectly tousled hair, sharp cheekbones, and dark green eyes. From the tailored lines of his uniform, she could tell he took care of himself. There was something about him that made Carter cautious. It was more than he knew he was good-looking, it was that he seemed the type to enjoy breaking hearts.

Before her mother had left, Carter used to read Teen Fiction books. But after they seemed shallow to the pain she faced and hated the cheap happy endings. Looking at this new classmate, Carter felt there was only one tag to attach to him: cliché bad boy.

As if to prove this, he strolled down the aisle towards the empty seat next to Mason, a slight swagger in his step.

"Mason," the guy said.

Mason raised his head from his phone and nodded to the newcomer. "Jamison. What are you doing in this class?"

"My schedule got rearranged so I got bumped to here." Jamison's eyes trailed away from Mason to Carter. A slow crooked smile overtook his face. "Hi. I don't think we've met, if we had I'm pretty sure I'd remember."

Carter stared back at the guy, baffled. She knew that her uniform from last year fit differently due to more development, but she seriously didn't think she merited his notice.

"Oh, this is Carter Owens," Mason said like she was no one of consequence.

"I'm Jamison," Jamison said, still wearing his crooked smile.

Carter wondered if as a sophomore she should be flattered by his attention but she wasn't. Though she could admit his smile was disarming, she wasn't drawn to it. This guy was not her type. She didn't care for cocky.

"Okay," she said.

The unfazed remark made Jamison's smile quirk with surprise and curiosity. Before he could say more, the final bell rang and class began. Carter put Jamison out of her mind as she took notes. When class was released, she shouldered her messenger bag and joined the tide in the hallway.

A second later, Jamison caught up to her.

"Where are you running off to?" he asked.

"What aspect of my casual stride would you equate to 'running off'?"

Again a flash of curiosity darted through Jamison's expression.

"Figure of speech. Where are you headed, I can walk you there?"

"You know, as feeble as I am as a girl I think I can manage to make it from point A to B without a male escort."

Jamison laughed a warm teasing sound that attracted surrounding gazes, including a few girls who threw Carter baffled looks. Yeah, she didn't understand why he was walking with her either.

"You're cute," Jamison said.

"Okay."

Why was he still following her?

As Carter cut away from the mass of students and towards the doorway of her A.P. Euro class, Jamison blocked her path, putting one hand on the doorframe.

"Look," he said, his green eyes locking with hers. "What do I have to do to get your number?"

"Nothing."

Jamison smiled, pleased.

"Because I'm not giving it to you. I'm not interested in whatever you're offering."

Ducking under his arm, Carter slipped into her classroom. As she took her seat, Jamison stuck his head inside.

"You aren't getting off that quickly, Carter Owens," he said.

With a final flash of his crooked smile, he disappeared. A few girls around Carter stared at her, but she pretended to not notice, hoping that her lack of interest in Jamison would make them ignore her. And hopefully make him give up as well.

Carter had no such luck. As she sat in her living room, textbooks strewn about her, her phone buzzed. Captain sat at the dining table, on the phone as he inspected a file. Carter dug through the mess around her until she found her phone. The number was unknown.

Her heart jumped. Was it her mother? It had been less than a year since she'd left but maybe she just needed time and space. Maybe she'd missed Carter.

"Hello?" Carter answered, hating how much she wished to hear her mother's voice.

"Hey, beautiful."

Carter's heart deflated. For a second, she sat there trying to convince herself that it didn't matter.

"Hello?" the male voice on the other end said.

"Who is this?" Carter asked.

A light laugh. "You know you don't have to pretend."

Carter pulled the phone away from her ear and hung up. She didn't know what game was being played but she wanted no part of it.

"Who was that?" Her father asked his own phone call down.

She hated that she heard a note of hope in his voice as well. At least she wasn't alone in wishing one day it would be a call they both wanted.

"Wrong number," she said.

Her phone pinged.

Unknown: *Hanging up on a guy, that's cold.*

Carter: *How did you get my number?*

Unknown: *I have my ways.*

Carter: *Stalking is unattractive, just so you know.*

Unknown: *Haha it's not stalking if Mason willingly gave it.*

Carter was going to kill Mason Douglas. She didn't even care if she went to jail for it, at least she'd rid the world of such an irritating person.

Unknown: *Are you mad at him now?*

Don't be, I'm hard to say no to

You'll find that out soon enough

Are you ignoring me now?

You understand playing hard to get is pointless, I'm not hard to get

I'm right here, waiting and willing

Carter?

You there?

Carter continued to ignore the pings of her phone, focusing on homework. His attention span had to die off soon enough.

***

The next day as Carter approached her locker, she slowed her steps. A circle of people had formed around it. Scowling, she elbowed her way through and stopped dead in her tracks. A red rose was taped to the outside of her locker with a note hanging from a ribbon around the stem.

Morning beautiful. - Jamison

Ignoring the rose, Carter got into her locker and dumped her notebooks inside. She closed the locker as a group of girls appeared beside her.

"That's sweet of him," one of the girls said. "But you understand he's out of your league, right?"

"Doesn't matter," Carter said. "Like I told him, I'm not interested."

"You don't have to play the denial card with us. Everyone girl has fallen for him at least once."

"Not denial," Carter said, ripping the rose off her locker.

As she strode off, the girl called out to her. "You aren't fooling anyone!"

Why would no one take her word? Shaking her head, Carter kept moving. When she spotted Mason, she stormed over to him. She snatched his phone out of his hand and shoved the rose into it.

"Someone left this for you," she said.

As Mason eyed the rose, confused, Carter got into his contacts and deleted her number. If they ever had to work together on a project again, they could find some other way to communicate. She gave him back his phone.

"Give my number out again and I'll break your face," she said.

"Owens, always so violent," Mason said, walking off. "Hey Tiffany, I have something for you."

Carter forced her annoyance at Jamison out of her head for the rest of the day. That was until she sank into her seat in math class. Flipping open her textbook, she started to work out the lesson for the day and then went to the homework. She'd barely started when Jamison put a hand on her paper, forcing Carter to look up.

"You gave away my rose?" he asked, with genuine hurt in his voice. He put his hand over his heart. "Are you trying to break my heart?"

"If in the span of half a day of you knowing me you've given me the power to break your heart, you're really not that smart. Also, it would show a tendency for being impulsive and flaky. Not great qualities."

Jamison crouched down so that he was at eye level with Carter. His green eyes seemed to sparkle as they took her in. Carter understood how attractive he was, she wasn't blind. But since telling him she wasn't interested all he'd done was push past her refusal and that took all attraction away from him.

"Give me a chance to show you my better qualities," he said.

Though his tone was sincere, Carter wasn't versed enough to know whether that sentence had a second meaning. Either way, it made her more wary of him.

"No," she said. "Go find someone else to bother. I said I wasn't interested and I meant it."

"How can I when you seem to be the only girl I want to bother?"

He sent her a teasing grin and Carter knew he expected her to melt. But his pushiness only hardened her to him. Why couldn't he understand her 'no'? Did he seriously think continuing to flirt with her when she turned him down would win her over?

The bell rang, saving Carter.

***

By the time Friday came around, Carter didn't understand how many more ways she could say 'no'. Clearly, the word wasn't in Jamison's vocabulary because he kept finding reasons to talk to Carter. Each time the eagerness in his expression grew. His smile almost never left his lips and there was an amused light in his eyes.

As Carter headed towards the school exit with the rest of the students, a girl bumped into Carter. She was one of the group that thought Carter was in denial. Carter didn't understand them at all.

"I have to say I'm impressed," the girl said. "Making Jamison wait this long before getting a date is gutsy of you, he might have moved on by now."

"I wish he would," Carter muttered.

"You should really just give in and admit you like him, he always gets his way eventually."

Carter hated that. How was that okay, at all? She didn't want him. She didn't want to date him. Yet the whole school somehow believed that she had no opinion on the matter. He was good-looking and came from a rich family that seemed to mean everyone would want to jump at the chance to date him. So his pestering, which he thought as flirting, was what? Supposed to simply be endearing? But it wasn't, it was getting on Carter's nerves.

Carter didn't respond to the girl, instead she pushed through the doors and into the cool fall sunlight. Finding a secluded spot, she waited. The parking lot emptied and the noise around Carter slowly vanished. Her father said he'd pick her up and they'd go see a movie. Carter didn't mind waiting, it gave her peace and quiet.

Unfortunately, it didn't give her peace and quiet for long. The front doors opened and Jamison strode out. He glanced around and when he spotted Carter, he grinned. Carter wanted to melt into the wall and never be seen again. This guy was intolerable. But at least Captain would be there soon and she could get away.

"Do you need a ride?" he asked, leaning his shoulder against the wall near her.

Too near for Carter's liking. She shifted away from him.

"I don't, so please leave."

"I can't."

He could, he didn't want to. Carter didn't look at him.

"Carter," he said, his voice low, earnest. "Look, I know that you think I'm some flirt who can't be serious about anyone. But the way you've knocked me down a notch this week...well I don't know, it's been refreshing. They say it takes the right person to make someone change."

He couldn't actually be serious about this? How stupid did he think she was? Very stupid, clearly, if he thought she actually bought all the crap he was spewing.

"Why in the world would you think that's me?" Carter asked. "You don't know me, at all. You've flirted and I've not responded."

"But you're unlike any girl I've known before," he said.

"How few girls have you known in your life then?"

Jamison simply laughed. A breeze kicked up and stray strands of Carter's hair blew into her face. Jamison reached out and caught hold of them, tucking them behind Carter's ear. A chill ran down Carter's spine. She gripped his wrist, pulling it away from her face.

"What made you think I'd be okay with you touching me?"

Jamison stared into Carter's eyes, his whole manner sober.

"Carter, you don't understand. I can't stop thinking about you."

She flung his wrist away from her. "I can see how that would be devastating to you since usually you only think about yourself."

In a blink, Jamison stood before Carter, both hands pressed against the wall beside her head, pinning her there. Carter's entire body reacted.

She went rigid even as adrenaline spiked through her. Jamison was a head taller than her and a whole sixty pounds heavier. Carter was shockingly aware of the emptiness around them, no other students, teachers locked away in their classroom with headphones on. They were completely alone.

"Can't you see the connection between us?" he asked.

All Carter felt between them was a lack of space. Jamison glanced down at her lips and another shot of adrenaline surged through Carter. She knew how to defend herself, but would his strength counteract everything she knew?

As he leaned in, Carter thought of all the other girls who could have been in this exact position. Did they convince themselves that the frantic beating of their heart was from desire instead of fear?

Did they want Jamison or were they badgered into thinking they did because of his attention and everyone else's constant statements that they did?

Fury tore through Carter, not only for the violation she was feeling right then, but for all the other girls as well who might have been in her place.

When Jamison cupped her cheek and leaned in, Carter jammed her palm upward and broke Jamison's nose. He let out a cry and staggered back, clutching his face. He swore at her, but Carter didn't care, she was racing away from him.

As she sprinted down the front steps, her father's SUV pulled up. Carter didn't have time to open the door before her father stood there.

"Carter, what's going on?" he said, urgent.

"I broke a guy's nose," she said. "He tried...he was going to..."

Only as she spoke did Carter realize that her whole body was trembling. Nothing had happened to her but that didn't matter, her mind played out all the things that could have.

"Is that him?"

Carter glanced back to see Jamison swaying towards the parking lot, his nose bleeding all over his white oxford shirt.

"Yeah."

Her father stormed over to Jamison as Carter crossed her arms, trying to get herself to stop shaking.

"Carter," her father said.

She climbed the steps towards him and let out a breath as she saw the firm grip he had on Jamison's arm. Jamison no longer looked cocky, instead he looked pale and ready to puke. Carter knew even then he wasn't feeling the fear she'd had, what guy ever could?

"Come on," her father said, pushing through the school doors.

Carter walked beside him, feeling the anger coming off him. She knew he wanted to pummel Jamison but had a clear enough head to hold himself back. In Principal Withers' office, her father shoved Jamison into a seat.

"I want this kid expelled for sexual harassment," her father said.

Principal Withers looked rattled but calmly gathered the facts. With her father's statement from seeing them and the footage from the camera's outside the school, Withers got on the phone and rang up Jamison's father.

An hour later, Carter walked out of the school with her father. Jamison was getting sent to military school, something he'd already been threatened with and Carter wasn't going to be punished for breaking his nose since it was a gut reaction.

At the car, Captain hugged Carter tightly. She hugged him back, feeling as tears built but kept them at bay. She would be stronger than some guy scaring her.

"Are you okay?" her father asked.

Carter nodded, she would be. When Captain pulled back, he placed his hands on Carter's shoulder.

"I'm really proud of you for protecting yourself," he said.

"Thanks, Captain."

He kissed the top of her head and opened the car door for her.

"Come on, we're going to skip the movie," he said.

"Why?"

"Because I'm going to teach you tactics for taking down guys twice your size. I never want you to feel afraid or be unprepared for the type of situation again."

The Anniversary

Carter gripped the edge of her PE locker, wanting to slam it closed over and over again.

"It's so cute, every time we're in science he's always trying to sneak glances of me. But when I look back he looks away."

Didn't this girl get it? Hope was stupid. Hope was vengeful. It played with emotions, bringing them to the highest point only to send them crashing down. How could she not see that having hope was the most dangerous thing a person could do?

"He still hasn't made a move though."

"Ask him out. Go for it."

"Should I?"

No! Carter slowly closed her locker because if she didn't do it that way she'd slam it.

"Don't do it," she said.

The girls behind her stopped talking.

"What did you say, Owens?"

Carter turned around to find the girls already regarding her with judgmental looks. Looks that Carter had gotten used to over the last year. But still, she couldn't let this girl make a move that would end up humiliating her.

"Don't ask him out, Amber," she said. "He's not looking at you, he's always looking at Kira. You just sit right in his sightline. I know because I sit behind him."

And she'd noticed how Amber glanced back and Levi always looked uncomfortable when she did. This girl hoped in the wrong thing.

Amber crossed her arms and jutted out her hip. "Owens, you're wrong. You know how I know? Because no one has ever wanted you."

Carter curled her fists, the words hitting a place in her heart already torn to shreds. Amber smirked and turned away.

Shaking with fury, Carter yanked her bag off the ground and stormed out of the locker room. The bell was a minute away from ringing, ending the day. She wished the day would be over completely. It was one day...but it wasn't. It was the... It was one stupid day!

Mason walked out of the boys' bathroom and right into Carter's path.

"Owens, you look poetically like a thunder cloud today. Is it a special occasion?"

"Mason, shut up!" she shouted. "For once in your life can you not be self-centered!"

Mason took a step back, shocked.

"Woah, where is this coming from?" he asked.

"What? You think it's odd that someone would want you to stop talking? Clearly, you misread every interaction you have."

Frowning, Mason studied her. "What's going on, Owens?"

"Why does anything have to be going on for me to not want to talk to you? Seriously! You constantly get on my nerves and I'm sick of it!"

"Then you are free to leave. It's not like I enjoy talking to you."

"Great!"

Carter took off, pushing hard against the school front doors as the bell rang. Behind her, the hallways flooded with students and she quickened her step. She needed to get out of there. Despite the cold, Carter didn't go to the Metro. She couldn't stand being packed with other people.

By the time she made it to Maggie's, her face was freezing and her nose was bright red. Maggie hurried out from behind the counter when she saw Carter.

"Hon," she said. "Are you okay? Did you walk all the way here?"

"Yeah."

"Carter, it's freezing, you could get sick. Are you okay?" she asked tenderly.

"I'm fine, okay! You don't have to worry about me."

"Of course I do," Maggie said with a smile. "I care about you."

She reached out to Carter but Carter jerked back.

"Well don't, okay! I'm fine! I don't need a mom. I'm fine without one! So back off!"

"Carter-"

Carter raced out of the deli and sprinted across the street. In the apartment, she kicked the door closed and stood just inside. She was everywhere. She was everywhere even when she hadn't been there for a year.

Tearing off her bag, Carter flung it at the couch. She moved to the closest wall and yanked the first picture frame off the wall. One of all three of them smiling.

A happy family.

A lie.

Photo after photo, she removed them all. Even the ones of only her and Captain. They were always laughing or smiling. That was no longer them. She stuffed the frames in the back of a closet and went to the couch. She ripped the decorative pillows off and jammed them on top of the frames and slammed the door closed.

It wasn't enough.

Carter went to her room, grabbed her boxing gloves. She hit play on the only band she listened to anymore, 7 Ships. The only band she felt she could listen to and not want to throw up over its sweetness.

She jerked on her boxing gloves and savagely punched the bag. She didn't think about technique, stance, or follow-through. All she thought about was hitting and kicking the bag with every ounce of strength she had.

When her wrists ached, her knuckles throbbed, she yelled.

"Why didn't you come back! Why did you leave me! What...what did I do!"

Over and over again she attacked the punching bag hating that it didn't break or crack like she was.

"Why didn't you call!"

The apartment door opened but Carter didn't care. It wasn't her so what did it matter. She stopped punching and simply slammed the sides of both her fists into the bag.

"Carter."

Carter didn't stop. She wanted the bag to do something other than swing slightly.

"Carter."

A pair of strong hands took hold of her arms and she struggled against them.

"No!" she yelled.

She kicked at the bag. Before she could do it a second time, her father turned her around. She fought him, trying to break out of his hold. He didn't let her go.

Finally, she lost her fight and crumpled. But her father held her up, pulling her into a hug. She clung to him.

He was the only certainty she knew.

"Please, please don't leave," she cried. "Don't leave me."

Her father kissed the top of her head. "I'm not going anywhere, Sarge. I'm not going anywhere."

***

Carter didn't look in the mirror. She didn't want to see how awful she looked. What did it matter anyway? Everyone at school already dismissed her, today would be no different.

When she left her room, she found Captain sitting at the kitchen table, two smoothies before him. Carter took a seat and sipped the power shake.

"How are you doing?" Captain asked.

Carter shrugged. She felt exhausted even though she'd fallen asleep early last night. It was the type of exhaustion that didn't go away with a good night's rest.

"I yelled at Maggie yesterday," she said, turning her cup in a slow circle and not looking at Captain.

"I know. She called me."

Carter swallowed hard. "Do you think she'll forgive me?"

Captain leaned forward and Carter finally looked at him. "She already has. She understood what yesterday was. She said she'll have a cookie waiting for you after school."

Tears formed in the back of Carter's eyes and she blinked hard.

"Okay."

"Are you ready to head out?"

She nodded and finished off the last of her smoothie. With a quick brush of her teeth, she snatched up her bag and walked back into the living room. Captain stood looking at the empty wall. Carter didn't look at it.

"I can put them back," she said.

He looked at her. "Only if you want to. I did like the one of you with your face smeared with ice cream."

That one had only the two of them in it. It was from when Carter was three-years-old and her father looked so young at twenty-four. She might be okay with that one going back up.

When they pulled up in front of her school, Carter reached for her door handle.

"Maggie said this was for lunch," Captain said, giving her a brown paper bag.

Carter took it then slid off her seat.

"Sarge."

She turned back, seeing the caring blue eyes that were always there for her.

"I love you, Sarge."

"I love you, Captain."

She held onto the door frame, not wanting to let go or leave him. Captain looked at her intently.

"Sarge, do you want to know something?" he asked.

She nodded.

"No matter what happens, I will always find you. That's a promise."

The words comforted Carter and she let go of the door. At the top of the stairs, she watched his car disappear. The noise of the school washed over Carter as she headed to her locker. She opened it and set the brown bag inside but paused. Opening it, she saw the sandwich with a bag of chips. Tucked beside them was a folded piece of paper.

All I ever want to be to you is your friend if you'll let me. I hope you have a good day. Love Maggie.

Instead of putting the note back, Carter folded it up and slipped it into her pocket. She wanted to have it close.

"Owens...uh...are you okay?" Mason asked.

Carter remained focused on her locker. "Mason, I heard the boys' bathroom got a new full-length mirror installed, isn't your reflection missing you?"

Mason sagged against the lockers. "Good, you're normal again. You scared me yesterday with all the shouting. Nothing was witty." He cocked his head. "You're time of the month?"

Carter closed her locker door and stared at Mason.

"Mason, only you would think that just because a girl yelled at you means she's on her period. I have no doubt countless girls want to yell at you on a daily basis."

"A lot of girls yell at me, but it's because they are behind a line of Secret Service agents and trying to get my attention."

"It amazes me how you can take the scream of protesters and completely reframe it in your mind." She slow clapped. "Well done, Mr. President."

The bell rang and Mason grinned as he took a step back from Carter.

"I'm glad you're no longer broken, Owens. You had me worried."

"Only one of us is damaged and it's not me."

"You keep telling yourself that, Owens. But face it, we're both messed up."

He walked away with that parting shot. He was right but Carter knew one thing: she still had Captain and that's what mattered.

Donovan's Life

Retaliation

Donovan slammed the magazine into the paintball rifle before slinging it over his shoulder. The house around him lay silent as if taunting him as his brothers had. Their parents had gone out on a date leaving all four boys at home.

But that's not where they all planned to stay. After an hour, Brock announced to Donovan that he had to stay home while the rest of them went out. Donovan protested loudly, but the counterargument was that he was too young. Donovan shouted that he was only two years younger than James but he knew there was more than that.

At fourteen, James had already hit a growth spurt and looked more man than boy. At twelve, Donovan still stood on the skinny side and so his brothers had left him behind with the threat of a beating if he tried to follow them.

So Donovan stayed behind, but he planned to show his brothers that it was a terrible mistake. Dressed in all black, Donovan headed out the front door. The night spring air held the scent of dirt and a bit of the sea. A chill swept across the base, stirring up clouds of dust.

Rifle secure, Donovan climbed into the railing of the porch. He reached out and grabbed the lip of the roof. Adjusting his grip, he let his body swing, holding himself up only by his fingertips. Pressing one boot to the railing, he hoisted himself onto the roof ledge. James had sprained his ankle trying to climb to the roof that way and falling. Since then it had been forbidden for them to climb into the roof. Donovan didn't care. This was war.

Donovan crawled across the rough roof shingles, up to the apex. At the top, he flipped over to the other side and positioned himself for an attack, rifle snug against his shoulder, his sights aimed at the road to their house. He didn't know when his brothers would be home. His parents varied when they returned, so he knew his brothers wouldn't stay out too long so they wouldn't be caught. It meant Donovan had maybe two hours to wait, but again he didn't care.

It was almost an hour later when Donovan spotted his brothers making their way back. Wispy clouds drifted across the face of the moon, but they weren't strong enough to block out the light. He could perfectly see his brothers' silhouettes and shifted the gun, aiming for them.

When they were a few feet from the front gate, Donovan fired. The shot hit Brock in the chest and he let out a grunt of pain. Using the moment of shock, Donovan aimed for James hitting him in the shoulder. But when he swiveled to Clint, the second oldest was already diving for cover behind a hedge, closely followed by the other two.

"Donovan! What are you doing?!" Brock yelled.

Donovan didn't answer. He waited. When Clint made a dash for another hedge, Donovan fired, nailing him in the leg. James darted towards the gate, but Donovan pelted him with two shots to the stomach, making his brother stagger and fall behind the fence.

Donovan knew that with their numbers, their best strategy would to be flank him and he had no intention of letting that happen. So he whipped the rifle from one side to the other, keeping them from getting close and doing more than taking cover.

When James burst from his hiding spot, screaming like a madman and running to the house, Donovan laid him out with so many shots his brother was going to be black and blue all over. At the same time, Clint vaulted over the fence, sprinting to get under the cover of the porch, but Donovan managed to get in a couple of hits on him.

Only when he felt a hand clamp over his ankle did he realize what James and Clint had been: a diversion. Donovan flipped onto his back, ready to fire on Brock, but his older brother ripped the gun from Donovan's hands.

"Not cool," Brock said.

"You were the ones who left me home! That wasn't cool!"

Brock called to Clint and tossed the gun over the side of the house. Donovan tried to scramble away, knowing Brock wasn't going to let this slid, but Brock caught him before he made it far. Donovan struggled but it was useless, his brother was eighteen and solid muscle. Gripping both of Donovan's wrists, Brock dragged him to the side of the house. Donovan fought with all his might, but still, he slid closer to the edge.

"Don't!" he shouted, panic bursting inside him.

Brock laughed and Donovan paled. It wasn't a pleasant sound.

"Mom will kill you," Donovan warned.

"Don't worry, two people are waiting to catch you."

"Brock! Don't!"

Donovan wanted to act brave, but terror seized him. Even though it was a one-story house, it was a far way to the ground below. He twisted and kicked at his brother, trying with all he had to break free.

"You ready," Brock called out.

"Send him down!" James said.

Donovan let out a wild scream as Brock tossed him from the roof. For a heart-stopping moment, he hovered then plummeted to the ground, stomach lurching into his throat. Two sets of arms caught him, but the force of Donovan's body sent them crashing to the ground.

Pain exploded in Donovan's arm as he landed on it hard. He bit back his cry, knowing he couldn't let his brothers see more of his weakness. It was the reason he hadn't been invited in the first place. White spots popped in his vision as he rolled off his arm, agony lancing up to his shoulder.

Holding his arm close, Donovan stumbled to his feet, hearing his brothers laughing at it all and making comments about Donovan's scream. When Donovan headed back to the house, James called out.

"What? I thought you wanted to hang out with us?"

Donovan ignored him and slipped inside. He touched his wrist. Blazing fire ripped through his arm and he gritted his teeth, fighting a wave of nausea. He guessed it was broken, but he wasn't sure. In his room, he climbed into his bed, putting his back to the door. Minutes later, James came in, but Donovan ignored him and his joking comments.

Eventually, James' snore filled the room. Donovan let out a shaky breath, his arm throbbing in pain. When he heard the sound of the front door opening, he got up and crept out of the room. In the front hall, his father removed his wife's jacket and hung it up.

Donovan moved towards them, holding his arm to his chest, tears of pain and exhaustion building in his eyes. His mother spotted him first and gave him a warm smile.

"How come you're up so late?" she asked.

Donovan swallowed hard, but couldn't speak. His mother's expression fell as she took in how he held his arm. Hurrying forward, she reached for him, but Donovan jerked back, knowing moving his arm would hurt. Worry played across his mother's face.

"What happened?" she asked.

Donovan's father took the spot beside Eleanor, eying his son. Despite everything, Donovan didn't plan on ratting out his brothers. They might be the reason for the pain, but he couldn't snitch on them.

"I hurt it," Donovan said. "I don't know if it's broken."

"What happened?" his mother repeated.

Donovan knew he couldn't lie to her, so he settled for saying nothing at all.

Eleanor exchanged a glance with Ted and Donovan felt as if they were talking without saying anything.

"Come with me," his father said. "We'll get that checked out."

Donovan was grateful he didn't have to answer any question but knew they would come later. In the car, Donovan stared out the window, not wanting to see his father's silent countenance and know that he wasn't pleased.

His father remained silent towards Donovan through the examination with the base's doctor. The injury turned out to be a sprain instead of a broken bone. Donovan took pain killers and held still as his hand was wrapped up.

Only when his father parked the car outside of their house, did he talk.

"I know you're not telling me what happened because your bothers are involved," he said. "I respect the fact that you want to stay loyal to them. But there are some lines that when crossed loyalty no longer matters. The truth is what matters."

Donovan stared down at his bandaged hand, hating being torn between his brothers and his father.

"I shot them with a paintball gun from the roof and they...weren't happy."

His father nodded and climbed out of the car. Donovan trailed behind him, knowing he should tell him all of the situation but knew what he faced would be ten times worse for Brock.

But it didn't seem to matter, because when they entered the house all the lights were on, his brothers cowered on the couch in the living room, and their mother stormed before them. Donovan couldn't remember a time when his mother looked angry.

"You want to be soldiers but you treat your brother like this! What does that say about you? He didn't give you up when he should have told us from the beginning! His arm could be broken and because of your stupidity, it could have been worse. You're his big brothers, your job is to protect him! To have his six."

To Donovan's surprise, all his brothers looked on the verge of tears. When Brock met Donovan's gaze, Donovan dropped his, not able to handle the broken spirit of his older brother.

"El," Ted said, announcing their presence.

Eleanor spun around and noticed Donovan's bandaged wrist. "Not broken, thank goodness."

She wrapped Donovan up in her arms and kissed his head. Still holding him, she talked to her other sons.

"All of you go to bed, your father and I will deal with you in the morning."

The chastened trio stood and shuffled to their rooms, each of them glancing at Donovan with regret in their eyes. After ten minutes of his mother's love and worry, Donovan headed to his room.

Stepping out of his boots, he got into bed. But before he could find sleep, his door opened and Brock and Clint entered. James joined his bothers as they all crouched beside Donovan's bed. For a long moment, none of them spoke.

"You didn't tell us you hurt your wrist," he said.

Donovan shrugged. "Didn't want you to think I was weak."

"Why didn't you tell on us?" James asked.

"Because your my brothers," Donovan said.

Even in the dim light, Donovan could've sworn they looked about to cry themselves.

"We failed you," Brock said.

"Even when you didn't fail us," Clint said.

"We aren't ever going to let that happen again," James said.

Donovan met each of his brothers' gaze, seeing the sincerity there. He felt like one of them again, no longer left behind.

"From here on out," Brock said, nodding with them all. "We have your six."

Invisible

The house was silent, but Donovan knew it wouldn't be that way for long. Glancing at the door, he hurriedly changed into a pair of running shorts and laced up his shoes. Straining to hear the entrance of his brothers, he went to the window and pushed it open. A dry, dusty wind whipped inside the room. Beyond the smell of dirt, the tang of the ocean could be detected.

Having grown up with this scent, Donovan didn't even notice it anymore. He climbed out and dropped to the ground, a cloud of dust puffing up underfoot. He eased the window shut and let out a breath. The day was settled into the warm glow of late afternoon, the sky hinting at a sunset to come and the sun backing off of its glare.

Feeling satisfied with his escape, Donovan rounded the house. He instantly jerked back, bumping into the corner.

Standing, waiting for him, were his three older brothers.

They were all copies of each other with individual markers that kept them apart. Brock leaned against the house, his arms crossed. He had their father's broad features. James had one elbow resting on Clint's shoulder. Though he was a few inches shorter than his quiet older brother, James' loud personality made up the difference.

"Where are you going?" James asked a laugh hidden in the dimple in his cheek.

Donovan shoved his hands into his pockets, hating that trying to lie to them was like trying to escape their mother's keen eyes.

"I was going to go for a run," he answered.

"Where to?" Brock asked.

"The beach."

All three brothers exchanged looks.

"Great, we'll go with you," James said.

Donovan fought down a scowl of annoyance, knowing it would betray him. Instead, he shrugged.

"Fine."

Removing their shirts and discarding them in Donovan and James' room, the four brothers took off. They crossed the front lawn and moved out onto the road that led through the Marine base. As they ran, the group all looked like echoes, though Donovan just two weeks past sixteen was still the smallest in size. They left the base and crossed the highway, taking it to towards the ocean.

The beach was narrow and occupied by very few people, the location too far for anyone to really bother with driving to. The group kept a tight two-man formation as they moved to the shoreline. Donovan made up one part of the pair at the front, Brock beside him. Despite himself, he was guiding the pack where he really didn't want to go but was pulled anyways.

As they were crossing the path of a lifeguard station, Donovan glanced over. He instantly regretted it and felt a sinking feeling in his gut. The girl sitting on the tall chair waved to him and called out.

"Hi, Donovan," she said.

She was in her late teens with brown hair speckled with blonde from the sun and deeply tan skin. Hating everything at that moment, he waved back.

"Hi, Ashley," he said.

She hopped down from her platform, obviously under the impression that they would have a conversation like they usually did. Donovan felt the familiar pang of attraction as she walked forward, the red lifeguard bathing suit doing everything to display her body to an advantage.

"Are these your brothers?" she asked, eying the group.

As if planned, the brothers fanned out, forming a crescent moon around the girl, Donovan ending up on the far edge. James leaned forward, his smile quick and flirtatious. At seventeen he had still yet to experience anything that was close to awkward. The world was his stage.

"Bond, James Bond," he said.

This was received with an appreciative giggle. Beside him, Clint showed no smile or any sort of descriptive expression.

"Clint," he said.

He said his name like he knew who he was with absolute certainty. It was a certainty that was wrapped in mystery just daring to be solved. The laughter in Ashley's eyes melted to something more awed. When her gaze naturally drifted to Brock, his smile was slow and full of secrets.

"Hey," he said. "I'm Brock."

It was because Donovan was watching so closely, that he saw the moment Ashley's breath hitched.

"Hi," she said, her voice promising she wanted to know every one of his secrets.

Groaning in annoyance, Donovan walked away. He wasn't worried about his absence ever being noticed. In the shadow of his brothers, he was rendered invisible. Lacing his hands together, he placed them on top of his head and stared out at the sea. The breeze whispered against his bare skin, but he barely registered it. A frown cut into his forehead, as he contemplated payback.

The light laugh that floated over the air irked him and he clenched his jaw. Only yesterday that same laugh had been because of him, now he was worth less notice than the sand. At least that played a part in keeping Ashley standing.

A shadow moved to stretch out before him, attached to it was Clint. His brother didn't say anything. He merely stood there, watching the ocean. In that regard, he took after their mother, silent until something worth saying needed to be said. It was a trait that easily gave Brock competition when it came to girls.

There was something about the strong, silent type that drew them to him. It was a persona Donovan wish he could emulate. But since Clint had perfected it, Donovan would only seem like a cheap knock off.

"She only ever saw you as entertaining, not to be taken seriously," Clint said.

Donovan kicked viciously at the sand.

"Shut up. You all suck."

Clint said nothing else, his gaze fixed on the horizon. Donovan hated how it looked deep and philosophical.

"I hate being the youngest," he said.

Clint faced him and placed a hand on his shoulder. Though only nineteen there was a gravity in Clint's gaze that made him seem ancient and endowed with wisdom.

"I know. But you're not invisible, no matter what it may seem like."

Donovan had no answer. It felt strange having his thoughts plucked from his mind so easily. It was exactly what his mother was capable of.

The moment of understanding was broken by James launching himself at Donovan and tackling him to the sand. Happy to let out his annoyance, Donovan rolled and began pummeling James's side. In return, James fought back, landing a few painful blows.

By the time Donovan's spirits were back to normal, both brothers were coated with sand. Jumping up, James held out his hand to Donovan, who grasped it and was hauled to his feet. Even if he was invisible when it came to girls at least he wasn't invisible to his brothers.

As if to echo this, Brock charged forward, grabbing Donovan and hurling him into the water. He crashed through the surface and was enveloped in a chill that was invigorating. He came up for air, sputtering.

Brock and James were laughing and before either of them were prepared for it, Clint was dragging them by the arms to the sea. The trio dived it and resurfaced close to Donovan, who attacked Brock, pinning him under the waves. What ensued was a madness of fists, water, and grunts.

Eventually, when the brothers were tired of choking on salt water, they pulled themselves out of the waves. Ashley was beaming at them, feeling pleased with the entertainment. Ringing out as much water as they could from their shorts and shoes, they took off. Ashley waved to them, her eyes only seeing Brock.

"See you Saturday," she called as if worried he would forget the date that had been set only an hour before.

Jogging backward, Brock offered a salute and wink that made Ashley go giddy. Donovan glanced back but didn't bother waving to her. There was no point in further humiliating himself. The run back to the base was awkward with sopping shoes and dripping shorts. By the time they reached home, Donovan's skin was sticky from the ocean. They all dumped their shoes on the porch, where the sun was likely to rid them of water.

A battle started up as they all raced to the doorway, calling dibs on the shower. They burst through the front door like a stampede, each one trying to trip the other and gain the lead. But at a sharp whistle, they all jumped to attention.

Standing in the living room was their father, alongside him was a man in his forties with neat blonde hair and in a tailored suit. His hazel eyes took in the chaos of the boys with a hint of amusement. It was a look their father did not share, but the sternness of his face didn't say they were in trouble.

"Boys, I would like you to meet an old friend of mine, Senator Douglas."

The brothers all offered murmurs of greetings.

Though the introduction had made it seem like the visit was of a friendly nature, there was an energy that contradicted this. Donovan felt it and tensed, wondering what was really going on. When his father's eyes landed on him, his stomach twisted.

"Donovan," he father said.

His brothers gave him room and Donovan stepped forward.

"Yes, sir?"

The older men seemed to study him as if confirming what had already been spoken about. With a glance at each other and a nod from Douglas, Donovan's father focused back on his son. Donovan got the sense he wasn't going to be invisible anymore.

"Donovan, Senator Douglas has a job for you."

Parting Words

Donovan folded his white shirt in half, pressing his hand along the edge, making a neat crease before folding it in half again and tucking it into his duffle bag.

"Nervous?" his mother said.

Donovan didn't look at her and reached for another shirt. "No."

They both knew he was lying. He was aware that his mother could tell the state of his nerves by the way he was packing his bag. It was all neat edges and control because right then he didn't feel in control. He felt on the edge of an unknown that was too great for him. Not wanting to deal with it, Donovan turned his mother's focus away from him.

"What do you think I should expect with Link?" he asked.

His mother sat in a chair beside his bed, legs crossed, posture comfortable. The sight of her sitting there was a familiar one. When she wasn't in the main part of the house or her office, she could often be found in her sons' rooms, talking to them, listening to all that they would share with her.

"He has only just learned who his father is. For anyone that would set their whole world on its head. It's harder for him since now his world is truly set on its head, he's had to move schools, change his appearance, and have you in his life."

A tinge of sadness entered his mother's eyes and Donovan paused in his work, unsure what the look meant.

"He will hate you," she said.

"I figured."

His mother leaned forward, resting a hand on Donovan's stilling his work.

"No, I don't think you do. It's not you that he will hate, it's his father, it's a life that he didn't ask for, it's the change that he now has to deal with, it's his mother lying to him. All of that will be put on you."

Donovan looked down at the pair of pants he was folding, already feeling the burden of so many emotions aimed at him. "Why me?"

"Because he can't hate his father because his father won't be there often enough, his mother is someone he has always loved so he won't want to take out his hurt on her. But you. You are the symbol of everything that is different in his world. For him, you will embody all the hurt he feels and since he doesn't know you, doesn't have a connection with you, he will hate you and take out his hurt on you."

Already weary, Donovan sank onto his bed and rested his face in his hands.

"How do I handle all of that?"

His mother dropped onto the floor before him, holding onto his wrists. "You take it one day at a time. And you build a connection. It won't happen right away and it won't be easy, but knowing how stubborn and determined you are, I have no doubt you can do it."

Wearing a small smile, Donovan pulled his hands away and met his mother's eyes. She stared back at him and brushed her hand on his face. It was such a tender touch that Donovan felt like a little boy again. He knew if his brothers saw how he let himself be comforted they wouldn't let him forget it, but right then he needed it.

He was leaving everything he knew. For all sixteen years of his life this house, this base, this coast had been his whole world. Now he was going to a world he had never experienced. His world was being turned on its head.

In the moment, he knew a little about how Link was feeling.

Donovan swallowed. "I'm going to miss you."

His mother smiled but there was so much sadness in it that it stole the beauty of it. "I am going to miss you more." She took his hands in hers. "Look, I want you to call me every day."

"You know I can't do that. They would never let me live it down."

"You're not calling for you, you're calling for me. My baby boy is leaving and it's breaking my heart. If you don't want me to die then you will obey and call me."

"Okay, I'll call."

They both knew it was for him. There hadn't been a day in his life when he hadn't talked to his mother, gone into her office when she was done with work, sat on the couch and asked her a million questions. She fed him knowledge like his brothers fed him adventures.

His mother cupped his face. "I love you so much and you are being so brave."

Donovan clenched his fists, already feeling homesickness for a home he hadn't left yet.

"I love you too."

His mother kissed his forehead and Donovan knew it was one of the last times she would do it for a long time. As she stood, Donovan's father appeared in the doorway. Donovan glanced up, not sure what his father's presence meant.

"Donovan," his father said, making a curt nod for his son to follow.

Donovan rose and his mother squeezed his hand. Following his father through the house, Donovan couldn't help but take note of everything that he was going to leave behind. The worn carpet, rows of family photos on the wall, nicks and dents in the walls of years of roughhousing, the smell of too many aftershaves with only a hint of their mother's flowery scent.

Outside, his father's truck was waiting. Without a word, Donovan climbed into the passenger seat. The pair drove through the base in complete silence.

Where people had facial expressions to betray their mood, his father had different silences. If you didn't know him, Donovan figured his father's silence would always feel the same, but it wasn't true. Donovan could tell the difference between a thoughtful silence and a disapproving one. He knew when his father wanted to say something and when his father was withholding his opinion for a reason.

Donovan knew the silence unnerved the other Marines. It's why his father made such a good commander, how did a person yell at someone who wouldn't yell back? You couldn't. And the man who was silent always looked in control, no matter what size the guy yelling was.

As they drove, Donovan didn't ask questions about what his father had planned. There was no point, his father would talk when he was ready. Instead, Donovan took in the sight of the line of barracks, mess hall, airfield, row of garages. Everything that would no longer be part of his life.

His father turned the car into a parking spot outside one of the gun range buildings, still Donovan didn't say anything, simply jumped down and followed his father inside.

After each getting a set of headphones, protection glasses, target sheets, clips, and guns, they walked into a room that was half a block long with divided sections. It was empty and Donovan wondered if this was for a reason. Knowing his father, it probably was.

Choosing one of the sections, Donovan clipped his target sheet up and sent it whizzing away from him, far enough away that when he hit it, his father would nod approvingly. He loaded his clip into his gun, but before he raised it, his father placed a hand on his arm.

"Disassemble it and reassemble it," he said.

Donovan dropped the clip out and started rapidly taking apart the gun.

"What is the number one rule of protecting someone?" his father asked.

"Always know where your charge is," Donovan said, his answer quick and concise.

"What do you do if you think someone is tailing you?"

This was an answer Donovan had thought basic a week ago, you use reflective surfaces to check, but he had been wrong.

"Stop, turn around, face them so they know that you could identify them. If unclear whether I am being tailed at all, this action will let me see if anyone quickly turns away or acts at all suspicious."

The gun lay in pieces on the table before Donovan and he reversed his work, connecting everything together once again. His father watched his progress without comment, his arms tucked behind his back.

"Three elements to spotting someone more than once?"

"Once is common, twice is coincidence, third is intentional."

"Protocol for walking with your charge in public?"

"Always keep them on the inside, that way my body is between them and a sniper or an attack from the street."

Donovan slid the last piece of the gun into place, raising it and aimed it at the target sheet.

"Again."

Donovan lowered the gun and repeated the act of breaking it down.

"What is your role?"

"Shield, protector."

"What is your main goal?"

"Keep my charge alive."

Donovan's fingers seemed to fly over the pieces assembling it again.

"What is fear?"

"A chemical reaction in my system warning me that danger is near?"

"What do you do with fear?"

"Use it to keep me alert for potential attackers."

"Can you erase fear?"

"No, but it can be used to make me faster, stronger, prepared."

"Whose life matters most?"

"My charge."

"If there is a bullet fired, who takes it?"

"I do."

Donovan raised the gun, aimed it at the target and fired three times, each shot finding its mark. When he dropped his arms, he felt his father's hand on his shoulder and faced him. For a long moment, they stood eye to eye in silence.

It was a silence that felt new to Donovan. It was one of pride, but of something more. There was a depth to it that spoke of his father's love for Donovan but something else, almost like sadness but not one of grief but of missing.

His father gripped his shoulder and Donovan knew right then he wasn't reading the silence wrong, his father was going to miss him.

Then the most shocking thing of Donovan's life happened, his father hugged him.

Donovan tensed, completely thrown, but then he hugged his father back.

The hug didn't last long before both of them backed away. His father placed both his hands on Donovan's shoulders and Donovan could feel the weight of what was coming next and knew that it would be what he needed to hear. Knew it would be the thing that would help him get through the hardest days with Link. Help him face complications head-on.

"I love you," his father said. "And I am so proud of you."

Leaving It All Behind

There was a foghorn in Donovan's room, blaring at him. It was a side effect of sharing a room with James whose snore could alert the coast guard hundreds of miles away.

It was a snore that Donovan had grown up with and learned to sleep through. It was a sound that a small part of him knew he would miss, but right at that moment all he wanted to do was smother James's face with a pillow.

Curbing the desire for the sake of his mother, Donovan crept to his window and opened it. There was no need for subtlety. James could sleep through the apocalypse without stirring. Donovan dropped to the ground and slid the window shut. Overhead a silvery moon watched over the Marine base and lit Donovan's path. It was late enough that he only encountered the gate guards who nodded at him.

At the beach, Donovan tugged off his shoes and dumped them onto the sand. Shoving his hands into his pockets, he crossed to the water's edge and stared out on the endless expanse. The moon shivered in the ocean's face, rippling on the waves. Letting out a breath, Donovan sank onto the dry portion of sand, draping his arms over his knees.

Tomorrow his life changed.

Tomorrow he left his home.

Tomorrow he left his family.

His brothers.

It would be the first time Donovan had ever traveled to the East Coast. There it wouldn't even be warm, it was still in the heart of winter. He would face so many unknowns. He didn't know what snow was like to live with. Cold was a thermostat that dropped down to 30 degrees at the worst. City life was nothing he had never experienced beyond a week's visit here and there.

He was about to deal with things he had never imagined he would deal with and he was doing it all on his own.

Donovan's throat tightened. He was alone, in the dead of night, if he was going to let himself feel anything or break it was now. Because he couldn't let himself break down around his brothers.

They had been raised around Marines, Marines didn't cry. They didn't show weakness. Fear. Or trepidation. His mom would say that crying was a way of releasing emotions and was good for him to do but he knew he couldn't. He couldn't cry.

Still, Donovan felt himself on the verge, overwhelmed by a weight of uncertainty that he would never admit to. What had been asked of him was a huge honor. It was a task that he should feel proud about. But all he felt right then was alone.

Before Donovan could give in to his weakness, he heard the shuffle of footsteps on the sand. Swallowing, he buried his emotions, blinking to keep from betraying himself. Clint plopped onto the sand beside Donovan, gazing out on the water.

The two brothers sat there, silhouettes in the night.

"I had to get out of there," Donovan said. "James was going to kill my eardrums if I didn't. I will not miss that."

It was a lie they both knew but Clint didn't point it out. Donovan dropped his gaze, digging his heel into the sand, making a deep grove.

"He's been such a pain lately," he said.

"He's jealous," Clint said. Donovan scoffed, disbelieving. "It's true. Of all of us are, you're the youngest yet the one to leave first. To have a job that any of us would love to have."

Donovan scowled, continuing to dig through the sand, not wanting to think about tomorrow. "It's only because I can pass as a twelve-year-old. I'm not sure that's something to be jealous about."

"Yeah, but James is only two years older, he thinks that he was the better choice because of maturity."

"Who's the mature one? He's been beating up on me more than ever and been a complete jerk."

The truth of it hurt Donovan in a way that he would never admit. Of all his brothers James and he were in someways the closest. Part of it was due to having to live together and being close in age. But over the last couple of weeks, James had acted like none of that was true.

"He's going to miss you," Clint said.

"I find that hard to believe. You've seen what he's been like."

"It's because of that. He doesn't know how to say goodbye. None of us do."

Donovan didn't say anything. It made sense but he didn't want to let James off the hook. Already when the fact that he was going to have to leave was weighing on him, his best friend had been making it worse by pushing him away.

Another pair of footsteps crossed over to them and Brock took the spot on Donovan's other side. His hair was a tangled mess and he was carrying something in his hand.

"What took you so long?" Clint asked.

"Do you know how hard it is to get anyone to give you alcohol when you're the commander's kid and they could be shot for their actions?" Brock asked.

Neither brother argued this because they knew it was true. There were many things they hadn't been able to experience because of the fear their father instilled in the other Marines. Still, Brock lifted two beer bottles, handing one to Clint who twisted off the cap.

"How'd you manage it then?" Donovan asked.

"Private Wilson is out seeing his girlfriend and so I snuck some from his room."

Clint took a drink and handed the bottle to Donovan. He drank. It didn't taste good but that wasn't the point of drinking beer anyways. They didn't talk for a while, listening to the lapping of the waves. The absence of James made the night harder to bear than Donovan thought it would.

When he decided that it was better to simply return home and try to sleep, he heard someone else approaching. He looked back and saw James making his wobbly way towards them, yawning as he did so. He fell to the sand next to Brock, almost falling backward.

"Why didn't you losers wake me?" he asked, snatching the beer bottle from Brock's hand.

"Like that's ever possible," Clint said.

James shrugged. "True."

Donovan relaxed. Even if his brother had been awful to him lately at least he was here. Though with his presence, the completion of their quartet brought back the tightness to Donovan's throat and he balled his fists shoving his sadness down.

"Remember when we executed an ambush on Commander and got grounded for a month?" Brock said.

The brothers all chuckled, playing out the memory in their minds.

"Or when Donovan tried to snipe us with paintballs from the top of the roof?" James said.

"What do you mean tried?" Donovan asked, taking the beer from Clint. "I nailed you all so hard you had welts for two weeks."

"Though we did repay that, didn't we?" Brock said.

They laughed as Donovan grimaced, taking a drink. They had. They had attacked him leaving him with a sprained wrist that their mother was furious over. Donovan hadn't complained, he had earned the payback.

"What about the time we stole Corporal Diego's stash of cigarettes and smoked them, nearly killing ourselves in the process," Clint said.

Donovan could still remember the livid glow of his father's face when he had found them. None of them had been teenagers at the time. Brock was the oldest at twelve and the mastermind of the terrible idea.

"Remember our attempt at making mom breakfast and almost burning down the house?" James asked, laughing.

"I told you we shouldn't have tried to make pancakes. We didn't even know how to cook eggs," Clint said.

The boys all fell into laughter, picturing their mother's amused smile as she put out the fire and finished the project they had started, all of them doing their part to clean dishes and set the table as a way of apologizing for their bad culinary skills.

As the moon drifted across the sky, they relived moments in their lives like they were trying to box them up so Donovan could take them with him.

When they had exhausted their store of antics, they fell into a somber silence, memories swirling in the air around them. Donovan blinked out on the sea, feeling the solid presence of his brothers surrounding him. Feeling how he was going to lose this.

"Hey Donny, maybe you'll finally get a serious girlfriend," James said, breaking the quiet.

"Everyone around me will be twelve or thirteen years old," Donovan said. "That would be disturbing."

James winced. "I do not envy you."

There was truth in his words that helped Donovan forgive his brother for the previous weeks.

"At least it's only for a few months," Brock said.

"Unless he gets elected," Donovan said.

"Then it's only fours years," Clint added.

"Unless he gets reelected," Donovan countered.

"Then it's eight years."

No one said anything, the scope of what Donovan was walking into settling on all of them. Donovan fiddled with the empty beer bottle, wanting to break it, watch it shatter.

"But don't worry," Clint said. "we won't let you have to only talk to middle schoolers all the time."

"Yeah," Brock said, voice quiet. "We have your six, doesn't matter how far away you are."

"You got us," James said.

Donovan gripped the bottle, dangerously close to breaking. He couldn't. He couldn't let himself leave his brothers with the image of him crying. He had to be strong like they were. He had to prove that he was going to be okay on his own though he wasn't sure he believed it.

Donovan's eyes stung and he could barely breathe past the lump in his throat. Needing to joke or make some comment that would keep him from crying, he glanced at Brock but what he was going to say was stolen from him.

Brock's eyes were glassy and he was blinking so hard that Donovan was sure he would break his eyelids. When Donovan looked to James, James was staring at the sand, clenching his fists as something slid down his nose and plopped onto the sand. Clint wasn't fighting it, accepting his emotions like none of the rest could and letting his tears spillover.

At the sight of his brothers breaking the rule of a Marine, Donovan bent his head to his knees and let himself feel the grief of having to leave them behind. None of them made a sound, because they couldn't let themselves go that far even though they were all aware of what the others were doing.

When Donovan raised his head, Brock clapped his hand on his shoulder, jostling him affectionately. "You better make us proud or we'll fly over and beat you up."

"Like you could do that?"

Donovan wrapped his arm around his brother's neck, pulling him into a chokehold. Brock fell sideways crushing Donovan beneath his weight and James dove into the fray, pulling Brock away but didn't get far as Clint barreled into James. The roughhousing continued until they were all covered in sand and their sadness had been concealed once more.

Laughing, sandy, and breathless, they all clambered to their feet. Brock slung his arm around Donovan's shoulders, James took the other side and Clint latched himself onto James.

Locked together the brothers made their way home as the sun began to rise on the new day.

The First Meeting

The black SUV pulled up to the curb and stopped. Washington D.C.'s downtown was bustling with men and women heading home. The sun dipped towards the horizon, stretching the shadows on the sidewalk. The gentle hum of the engine was all that filled the inside of the car. Donovan stared up at the apartment building, taking in the shine of the glass walls and the trim doorman out front.

Donovan's father cleared his throat, drawing his son's attention. At the sound, Donovan straightened and met his father's level gaze. For a moment, neither of them said anything. Then Ted placed a hand on his son's shoulder.

"I'm proud of you," he said, his voice gruff from years of shouting commands. "I know you are an excellent choice for this job."

Donovan gave a single nod. "Thank you, sir."

His father smiled. It was a look Donovan could count the amount of times he had seen.

"Call us."

"I will, sir."

After another pause, Ted removed his hand and Donovan opened the door. A rush of late summer air converged on him. The chaos of city noises assaulted him and he had to stop himself from glancing around to identify each one. The sound was a harsh contrast to the roar of humvees, gun fire, helicopter propellers and jet engines he had grown up with.

Collecting his bag from the back of the car, he returned to his door. His father was looking at him with a serious expression. Though it was familiar, Donovan still stiffened his spine in response.

"You can handle this," his father said.

"Yes, sir."

Not wanting to show any sign of weakness, Donovan closed the door and gathered up his bag. Without looking back, he walked to the apartment building. A gray haired man with a wrinkled smile nodded to him and opened the door. Inside the lobby the decor was minimalistic, a polished tile floor, simple potted plants by the entrance and a dark wooden desk at the center of the space.

Waiting at the desk was a woman in her late thirties with blonde hair, vibrant blue eyes and a welcoming smile. The second Donovan walked in, she moved forward.

"You must be Donovan," she said, hand out stretched.

"Yes, ma'am," Donovan said.

Her smile widened. "Please, call me Monica."

"Okay, Monica."

The woman was at eye level with him only due to a pair of high heels. She gestured to the elevators and in silence they climbed inside. Once the doors shut, she spoke.

"William told me how he knows your father," she said.

"Yes, they were both in the marines together, ma'am." Donovan cleared his throat. "I mean Monica."

She gave a light laugh. "Don't worry too much about it, I'm sure there is going to be a lot you'll have to adjust to."

Donovan gripped the handle of his bag a bit tighter.

"Nothing I can't manage."

"That is what both William and your father assured me of. They also mentioned you were sixteen?"

"Yes."

Monica glanced at him, as if trying to make sense of the figure beside her that looked barely older than her son with a very young face. In that look Donovan could see the mothering side of her coming out. It was not something he needed or wanted.

"I grew up on a marine base, I know how to deal with situations."

She nodded in understanding and let the mother side of her back off. The doors slid open, revealing a beige carpeted hallway. Monica led Donovan past an apartment.

"This is ours," she said, waving a hand to the doorway, "but before you meet Link, I'll show you to your own place."

When she opened the next door over and flipped on the light, Donovan found himself in a spacious apartment. It was fully furnished with TV, couch, coffee table, dining table and chairs. The color scheme was masculine with black and browns. The walls were bare. It felt as if it had been pasted from a magazine ad.

"The cabinets and refrigerator are all stocked with the basics," Monica said, taking a step towards the kitchen. "I make a weekly order so let me know whatever you need."

She turned once as if taking in the apartment. "I wasn't sure how you wanted it decorated and so I took the liberty of doing it for you. If you have a problem with anything just let me know and I can have it dealt with."

Donovan focused on Monica and realized she was staring at him expectantly.

"It all looks great. Thank you."

Relieved, she smiled.

"I'll let you settle in. Come over when you're done and you can meet Link."

"Alright."

The door clicked shut behind her and Donovan let his rigid posture relax. His bedroom back on the base could have fit inside the living room without taking out any of the furniture. Setting his bag on the coffee table, he unzipped it. Stacked on top of his clothes was a framed photograph of his family. He took it out and put in the table right below the TV.

Pulling his gaze away from the familiar faces, he looked over the apartment again. It felt too big and empty. There was no shouts from his brothers. He couldn't hear the telltale crush as Clint got annoyed and tackled James to the ground. Brock wasn't on the couch bent over a disassembled gun, cleaning it. The air was tinged with the scent of cleaning supplies when it should have smelled like gun cleaner, cooking food and dirt.

For the first time in his life, the world felt quiet.

Forcing away the sense of loneliness that was beginning to creep in, Donovan grabbed his bag and walked down the short hallway to what he guessed to be the bedroom. The color palette was the same, a black comforter was draped over a dark brown bed with pillows in black cases. A coffee colored armchair sat in one corner. Beneath the window was a glass desk. Barely taking note of it all, Donovan went to work unpacking his life.

In under fifteen minutes everything was put away and the apartment looked no different. Knowing it couldn't be put off any longer, he walked to the neighboring apartment. Monica opened the door at his knock.

"I'll get you a set of keys so you don't have to worry about knocking," she said. After a glance back at the hallway, she frowned, thinking. "Do you want me to introduce you? Or..."

"I'm fine on my own."

She smiled encouragingly. "He's in his room. Last door on the right. I'll be out here if you need me."

She shifted and Donovan could see the apprehension she was feeling. Following her directions, he walked to Link's room. The door was ajar and Donovan eased it open. On a queen sized bed was a twelve year old kid. His gangly body was curled together as he sat crossed legged. It almost appeared as if he could get lost in the depths of the bed. Long brown hair hung in front of his face and his gaze was fixated on his phone.

Donovan stepped forward, glancing at the walls and taking in the posters that decorated them. Link's light hazel eyes darted to Donovan and a scowl formed on his forehead.

"Who are you?" he asked, still not ready to ignore his phone.

"I'm Donovan Keller," Donovan said. "I'm going to be protecting you."

Link let out an annoyed huff and went back to his phone.

"I'm sure you've been debriefed on the situation and understand how this will work."

Link didn't look at Donovan but still managed to give off the impression of irritation.

"I will be with you when you leave the apartment," Donovan continued. "I'll attend school with you and any activities you may be involved in. Living next door will be the cover for our friendship."

Link let out a mocking snort. "We're not friends. I don't even know you."

"You will in time," Donovan said, his voice controlled and even. "I know this will be an adjustment and I can understand how it can be difficult."

"No, you don't!" Link snapped, his eyes locking with Donovan, anger simmering in them. "You don't understand anything! My life is complete crap! Not only do I have to deal with some random guy I've never met but I have to go to a new school! I have to leave everyone I know behind because now that I have freaking brown hair and wear glasses they would ask questions. So no! You don't understand and don't pretend to be my friend! I don't need you!"

Link scrambled off his bed and stormed past Donovan. Though he tried to knock Donovan with his shoulder, his lack of muscle only managed to do damage to himself. Biting back a cry of pain of his new bruise, Link left the room. Taking a breath, Donovan counted the years before him. Behind him, he heard Monica call out and the sound of a door slamming.

Rearranging his face into an impressive mask and strengthening his resolve, Donovan went after Link.

Becoming Friends

Donovan pulled his shirt over his head and reached for his bag. Around him, the boy's locker room was a chaos of sound. Boys jeered, taunted, challenged, mocked and laughed at each other. There was a loud crash and a weak groan as one kid was knocked sideways into the wall of metal. Laughter sprung up from the guilty party. As someone retaliated, a body stumbled into Donovan, knocking him into his locker.

A stab off irritation shot through him, knowing he couldn't pummel whatever idiot had bumped into him. Instead, he looked around at the younger kids who had done the pushing. The smiles on their faces faltered at Donovan's cold eyes and controlled expression. Having to deal with the immaturity of Link's classmates had not been one of the problems he had foreseen, but it was one that was the most frustrating. Compared to the twenty and thirty-year-olds he had grown up with, everyone was like kindergarteners.

Collecting his bag, he closed his locker, his eyes never leaving theirs. Scared, the boys shuffled back to getting changed, waiting for Donovan to leave before continuing their antics. On the opposite wall of lockers, Donovan found Link just opening his to get changed. When Donovan paused next to him, Link shook his head in annoyance.

"I don't need a babysitter to change," he muttered under his breath.

"I'll be outside."

"Like I care," Link said as Donovan walked away.

Beyond the door classes were still in session, the patter of voices humming in the air. Donovan stepped away from the door and leaned against the wall, shoving his hands into his pockets. Despite the couple months that he had been protecting Link, they seemed no closer than before. Though Donovan knew Link's anger wasn't meant for him, but for the man who had put him in this situation, it still didn't mean it wasn't tiring to constantly be fighting with the person he was charged to watch.

A steady stream of boys left the room, jostling each other as they raced towards the school entrance. Across the way, the girl's locker room door swung open. The buzz of gossip slipped out as a group exited. When the collection of girls noticed Donovan, they scurried away whispering and giggling together. One girl broke away from the group and approached him. She barely looked thirteen with lengthening limbs that weren't natural to her yet, a sweet round face and wispy black hair that she wore up high in a ponytail. Hugging her binder, she smiled at Donovan, a dimple appearing in one cheek.

"Hi, Donovan," she said, her voice high and innocent. "What are you waiting for?"

"Link. His mother drives me home."

"You live in the same building, right?"

He nodded.

"That's cool. So," she tucked a loose strand of hair behind her ear. "It's my birthday today-"

"Happy birthday," he said.

The well wish made her blush and her smile to widen. At the look, Donovan knew it had been the wrong thing to say. With each day he was learning the best ways to navigate this small world and more likely than not the best thing to do was keep silent.

"Thanks," she said. "Well, I'm having a pool party tomorrow and I didn't know if you wanted to come?" She pulled out a colorful piece of paper and handed it to him. Across it in bubble letters was information about the party. "You can bring Link if you want to."

Donovan took the offered paper. "Thanks."

Wishing for more of a positive response, the girl paused. But when Donovan said nothing more, she shuffled awkwardly.

"I hope to see you there!" she said, then joined her waiting friends.

As she was pulled into their fold, their voices rose and snippets of their conversation made it back to Donovan.

"I can't believe you actually asked him!"

"What did he say?"

"He's so hot!"

The last comment sent the girls into rounds of giggles as they hurried away. Donovan let out a sigh, trying not to feel annoyed at girls that were simply growing up. The door beside him opened and he looked over. It wasn't Link. From inside he heard the taunting remarks of someone pleased with their strength. Sensing that something was off, Donovan walked back into the locker room.

At the center of the room, a circle of five guys were shoving Link around like a ball in a pinball machine. Their laughter was harsh and their smile jeering.

"Where's your boyfriend, wimp," one asked.

"I don't have a boyfriend," Link growled back, trying to fight the strong grips that pushed and pulled at him.

"You should stop," Donovan said.

The boys around Link looked over. They were the ones that had already hit their growth spurt and easily stood as tall as Donovan.

"You worried we're going to hurt your special little friend?" one of the biggest taunted.

As Link tried to use their distraction to break out of the circle, one of them yanked his collar, jerking him to a stop. It was then his eyes found Donovan's and in them, he could see Link's fear, shame, and anger.

"Let him go," Donovan said, calmly.

A boy with a face made for scowling took a step towards Donovan.

"Or what?" he sneered. "You're going to make us?"

"Yes."

This made all the guys laugh, their eyes connecting as if to make sure none of them were going to ditch.

"There's five of us, idiot."

"Makes no difference, you're all equally stupid."

As if they had rehearsed it, the group charged at Donovan. When the first guy reached him, he stepped to the side and shoved the boy's shoulders, using his momentum to send him sprawling onto the floor.

A fist came from the left and Donovan caught the arm, twisted it and kicked the boy in the side, making him fall into a bench. Another fist appeared and Donovan blocked it while kicking another kid in the stomach. He flicked the throat of the guy who had tried to punch him. Choking for air, the boy clutched his neck. The final boy lunged for Donovan, letting out an angry cry. Donovan twisted and the boy collided with his other fallen companions. The fight was over in less than a minute. Link stared at Donovan wide-eyed.

"Can your mom still give me a ride home?" Donovan asked.

The question snapped Link out of his thoughts and he nodded. They left, Link glancing back at the moaning figures.

"Umm...thanks for that," he said, as they headed towards the entrance.

"Sure." After a pause, Donovan spoke again. "You're coming over to my apartment."

"Why?"

"Cause I'm going to teach you how to fight your own battles."

Facing Facts

As the elevator doors dinged open, Donovan hoisted the last load of wood onto his shoulder and stepped out into the hallway. After eight trips from the lobby to his apartment carrying the thick planks, his shoulder was aching. As he passed by Link's apartment, the door opened and twelve-year-old Link watched as Donovan walked by, neither of them saying a word.

Donovan nudged his apartment door open with his foot and hauled his load into his room, dropping with a loud bang onto the other pile of boards. Moving to his tool bag - sitting on his bed, he removed a measuring tape and a pencil and began making marks on the wall. He was determining the height when Link walked in. He stared at Donovan who was penciling in a line on the wall.

"What are you doing?" Link asked, scowling.

"Building a bookcase."

Link eyed the pieces of wood skeptically. "Why?"

Donovan turned around and had to stop himself from rolling his eyes. "Because I need a place to put my books."

Frowning more, Link surveyed the rest of the room, spotting a small bookcase shoved aside.

"Why not use that one?"

"Not big enough."

"You could just buy a bigger bookcase then," Link said.

Donovan could have, but he felt to help maintain his sanity he needed to build one.

"I could," he said, "but I know how to make one so I'm going to."

Donovan walked back to the tool bag and rummaged through it pulling out a hammer, a box of nails and L shaped brackets.

"How do you know how to make one?" Link asked.

Donovan wanted the kid to leave him to his work but since this was the most Link had talked since Donovan had arrived five months ago, he figured it would be a bad move to push him away.

"Two years ago," Donovan said, kneeling down by the pile of boards. "I broke the one in my room by overloading it. My dad said since I was a fool to break it, it was a good time to learn how to make one myself. One that was stronger. So he taught me."

"How old were you?"

"Fourteen."

Link sank onto Donovan's bed, his face crumpling. "My dad never taught me to build anything."

Donovan didn't reply. When Link wasn't taking out his anger over his father on Donovan, he was playing the pity card. In the first couple of months, Donovan had been sympathetic, but all that sympathy was dried up and he wanted to smack the kid out of his self-pity. But knowing his mother would kill him if he did, he simply said nothing at all.

Donovan had hoped teaching Link how to throw a punch would have bonded them, but when Link failed at it after one time, what connection Donovan thought he had created was gone. Now they were two people stuck together. Link wanted someone to hate and pity him and Donovan wanted to be left alone.

As Donovan was hammering two boards together, his phone rang. He raised his head as Link snatched the phone off of the bed.

"Who is James?" he asked.

"My brother."

Link's forehead creased and Donovan knew what was coming next so he went back to his work.

"Did you know I have a half brother. I didn't even know that until a few months ago. I've never met him. He doesn't even know I exist." Donovan banged away at the nail, not saying anything. "Does James know who I am?"

"Yes."

Before Donovan knew what Link was doing, the phone was answered and James's voice came through the speaker.

"Sup Donny?" James said.

Biting back his frustration at Link answering his phone without asking, Donovan sank back on his heels.

"James you're on speaker and Link is in the room."

There was a pause and Donovan knew James was trying to figure out why Donovan answered the phone and put it on speaker with Link there.

"Cool," he said. "How's life little man?"

Link hunched his shoulder's. "It sucks. I found out who my father was only a few months ago and have barely seen him."

Donovan didn't know what Link's plan was, have the whole world to know his sob story and get everyone to feel sorry for him or make his father pay by having everyone know how he failed?

"That's great," James said, surprising Link and making Donovan fight against a smile. "Look, Link, why don't you stop being a piss ant and taking out your issues on my brother. A lot of people have worse fathers than yours, ones that beat them half to death for no reason. So why don't you grow up and deal with it? Sound good?"

Donovan put his back to Link so he wouldn't see that Donovan was trying hard not to burst out laughing at Link's stunned expression. After a second, Donovan heard the phone thump to the mattress and Link leave. Sighing, Donovan grabbed the phone and set it beside him.

"You shouldn't have done that," he said.

"Yeah, well mom's love and patience tactic hasn't been working for you, I figured someone should lay it out for him. He'll be fine. Everyone needs a smack in the head once and a while."

"Thanks."

When Donovan had first arrived in DC he had tried to keep the worst of the situation from his brothers, but they knew him well enough that they could tell when he was lying and had pried the truth from him. Though Donovan hated to talk about Link to them since he was supposed to be protecting him, it had helped him not feel so alone.

"What are you up to?" James asked.

"Building a bookcase."

James's laughter filled the room. "You already break the one you have."

"No, but I would have eventually. It's a pathetic bookcase it can only hold about thirty books. I had to start piles along the walls."

"Of course you did. How many books did you read this week?"

"Nine."

James clucked his tongue in disappointment. "I knew this would happen. You go to middle school again and become a slacker."

Donovan smiled as he screwed an L bracket into one of the boards. "Give me some credit, two of the books were a thousand pages long."

"I still think you're falling behind."

"That's not what my teachers think. Yesterday I was sent to the principal's office for getting caught reading in class again. It's the twentieth time."

"I always knew you were a troublemaker. What did you do?"

Donovan lined the board he was working on against the wall and connected the other half of the L bracket to the wall.

"I told the principal to check my file. When she saw that even as a transfer student I had the highest GPA in the school she didn't really have much else to say to me. Even suggested I think about skipping a grade. I told her I would take it under advisement."

James laughed again and Donovan smiled, feeling how the sound made his apartment not feel like the barren place it usually did.

"How did your date with Rosa go?" Donovan asked, moving to the next section of planks.

"Great, she thinks I'm devilishly handsome and the funniest man on the planet."

"She hasn't texted you back, has she?"

"Shut up. You know the ladies love me."

"Only when they don't know you have two older brothers that are better in every aspect."

"You should picture me giving you a rude hand gesture right now."

"Okay, I'm effectively wounded by it."

"How's your love life?"

Donovan snorted. "It's great. Yesterday a girl came up to me already blushing, giggled before she said hi, giggled after she said hi; so if I play my cards right we might hold hands under the table during recess."

"Player player. Don't go breaking too many hearts, alright?"

"I will work hard to resist. How did the attack on Corporal Dalton go?"

When James laughed, Donovan knew he was in for a good story.

"Okay, so we roped Private Wyatt into the scheme. And you know the bunker on the east side? It was the perfect lookout."

As James laid out the story, Donovan worked, his smile slowly fading away. Everything James said, he could see clearly in his mind. But it was only in his mind. He couldn't smell the ocean in the air. Couldn't feel the heat of the sun on his neck. Couldn't see the reactions of all the men in on the plan. He was thousands of miles away in an apartment that never knew noise.

By the time James finished the story, Donovan was barely listening, finding it too hard. He gave the right response to it, but it felt hallow. Luckily, James was called away and Donovan didn't have to try to pretend for any longer.

"I'll talk to you later," James said.

"Okay."

"Got your six."

Donovan paused, the hammer hovering above the nail. "Yeah man, got your six."

The line went quiet and Donovan tossed his phone back onto the bed. Returning to his work, he let the focus of putting together the bookshelf be all that he thought about.

He was halfway through the project when Link walked back into his room, hands shoved into his pockets. Donovan glanced at him but went back to drilling a hole into the wall.

"Hey," Link said.

"Hey," Donovan said.

Link shuffled his foot and Donovan continued working, completely fine with ignoring the kid.

"I'm sorry," Link said.

Donovan looked at him, not saying anything. Link broke away from Donovan's gaze.

"Your brother what he said...I'm sorry...that I've...you know been getting mad at you and everything."

Donovan nodded in acceptance, grabbing a screw.

"Do you want help with your bookcase?"

Donovan stared at Link who shrugged and offered him a half-smile.

"Yeah," Donovan said. "You can help."

Getting In Trouble

The metallic bang of Donovan's locker door opening got lost in the noise of the busy hallway. Donovan put his social studies textbook inside his locker then stared at it. Social studies. He'd taken the class ages ago, but now he repeated history. It didn't get better the second time.

For a brief moment, Donovan wanted to take the textbook and rip it in half, just to feel the way the binding split in his hands. He didn't. Instead, he did everything he should, shut the locker door, and zipped up his backpack.

Out of nowhere, a hand grabbed Donovan, spun him around and shoved him against his locker. Stars popped in his vision as he hit his head against the hard metal. When he blinked the dizziness away, he found himself staring at Kyle Denton. A boy, though only fourteen, already matching Donovan for height and muscle. Kyle glared at Donovan with murder in his eyes.

"Stay the hell away from Lauren," he growled.

Donovan knocked Kyle's hand away from his shoulder.

"You're delusional if you think I even have a clue what you're talking about," Donovan said, passively.

Kyle shoved Donovan again and anger flared inside Donovan. The emotion raced through him, sparking every nerve, tensing every muscle. It felt good, it felt energizing.

"There's a rumor going around that you two were making out behind the gym," Kyle said.

Donovan knew he shouldn't do anything, should let this boy have his say and eventually leave. But Donovan needed this. Needed a fight. Needed action. He craved it.

So when Kyle went to shove Donovan again, Donovan slammed his palms into the boy's chest, sending him staggering back. Kyle stumbled, shocked at the strength and force of the hit. Donovan could feel the edge of his lips wanting to curl. He vibrated with energy. After a year of mind-numbing monotony, it felt good to have a change.

Fury sparked in Kyle's eyes as Donovan's reaction created a wall of onlookers. Students silently asked Kyle if he was going to take that kind of treatment. Kyle stormed forward, fists curled. He swung at Donovan with all the grace of a lumbering bear. Donovan wanted to laugh at the boy's lack of training. With barely a thought, Donovan blocked the punch and smacked Kyle on the side of the head, like he was reprimanding an unruly kid. The strike disoriented Kyle and he tottered to one side, clutching his ringing ear.

The crowd clapped and shouted their appreciation. Enough of them had been on the receiving end of Kyle's anger. Donovan stood, hands waiting at his sides, knees bent slightly, waiting for another chance to put this punk in his place. It felt amazing to move, to act, to fight. He willed Kyle to come at him again.

But Kyle didn't get the chance.

Before Kyle could charge Donovan again, a teacher cut through the onlookers and grabbed Kyle's arm and pointed at Donovan.

"Both of you are coming with me," he said.

At the stern command and twisted features of the teacher, Donovan crashed back into himself, struck by the stupidity of his actions. Had he really gotten into a fight with a fourteen-year-old? Grabbing his backpack, he trailed after the teacher, spotting Link in the crowd, eyes wide. Shame crept over Donovan. He wasn't a middle-schooler looking to prove he could take on the school bully. He was a Marine given a job. A job he'd ignored for his own selfish reasons.

The teacher deposited both boys in the principal's office. Principal Warren was a woman in her late fifties with a soft voice and an unyielding will. As both Donovan and Kyle took seats before the desk, Principal Warren thanked the teacher and looked to the two students.

"Which one of you wants to tell me what happened?" she asked.

Kyle crossed his arms and slouched in his chair, clearly not planning to speak. Donovan knew that in most instances neither boy would talk and the principal would be forced to give them equal punishments. But Donovan didn't plan on following that unspoken rule.

"After hearing a rumor that I kissed his ex-girlfriend behind the gym Kyle shoved me into my locker telling me to stay away from her. If he'd asked around at all he would have found out I don't date and barely talk to girls. But since he acted without thought it shows a sense of insecurity. As for the aggression he displayed instead of asking me about it, I have a feeling he also struggles with anger issues."

As Principal Warren stared at Donovan in shock, Kyle turned on Donovan, growling with anger, fist curling.

"Go ahead," Donovan said to Kyle. "Do something violent. It will only prove my point."

Kyle froze, caught between wanting to make Donovan bleed and proving his words incorrect.

"Donovan, why don't you wait outside while I talk with Kyle here," Principal Warren said.

Donovan left, slumping into a chair in the main office. The bell rang, emptying the hallways of students. Leaning over his knees, Donovan dropped his head into his hands. He struggled with the monster inside him, giddy at having acted out. He hated how good it felt to break from the constraint around him. Years of growing up on a Marine base surrounded by a million opportunities to get into trouble and be wild hadn't prepared him for this dull job.

Even during his homeschooling when Donovan would get antsy, his mother would send him outside to run two miles before coming back. She understood he'd been born a very physical boy who needed to move or he'd get in trouble. Donovan shook his head, he hadn't changed at all.

The office door opened and Donovan glanced up. Link stepped inside, hands buried in his pockets. At least the dullness of this life had meant even if Donovan left Link for a minute nothing was likely to happen. Link slid into the chair beside Donovan, looking at everything but him.

"What happened?" he asked.

Donovan stared at his laced fingers, the lines of his palms.

"Kyle thought I made out with Lauren."

Link snorted, then tried to cover up the sound.

"Sorry, it's just...you never talk to girls, why would he think you'd do anything with one."

Donovan almost smiled. "Because he's insecure."

Link laughed and scuffed his shoe against the floor.

"How'd you get out of class?" Donovan asked.

"Faked a stomachache."

Donovan nodded. As the office door opened again, both boys looked over. Donovan's stomach dropped as Brock strode in, grinning.

"What are you doing here?" Donovan asked, standing.

"You seriously got in a fight?" Brock asked, not at all masking his amusement.

"What are you doing here?"

The grin widened and Donovan felt the urge to start another fight right there in the office.

"As your guardian, I was called and told to come by since this is a serious matter."

But from the way Brock appeared on the verge of laughter, it wasn't a serious matter to him.

"Did someone steal your lunch money?" he asked.

"I'm going to kill you," Donovan growled.

"Hey now, you already got into one fight, don't go picking another. I'm not some preteen you can beat up. I'll wipe you out without blinking."

"You sure about that?"

Donovan said it but held no delusions about what the outcome of a fight between Brock and him would be. Brock had fifty pounds on Donovan, all of which was pure muscle and Donovan ran five miles each morning to keep himself looking thin and younger.

Principal Warren appeared in her doorway, letting Kyle out and motioning for Donovan and Brock. At the sight of the Principal, Brock's entire demeanor changed, becoming serious like the responsible guardian, he supposedly was. When all three of them were seated, Principal Warren laid out the issue to Brock.

"As this is the first time we've had a problem with Donovan and since he was provoked by Kyle I'm only going to suspend him for the rest of the day. I wanted you here so Donovan would understand the seriousness of the situation. We don't tolerate violence in this school."

"I'm firmly against violence as well," Brock said.

Donovan fought against kicking his brother hard and bursting out laughing. Brock had once thrown Donovan off a roof. Half of the scars Donovan had were because he got into scraps with his brother. But still, Principal Warren believed Brock's sincerity.

"I'm glad to hear it. I appreciate you stopping by."

A few more words were exchanged then Brock led Donovan out of the office with one hand on his shoulder, ever the stern guardian. Once the door closed behind them, Donovan shoved Brock's hand away which only made him smile. Signing Link out, the trio headed out of the school. As they walked down the front steps, a girl with honey blonde hair rushed up to Donovan, worried. Without having to ask for her name, he knew her.

"Look, Donovan," Lauren said. "I-"

Donovan cut her off with a steely glare. "Next time you make up rumors to boost your social standing and piss off your ex-boyfriend leave me out of it."

Lauren opened her mouth to reply, but Donovan kept walking. Only a minute into the drive home Donovan wanted to fling the door open and dive out because of Brock cracking jokes at Donovan's expense and Link's overblown account of the fight. From what Link told it had involved blood and broken bones.

Telling Link to go home, Donovan escaped to his apartment the second Brock turned off the car. Donovan's peace lasted half a minute before Brock walked into his living room.

"Go away," Donovan said. "I don't want to hear any more jokes. Go call Clint or James, annoy them. I don't care."

"I'll go," Brock said. "But first I wanted to see your face when you got the call."

Dread washed over Donovan.

"What call?"

As if in answer, Donovan's phone rang. He thought of ignoring it but knew he couldn't outrun whatever waited for him. Scowling at Brock, he dug out his phone. It was his mother.

"You told her!" he shouted.

"Yup, on the way to the school."

Donovan grabbed the rubber ball from his coffee table and hurled it at his brother. Laughing, Brock dodged the ball and slipped out the door.

"Good luck!" he called back.

Donovan sank to the couch, staring at his screen. He had to answer. He knew he had to. Closing his eyes, he put the phone to his ear. He said nothing.

"Ah, so it must have been really bad," his mother said.

Donovan clenched his fist, Brock needed to die. A slow painful death.

"Talk to me," his mother said.

Her soft voice reminded him of countless moments when he'd misbehaved and she sat beside him, one arm draped around his shoulders, asking him what was going on. It cracked the shell around him that everyone else saw. A shell that protected his inner thoughts and fears.

"I can't," he said.

His mother hummed in thought. He didn't know how she did it. Even when he barely spoke she understood things that no one else would. It might have come from being a therapist to some of the toughest and closed off Marines or because she knew him. Most likely a mix of both.

"It felt good to get in a fight, didn't it?" she asked.

Donovan curled and flexed his fingers, saying nothing.

"My troublemaker," she said with a gentle laugh.

The sound teased the truth from him because she didn't blame him or judge him.

"I want..." He swallowed hard, the words concrete in his throat. "I want to quit."

The statement felt like a sledgehammer to everything he'd grown up believing. Marines don't quit. Yet he wanted to.

"I know you do," his mother said.

"You do?"

Donovan didn't know why he was shocked.

"Of course. I've heard it in your voice for the last three months every time we talk. I knew this job would be a challenge. You don't have Clint's patience, James' friendliness, or Brock's determination. But," his mother said before Donovan could feel less than. "You have a loyalty that is stronger than you know. You feel like quitting, but I know you won't because you've grown loyal to Link. That's what you need to focus on."

The truth bolstered Donovan, but still that monster that needed to do more than die of boredom growled inside him.

"I don't know how I can keep doing this without wanting to get in trouble just so I'm not bored. Books aren't cutting it anymore."

He'd lost count of how many books he had read that year. Though they brought a distraction to the dullness of classes, they also reminded him he sat stuck in a classroom when more waited outside.

"Well, I think I have a solution for that."

"What?"

"I think it's time you graduate middle-school and go to college."

Stepping Out

The school hallway rang with conversations and laughter. It buzzed around Donovan, but he wasn't a part of it. Leaning against a set of lockers with his hands tucked into the pockets of his coat, he was the proverbial fly on the wall, seeing and hearing everything without taking part in it. Outside the front doors snow swirled in small tornadoes, the coldness at odds with the warmth of the school.

Donovan watched the awkward pair across the way with little hope. At fourteen, Link was lanky, bashful, and self-conscious. The girl he talked to appreciated his attention but held a self-satisfied air, believing if one boy paid her attention others would. Link was doomed.

Even from where he stood, Donovan knew that Link's attempts at flirting were poor, but Donovan also knew that if he was by Link it would be worse. He knew that when he stood by his friend, no one seemed to notice Link.

Donovan's focus was diverted when a senior girl approached him. He knew who she was. Everyone did. Kia Mitchell: Valedictorian and Student Body President.

On top of that she was pretty, confident, and driven. She was the type of girl you expected to be President or run her own company. Recently turned eighteen, she was also one of the few students who was the same age as him.

She stopped in front of Donovan with a straight-forward expression. There was no wistful, enamored glint in her chocolate brown eyes. Instead, she looked like she planned to take on an army.

"Hi, Donovan," she said.

Donovan greeted her with his customary silence. Just because she didn't gaze at him with the longing other girls did, didn't mean anything. He'd learned saying nothing at all worked best.

"Okay," she said, not at all offended or fazed by his lack of response. "So I'm going to ask you to go to Winter Formal with me tonight and I know that your answer will be no, but I need to ask it anyways."

This surprised Donovan, but he didn't show it. Kia waved her hand as if he had commented on the strangeness of her statement.

"It's because I wasn't asked to Winter Formal." Donovan had a feeling it wasn't for Kia's lack of attraction, it was that she intimidated most guys. "When I told my mother this, she said,'well you're a feminist, that doesn't mean you can't ask a boy yourself'.

"Which I think is stupid because if I really am a feminist can't I just go by myself? But she doesn't seem to think that's an option. Anyways, I know you'll say no when I ask you and that means I can return home and tell my mother that I asked someone and they said no."

Donovan almost wanted to smile at the explanation. The past two weeks he'd been asked fifteen times. Each time it was an older student and he knew they felt he would be flattered by the offer since he was a freshman. All of them had left disappointed. But Kia's offer was definitely a first.

"Okay, so Donovan will you go to Winter Formal with me?"

"Yes."

"I knew you'd say no and I appreciate...wait what?"

Donovan held her gaze and she frowned. "I don't think you understand. You were supposed to say, 'no'."

"I know."

Kia crossed her arms and huffed, clearly annoyed.

"You're friends with Aubrey Troy," he said.

"Yes, I am."

"Does she have a date tonight?"

At this Kia, rolled her eyes. "No, cause she turned down every offer hoping that Trevor would ask her. Which he didn't."

"If I went with you to Winter Formal, would she go with Link?"

Kia relaxed, understanding what he was getting at. "So you want to go with me, just so your friend will have a date, is that it?"

"Yes."

Donovan knew Link would strike out with the girl he was flirting with and wanted to give him hope. This was the best he could do.

Kia regarded Donovan with pursed lips, trying to figure him out. But he gave nothing away and she slowly nodded.

"Okay, it's a date."

"Does that mean you'll bring me a corsage?" The comment slipped out before Donovan could take it back.

Kia laughed. "No, I don't like you that much. Do you want us to pick you up or meet you here?"

"We'll meet you here."

Kia flashed him a mischievous smile. "Okay. Wear something pretty."

As she left, Donovan found himself watching her. For the first time, in a long time it felt like he'd met someone who was on the same level as him. He both wanted more of it while knowing he couldn't let it last. When Link trudged over to him, head down, Donovan put aside his own emotions to deal with the ones of his friend.

"Wanna talk about it?" he asked.

"Not really."

"Okay, then let's head home. You have a date to Winter Formal with Aubrey Troy tonight."

Link jerked his head up, shocked. "Really?"

Donovan smiled. "Yeah, let's go see if we can find something to wear."

***

"I think I'm going to throw up," Link muttered as they walked up the school steps.

Even from outside, they heard the thump of music emanating from within. Light shone out the front windows, beckoning everyone inside. Students laughed and rushed for the front doors, dressed up and ready to undo all their hard work with endless dancing. As they entered, Donovan's phone rang and he pulled Link out of the foot traffic to answer.

"Take deep breathes," he instructed Link, before saying hello to the caller.

"Donny, everyone's in place, where are you and Link?" James asked.

Donovan turned his back to the flow of sparkling dresses and button-down shirts paired with slacks. He closed his eyes, already regretting his words.

"We can't play a heist on GTA tonight," he said. "...We're at Winter Formal."

James' laugh made Donovan wince.

"Are you serious? Winter Formal! Oh you poor high school boy."

Donovan wished James stood beside him, so that he could throw his brother out a window.

"Did you ask someone to go with you? Please tell me you made a cute sign that said 'Brittany will you go to Winter Formal with me?' No, better yet did you go on the school speaker system and ask her during first period?"

"I hate you."

Donovan hung up on his bother's laughter, wishing he could strangle James. But when he faced Link, all his annoyance with his brother vanished. Link looked ready to pass out. He gripped Link's shoulder.

"It's going to be okay," he said. "Just tell her she looks beautiful. Don't worry about stammering, it will make her like you more."

Link nodded, but still looked nervous. Knowing there was no way to ease his pain, Donovan led him to the gym. Waiting for them in front of the doors were Aubrey and Kia. Both girls looked beautiful in bright dresses, updos and simple make-up. When the two pairs met, Link swallowed, eyes-wide.

"Wow, you look...wow," he said.

Aubrey beamed under the praise. "You clean up nicely as well."

With Donovan's help, Link did look good in a green shirt that enhanced his hazel eyes and slacks. Donovan went for all black, hoping it would help him disappear into the background. But Kia smiled at him, showing that his tactic wasn't going to work.

"Aren't you going to say I look pretty?" she asked.

Again Donovan was struck by how she didn't stare at him with desire. It was relieving. And for that reason he let himself relax a fraction.

"I'm your date," he said. "I believe it's your job to tell me I look pretty."

Kia's smile widened as a curious spark flashed in her eyes. "Don't be cute."

"I thought I was supposed to be pretty?"

She shook her head. "I'm serious. Don't be cute. In the fall I'm leaving for Harvard and I don't want to think that I'm leaving behind something wonderful when I go."

Donovan slid his hands into his pockets, admiring this girl's bluntness.

"Candid. I respect that."

Kia laughed. "Candid? What are you an eighty-year-old man?" She held up her hand. "Wait, please don't tell me you're a hundred-year-old vampire? Cause you should know I like the sunlight and I don't want you to change me."

"I get the feeling that no one could change you."

Kia shook her head. "Oh, this night is going to do me in, isn't it?"

A hint of a smile touched Donovan's lips. After two and a half years of being surrounded by immature kids, years younger than him, it felt strange to find someone who was on equal footing as him.

"Do we want to head inside?" Aubrey asked the group.

To Donovan's complete astonishment, Link held out his arm to Aubrey. Giggling with delight, she took it and Link led them into the gym. The setup was as Donovan predicted for a school dance and so didn't give it more than a single cursory glance. Already in the center of the gym students danced.

Before anyone could say anything, Aubrey pulled Link towards the dancing mass. Donovan watched, happy to see that Link wasn't completely helpless. In fairness, he danced better than Donovan imagined he himself would. Dancing had never been an activity that he performed growing up.

"Wanna dance?" Kia asked.

"No."

Despite the bluntness, Kia merely smiled. "So you really did say yes because you wanted Link to have a date for tonight?"

"I did."

Donovan could feel Kia scrutinizing him but didn't return her gaze.

"You know that no one can make you out?" she said.

"I wasn't aware that I was a common conversation topic."

That was a lie. Donovan couldn't help notice that eyes followed him at times, baffled by his choice in friend and lack of desire to be part of the 'In crowd'.

"You are," Kia said, clearly enjoying that she got to be the one to break this news to him. "You see you don't make sense. Your looks mean you could be one of the popular kids. You look athletic enough to be part of a sports team, but you're not. You seem to have only one friend and I'll be frank he comes off as awkward and a nerd. You barely talk to anyone. It's said you have the highest grades in the school even though most of the time you're in class you're reading."

At the last comment, Donovan wondered if he should give up the habit. It might make people question how he could have the highest grades without doing any work. He hated the thought of having to bear high school classes for a second time, but he couldn't risk too many questions.

"Is that all?" he asked, uncaring.

"The final thing is everyone is speculating that you are an extremely shy person. It would explain most of the factors, except that it's hard to look at you and think 'shy'. Somehow it doesn't fit."

Donovan nodded. Being shy did make sense of all the oddities he displayed. He wondered how many people would believe that he was shy if he told them.

"I like to keep to myself is all," Donovan said.

"How do you explain your friendship with Link then?"

In the midst of their back and forth, the pair had found themselves drifting to a table and sitting down. At the question, Donovan leaned back in his seat, watching Link move in closer to Aubrey, his confidence growing.

"Our friendship is one of those things that happened by necessity. I moved into the apartment right next to his and he was a transfer student. I became his only friend. It wasn't a easy transition for him. You could say I feel protective."

Kia shook her head and Donovan could see the beginnings of feelings emerging.

"Donovan Keller, you are something else. Where anyone would take the chance to improve their social standing when they hit high school, you've stuck with your friend." She sighed and Donovan could see her trying to reign in her admiration for him. "You're loyal and I hate you a little for being that way."

Unable to help it, Donovan chuckled, but not for long and not very loud. "Why? I thought loyalty was a good quality to have?"

"It is. But it's making me like you more than I should." She twisted in her seat so she faced him. Her expression sobered and Donovan paused, not sure what was coming next. "After tonight, I can't see you or talk to you."

Donovan raised his eyebrows. "Why?"

Thinking through it, he could understand why. There wasn't a more dedicated and focused student than her. She would leave this school and make a name for herself. A boy would get in the way. And one that was three years behind her. But still, he liked how easy it felt to talk to her and didn't wish for that freedom to go away.

"I don't want a boyfriend," Kia said, confirming what Donovan thought. "They are distracting and too much work. And if I talk to you longer than tonight I might rethink my stance and I can't do that."

"Okay," Donovan said, retreating into himself, knowing he needed to pull back before he could realize how much he missed finding connection with someone beyond his brothers.

Kia held his gaze, almost sad. "You're respectful too. You're really making it hard."

"I could tell you you look ugly and be condescending if that would help."

She laughed. "But I would know it wasn't real."

The sound died away and she sat there, staring at him. After a breath, she shook her head and Donovan knew she'd come to a decision. Disappointment seeped into his chest. Two and a half years felt like an eternity and there still lay before him six more.

"I can't even stay here with you tonight," she said. "I'm going to lose my head over you."

Donovan gave her a sad smile because he knew she would leave. "Can't have that. I think your head looks best right where it is."

Kia leaned forward and kissed Donovan's cheek. "Someday you are going to make some girl very happy."

"Just not you."

She stood and he could tell it took a lot of effort. "Just not me."

When she walked away, Donovan watched her go, feeling the emptiness of the chairs all around him. He might make some girl happy someday, but that day stood so far away he couldn't imagine it ever being true.

A Single Lie

Donovan pulled the car up to the curb outside a classic two story house and cut the engine. The keys had barely been yanked out before he was out of the car. He slammed the door but the sound was lost in the pounding bass that escaped through the open windows. On the lawn were clusters of students in grades above his, laughing and leaning against one another. By the time Donovan made it to the front door, his frustration was dangerously close to anger.

When he walked in, he was hit with the full force of the party and the noise that indicated it was not likely to stop any time soon. A brunette in a tight black dress turned and beamed when she spotted him.

"You came!" she said, her pink nails curled around a red cup, her lipstick left on the rim.

"No," he said. "I didn't."

Before she could question his response, he was diving into the chaotic scene. Cups littered the floor and hands. The smell of alcohol was heavy in the air and only intensified as he pushed his way further into the house. Couples were plastered to the walls, their bodies pressed against each other, oblivious to any sense of privacy. With each search of the bottom floor rooms, Donovan came up with nothing. Growling in irritation, he moved to the kitchen.

The space was packed with kids pouring drinks and shouting at each other over the music that hammered away on their eardrums. In a far corner, Donovan spotted a familiar face and cut his way to it. The bored looking guy nodded as Donovan approached.

"Derek, where is Link?" he asked.

Derek opened his mouth, but a sharp laugh sliced through the noise. Before Derek could offer up an answer, Donovan was gone. He made his way to the backyard. The air was breathable out there and it felt like the temperature had dropped ten degrees.

The sky was dark and the stars had been blotted out by strips of thick clouds. Past the patio, a group had formed, some cheering while others looked on without comment unable to stop watching. Donovan shoved his way to the center. What he found flared his emotions.

Laying on the ground was Link, a guy bigger than Donovan kneeling beside him, his fist raised. A redhead was crying beside them, yelling at the attacker.

"Brent! Stop! Please!"

Before Brent could strike Link again, Donovan yanked him off and flung him to the ground. The crowd shuffled back but made no sign of leaving.

Brent barely had time to register the turn of events, before Donovan was gripping his shirt front and punching him in the face. Brent's head snapped back, but Donovan held tight, keeping him in range. With the next hit, Brent's eyes rolled and there a sickening crunch. The sound snapped Donovan from his anger. The presence of the crowd and the voices that scattered speculations rushed in around him, grounding him.

"Listen," he said, giving Brent's shirt a shake. "Hit my best friend again and I'll end you."

When Donovan released Brent, he slumped against the grass. Donovan turned back to Link, who was still laying on the ground, one hand pressed against his side. The beginnings of a black eye had pushed his lid shut and Donovan made himself walk forward instead of doing more damage to Brent. The weeping girl knelt beside Link, her hand on his shoulder.

"Move," Donovan said.

The girl stumbled back and Donovan eased Link up, wrapping Link's arm around his shoulders. With the motion, Link winced and Donovan hoped it was a sprained rib instead of a broken one.

The crowd parted as he led Link back through the house. Eyes followed them, whispers picking up behind them. The redhead trailed behind them and even followed them out to the curb. Donovan helped Link into the passenger seat. When he rounded to the driver's side, the girl leaned against the door.

"I'm so sorry, Link," she said. "I really am."

Link managed a nod and Donovan started the engine, making it clear that this was the end of the conversation. The music of the party faded behind them and nothing but silence was left in its place. Donovan never once looked at Link. Link, feeling all too keenly the weight of Donovan's silence, sank deeper into the seat.

"I'm sorry," he said, sounding like a little kid.

For a long moment, Donovan gave no sign that he had heard. His face was hard and there was no sympathy in his eyes. When Link let out a tired breath, Donovan slammed his hand on the steering wheel.

"What the hell were you thinking?" he said. "You lied to me! On top of that, you decided to get involved with Brook. How stupid could you possibly be?! Brent's possessive even as an ex-boyfriend and has anger management issues. He's been sent to the principal's office three times in the last month because of fights he started. How could you carelessly put yourself in so much danger!" Donovan gripped the wheel. "I can't protect you if you're going to be an idiot! Why would you do to something so completely stupid?"

After the fury of the words had diminished, Link answered.

"I wanted to be normal," he whispered.

At the sadness in Link's voice, Donovan's fear and anger dimmed. He looked over at Link. At fifteen he was scrawny, still growing into his body. Sighing, Donovan ran his hand through his hair.

"I get it. But there's nothing I can do to change that. What I can do is make sure you don't get your ass kicked. But only if you let me."

Link nodded and stared out the window, taking in the blurring scenery.

"How'd you find me?" he asked.

"Find My Friends app."

Quiet filled the car but this time the tension from before was no longer a part of it.

"Did you mean it?" Link asked.

Donovan glanced over then back at the road.

"Mean what?"

"Mean it when you called me your best friend?"

Donovan rested back into his seat, the last of his frustration vanished.

"Yeah, Link, you're my best friend."

A weak smile slid onto Link's face. "You should know you're my best friend."

Despite the state Link was in and the events of the night, Donovan smiled.

Reelection

Donovan felt made of stone as he watched the tv, waiting. On the couch, Monica sat with her fingers relaxed on her legs, seemingly completely untroubled. Beside her, Link couldn't stop moving. His leg bounced and he kept repeatedly curling and flexing his fingers.

Despite there being only the three of them in the apartment, Donovan felt like he could feel the whole city, the entire country waiting for the announcement.

This was it. This moment right here could be as defining to Donovan's life as the one where his father introduced him to Senator Douglas. One moment that had set his life on a new path. Now here he was again.

Monica reached for Link's hand to be a comfort to him but Link pulled away, running his hand through his unruly hair. Donovan said nothing, offering nothing. They were both in limbo but in vastly different ways.

Finally, the woman on screen finished her short break down and announced, "William Douglas has won the Presidential election."

Everyone on screen rose and started applauding. From beyond the apartment, Donovan could hear the cheers of other tenants. Even outside he heard the faint shouts of people excited about the announcement.

But inside the apartment was completely silent.

Four more years gone. That quickly four more years of Donovan's life were solidified. No going out to get a job. No moving on. Remaining here.

For four more years.

Link stopped moving. He sat as still as Donovan, staring at the screen. Donovan knew he should say something. Say anything to be there for Link, but right then he felt trapped in his thoughts.

The past two months he'd mistakenly hoped for an end of his job. He'd seen how close the race was and Donovan had thought that maybe...

Link rose without saying anything and walked into his room, shutting the door behind him. Monica looked after him, worried. She looked to Donovan and he broke from his stunned state. She rose, but Donovan held up a hand.

"It's okay," he said.

He knew what he needed to do. He knew what role he needed to play. Monica could give a mother's comfort. But it was Donovan's reassurance that he knew Link needed.

Shoving his emotions away, he moved to Link's door. When he knocked, Link didn't answer.

After a second, Donovan walked in and took a seat at Link's desk chair. He swiveled this way and that, portraying an easy comfortableness.

"Seems like you're stuck with me," Link said.

"Pretty sure I was supposed to say that," Donovan said.

Link looked over and Donovan gave him a half-smile. It had the desired effect, Link relaxed. Though they had become close over the years, Donovan knew Link worried Donovan wanted to leave.

Donovan would never let Link see what he wanted. His job was to protect Link, Donovan took that to mean in all forms: physical and emotional.

"You know," Link said, placing his laced fingers behind his head. "I really wanted him to lose."

Donovan continued to slowly rotate in the chair as this was just one of the many normal conversations they shared.

"I thought..." Link rubbed his eyes. "I thought if he was no longer President that it might be different...That, I don't know, I could... see him more. Possibly meet Mason..." He shook his head. "Now it all sounds stupid."

"Wanting something is not stupid," Donovan said.

Link looked at him, completely open and vulnerable. Despite how much he'd grown since they first met, he seemed so young to Donovan at that moment.

"It's only four more years," Donovan said. "You could still have that. It's merely postponed."

Link nodded, staring up at the ceiling. A stretch of silence passed between them. Donovan could see how Link settled into the old reality: rarely seeing his father and not knowing a half-brother. He sighed deeply.

"It means four more years for you as well," Link said, coming out of his thoughts.

He could tell Link was now wondering how Donovan felt about it. For his part, Donovan showed nothing of his inner turmoil.

"Then it will be another good four years," Donovan said with a quick smile. "Do you know how easy it is to do homework when you already know the answers?"

Link laughed. "Yeah, true." He sighed again but it was filled with relief and contentment. "I'm really glad I won't have to finish high school without you."

"Only because I'm your personal tutor."

Link met his gaze, earnest. "No, because I'll have my best friend with me."

"I wouldn't have it any other way," Donovan said back, ignoring the twisting in his gut. He stood and slapped Link's shoulder. "Go talk to your mom, she's worried about you."

Link sat up. "Where are you going?"

"For a run and you're too slow to keep up."

"Also not insane to go out in this weather."

Donovan snorted. "Barely cold enough to call it weather. Go talk to her."

Donovan nodded to Monica as he left the Evans' apartment. She smiled gratefully at him and invited him to stay for dinner but Donovan needed fresh air.

He hurriedly changed into workout clothes and grabbed his phone before dashing down the stairwell. He hit the sidewalk and took off. His head pounded with scenes he'd had to endure over the last years. Scenes of mindless stupidity and immaturity. Endless days of mind-numbing dullness.

Four more years.

Four more years.

Donovan ran harder as if he could outpace the future. But he couldn't it. It was everywhere around him in the shouts of celebrations and loud toasts for what was to come with Douglas still as President. Some shouted with anger but their voices were drowned out.

Four more years. He couldn't do it. He couldn't face all those years of loneliness. Of boredom. He couldn't do it. He couldn't.

He made it to the Mall and the reflecting pool before he exploded. He screamed, loud and long, forcing every bit of frustration, emptiness, and despair out.

He sank to the ground, draping his arms over his legs. No one came to see if he was all right. No one even cared that he'd screamed.

Donovan sat there breathing hard, hating how much he wanted to sit there and never return.

His phone buzzed and he retrieved it from his pocket. Only then did he realize how many messages and calls he'd missed. All from his brothers. Two miscalls from his parents.

James: *Thought I rigged the election, seemed I didn't rig it the right way.*

Clint: *How are you?*

Brock: *I have a sniper rifle and gear, say the word.*

James: *are you crying out of happiness because you get to keep your cushy job?*

Clint: *Donovan, answer*

Brock: *Bad joke.... or was it?*

James: *Dude, answer*

Clint: *Donovan come on man, talk to me*

Brock: *Donovan, respond.*

James: *DONNY WONNY!*

Clint: *I called.*

Brock: *Now you're making me worry and I hate that.*

As Donovan scrolled through the mess, his phone lit up with all three brothers calling. With a sigh, Donovan answered. He didn't say anything, only fell back on the cold grass.

"Donovan," Brock said, concerned.

"I'm here," Donovan said.

But he didn't want to be. He wanted to be home with his brothers. But technically they weren't even home anymore. They all had jobs and lived in other states. Even Brock who lived in DC was currently on a job in Seattle.

Donovan was alone.

"So are we," Clint said as if he read Donovan's thoughts.

"I can't do it," Donovan said. "I can't do four more years. I..."

"Then don't," James said.

Donovan let out a derisive laugh.

"I'm serious," James said. "You signed on for one term with Link. There was a possibility of a second but it was never settled on. You could give up this job. Someone else could take your place."

"He has a point," Brock said. "You were sixteen when you signed on. Asking for a full eight years wasn't in the agreement."

"We would back you up with Douglas," Clint said. "You don't have to figure this out alone. If this is what you need to do, then we support you."

Donovan couldn't say anything, overwhelmed by his brothers' support as well as the idea that maybe he didn't have to endure another four years. He thought of the freedom, the ability to choose what he wanted to do. The relief it would mean to break away from high school.

How amazing would it be to be able to connect with people his age? How wonderful would it be to have the liberty of talking to a girl? To be able to date a girl.

The hopefulness of it all wrapped around Donovan until he knew with complete certainty that this was what he would do. He'd quit and be able to live his life.

A single image stopped him in his tracks: Link looking young and vulnerable.

Link saying Donovan was his best friend.

Donovan's daydream shattered.

"I can't," Donovan said. "Link."

None of his brothers argued. None of them said anything.

They knew Donovan. And they knew Link. How much he'd grown over the years. But also how much he still relied on Donovan. How much Donovan cared for Link.

Slowly, Donovan sat up, his resolve solidifying.

"We're proud of you," Clint said.

"And we're here for you," James said.

"We got your six," Brock finished.

"Thanks," Donovan said.

With the encouragement for his brothers still with him, Donovan headed back.

Link: the one reason he was okay with giving up his freedom.

Naturally

Link popped up beside Donovan as he was shoving his textbook into his locker. Donovan glanced at Link.

"Will you skip lunch and go to the drama class auditions with me?" Link asked.

Donovan returned to fitting his books together. "Kelsey Knight isn't going to date you."

"How do you know?" Link asked.

Donovan closed his locker and leaned against it, facing Link.

"Because she's a junior and you're a sophomore. Also, Ethan Jacobs is in drama and he looks like the next Chris Evans."

"I still want to try," Link said.

"It's a musical. You are tone-deaf."

"Then I'll be in the ensemble."

Donovan stared at him and Link looked back, clearly determined to go despite the evidence pointing to the fact that it was futile.

"All right," Donovan said. "Let's go."

Grinning with victory, Link led the way to the school's theater. It was a lavish auditorium with plush velvet red seats and a large, empty stage. Already crowding the first few rows were the hopeful auditioners. Kelsey stood next to Mrs. Hartley, the drama teacher, who welcomed all the eager students. Donovan and Link quickly claimed seats in one of the empty rows.

"This is just the singing portion of the audition," Mrs. Hartley said. "We will get through as many as we can before the bell. When your name is called go on stage and give us all you got."

Kelsey called out a girl's name and a perky girl leapt from her seat and scurried up the steps to the stage. Once there she announced her name and the song she planned to sing.

Before she began, she lifted her gaze to the rest of the theater's audience. When she noticed Donovan, she froze and her face flushed red.

"Any time you're ready," Mrs. Hartley prompted.

When the girl continued to stare at Donovan and he stared back, Kelsey too glanced his way, which encouraged others to do as well until half of the students had found Donovan sitting behind them.

Finally, the girl on stage managed to start singing, though her voice shook and wasn't very loud. When she finished, Mrs. Hartley thanked her and the girl hurried off the stage.

As the next student took the girl's place, Kelsey slipped from her spot and trailed back to where Donovan and Link sat. Sitting on the armrest of the chair in front of Donovan, she leaned in.

"Hey, Donovan," she said.

Donovan greeted her with his customary silence.

"Are you auditioning?" she asked.

Donovan shook his head.

"Okay, then do you mind leaving?" she asked.

This surprised Donovan. "Why?"

"Because some of the girls are nervous about auditioning with you watching."

"But aren't they supposed to be used to people watching them?"

"Yes, but there's apparently something about your intense blue-eyed stare that flusters them. Also, they're okay with average-looking audiences and well..."

Donovan thought this was ridiculous, but looked to Link. Link was looking at Kelsey, resigned.

"I never would have gotten your notice, would I?" he asked.

Kelsey looked at him like she was surprised someone was sitting next to Donovan.

"Sorry?" she said.

"Whatever," Link sighed and stood up.

Donovan followed him out of the theater and towards the cafeteria.

"Look on the bright side," Donovan said. "Kat Martinez takes pottery, you can join that."

Link rolled his eyes.

"Lynn Satō looks good in tights, you can join ballet. Maybe you look good in tights."

"Shut up."

Donovan laughed at Link's annoyance. But when a group of girls nearby cut off their conversations at the sound, Donovan swallowed his laughter and dropped down a blank face. It hardly worked, their whispers not low enough for him to avoid hearing his own name. When they were far enough away, Donovan jostled Link's shoulder.

"You shouldn't worry," he said. "You'll meet someone and it will be in a natural way."

"Yeah, like what?"

Donovan shrugged. "You're in the library and you both are looking for the same book."

Link simply looked at Donovan like he was ridiculous.

"Easy for you to say," Link said, as they claimed their normal lunch table. "All you have to do is look at a girl and she won't just join a class for you, she'll walk right over."

"That is not true."

"Really? You want proof." Link pointed to a girl in a cheerleading uniform walking away from the lunch line. "Look at Summer, the girl who is out of pretty much everyone's league, and see what she does."

"Just look at her."

"Yup, just look at her."

Donovan shook his head but did as Link wanted, focusing his gaze on Summer. For a few seconds, she didn't notice his stare but when she did, she paused for a fraction.

Donovan thought she might simply smile and wave but instead, she redirected her steps towards his table.

"See," Link muttered as Summer stopped in front of them, smiling.

"Hey, Donovan. You beckoned," she said teasingly.

"Sorry," Donovan said. "I didn't mean to stare."

"It's okay. I didn't know if you wanted to come sit at my table with me but weren't sure how to ask it so figured if you looked at me I would come over here and invite you."

Link snorted behind his hand.

"I didn't realize my eyes said so much," Donovan said.

"A lot more than you normally do. So is that a yes?"

"Sorry, I'm good here."

"Okay, well know that the invitation is open. If you can't speak then just look my way and I'll wave you over."

She spun around, her high ponytail swishing behind her back.

"See," Link said. "Proof."

Donovan let out a sigh. "It seems we both aren't going to meet anyone in a natural way."

"Yeah," Link muttered. "We're on opposite ends of the same boat."

"It seems so."

Hooky Day Reflection

Donovan rested against the bathroom wall feeling a sense of dread, though he let none of his emotion show on his face. Link leaned towards the bathroom mirror, fastidiously fixing his hair.

In the last couple of months, he'd hit a growth spurt and the oversized uniform now fit his fifteen-year-old body better. The height change had given Link a boost of confidence, one Donovan didn't feel.

Link pulled back and inspected himself then frowned.

"I don't know," he said.

Donovan moved forward, though he knew it wouldn't make a difference he wanted to help. In the reflection the contrast between them both was clear. Donovan knew it wouldn't matter what Link did, height wouldn't change the fact that Donovan's entire image was meant to draw attention away from Link. But still...

"Turn around," Donovan said.

Link did, looking uncertain.

"Take off your blazer," Donovan said.

Link did as instructed and Donovan stuffed it into Link's backpack, making sure it hung out. It gave the blazer an air of careless rebelling, not that Link was a rebel but maybe it would help. Donovan then loosened Link's school tie, unbuttoned the top button, and roughly rolled up his shirt sleeves.

"Tuck in your shirt more to take away the excess material," Donovan said.

Again, Link did as he was told. The end result was a naturally careless appearance. With Link's messy hair the image wasn't entirely a lost cause.

"Not bad," Donovan said.

Quickly, Link spun around to get a view of himself. He nodded, pleased with the rebel-type vibe his messed up uniform gave off, even if his boyish features contradicted the truth of his appearance.

"Okay," Link said. "Let's go."

Link picked up his backpack and hoisted it onto his shoulders. Donovan instantly tugged at one of the straps and Link unhooked one arm, leaving the bag dangling from one shoulder. Donovan nodded and Link perked up, encouraged. Donovan still couldn't match Link's hope. He'd interacted with Lexi Cummings before and he had little hope that Link's improved look would make a difference.

They left the bathroom and cut through the hallways to the library where their study group already sat ready. Link slowed as he took in the table's occupants.

Lexi sat at the head, casually scrolling through her phone. Honey blonde curls effortlessly cascaded over her shoulders, her beautiful face highlighted by natural-looking makeup, and her uniform perfectly fitting her slim frame. Link swallowed and stopped walking altogether, his confidence from his bathroom transformation seemingly disappearing at the sight of Lexi.

"Breathe," Donovan said under his breath, nudging Link forward.

Link shuffled forward counteracting all the work on his new look. Donovan directed Link to a seat adjacent to Lexi and took the spot beside him, nodding to their other two team members. Lexi raised her gaze from her phone, glanced at Link, and quickly skimmed over him setting her eyes on Donovan.

Donovan felt his heart sink in his chest at the disregard for Link. He could sense Link's disappointment emanating from him.

"Good you're here," Lexi said, offering a warm, inviting smile. "Let's get started. I don't want to fail this test."

Donovan didn't hold her gaze, instead drew out his notebook and pencil. He avoided Lexi's bright blue eyes, acting as if all he could see was his open notes.

"I've divided up the work study topics and figured we can work in pairs to do the research and then share it with each other. I thought I could work with-"

"I'll work with Link," Donovan said, still not looking up. "Unless you wanted to?"

Finally, he lifted his gaze to her in question. Lexi looked to Link, who sat slouched in his chair, not in a rebellious manner but in one of dejection. Donovan knew the state of his thoughts when he didn't even give Lexi a hopeful look.

"Actually since you and I both wrote our essays on one of the topics, I thought it would be more efficient for us to be paired since we already have an understanding of the subject. Link can work with Anthony since they both shared the same topic as well. That leaves Madison to work with Emilio. Does that work for everyone?"

As everyone nodded in agreement, Donovan looked to Link. He toyed with his pencil and Donovan made a decision right there. It might be a stupid decision but he hated seeing his friend so low.

The hour of study went by slowly in Donovan's mind as he focused on the work material and interacted as little as possible with Lexi. To her credit, she followed his lead doing the work, though she did take opportunities to lean in close to him under the guise of reading over something he'd found. When she did, Donovan caught Link glancing at them.

By the time the hour was up, Donovan had inhaled enough of Lexi's perfume to have a headache and had reaffirmed his plan. As everyone packed up, Lexi sidled closer to Donovan.

"Hey," she said. "If you're free this weekend I would love to work some more, you're very efficient and I appreciate that."

Donovan kept his focus on loading up his stuff. "Sorry, I can't. We can stick to working during free period."

"Oh, okay. Well, if you change your mind here's my number. See you."

Lexi left a piece of paper right beside Donovan's backpack and left.

"What's that?" Link asked.

Donovan grabbed the paper and stuffed it into his pocket. "Trash."

Link looked at him and Donovan knew he was aware of the lie.

"Come on," Donovan said. "We're leaving."

Link followed along, only realizing what Donovan meant by leaving when Donovan guided him out of the school and towards the front gates.

"Wait!" Link said, looking back at the school. "We still have two classes we need to go to."

"Not today," Donovan said. "There are no tests in our last two periods and I can teach you the material that's covered. We're playing hooky for the day."

Despite the nervous glance Link threw over his shoulder again, there was a bounce to his step. Donovan fought a smile. Link needed to get away, and Donovan needed to as well.

The Metro took them close to the Mall and Donovan felt pleased when he saw the mass of people wandering around the Reflecting Pool and the memorials. At the height of cherry blossom season, the tourists were out in droves and school field trips were in full swing. Everywhere he looked he saw teenage girls laughing and taking pictures of each other. It was the perfect spot for what Donovan came to do.

Link gazed around, surprised by the number of people and completely oblivious to Donovan's plan. Donovan strolled around, letting Link take his time adjusting to the sheer amount of girls around him. They walked up the Lincoln Memorial steps and stopped to take it in.

"Can we really do this?" Link asked.

"It's fine," Donovan said. "You needed a break. It will be fine."

Link relaxed with the words. Donovan found a spot from where to start their task and headed towards it.

As he descended the steps, he looked around, his eyes landing on a pair that made him hesitate a fraction.

He instantly knew who the blonde-haired boy was: Mason Douglas. Donovan looked for the Secret Service agent that should be nearby but couldn't spot one.

He looked at the girl next to Mason but couldn't imagine her playing the role of bodyguard. She looked about fifteen with messy brown hair pulled into a ponytail and a uniform wrinkled, possibly on purpose.

The girl met his gaze with a pair of blue eyes that stood out against her light brown skin tone. She seemed an odd contrast with the First Son who looked polished and put together.

Donovan looked away first, searching the area again for the agent that should be there while also putting himself between Link and Mason. Seeing his half-brother was not the thing Link needed right then.

As they headed away from the memorial steps, Donovan spotted two men in black suits striding towards the steps and he relaxed. Mason had his agents, Donovan's concern wasn't needed anymore.

He put Mason and his female companion out of his mind.

"Okay," Donovan said. "Today you are going to flirt with girls."

Link whipped his head towards Donovan.

"What?"

"It's a perfect place for it," Donovan said. "These girls don't know me or you, you can be anyone and if it fails, walk away."

"I can't...I'm not...I can't do this."

"Yes, you can. The more you try the easier it will become."

Link breathed rapidly and Donovan could see him edging towards panic. He put his hands on Link's shoulders.

"It's fine," Donovan said. "All you need to do is go up to a group and be yourself. Tell them you are trying to find your group and point out your maroon blazer. Use that as an opening to say hi and introduce yourself. You can ask where they are from? There are a lot of school groups here, most likely they've come from some other state. You need to simply work on talking. You can do this."

"I really don't think I can," Link said.

"You can. You have the rebel vibe going for you. It will be okay."

"Can't you come with me?"

"No. We know how that goes."

Link scowled but nodded in resignation.

"I'll be on that bench over there," Donovan said, pointing to a spot under a tree. "I'll watch you. If it doesn't go well with one group keep moving. Find girls that are in twos or threes, a bigger group will be harder. Smile. It will be okay. You can do this."

Link didn't look like he believed that and Donovan wasn't feeling all that confident either but knew the more Link got out there the more he'd learn.

"Go on," Donovan said, shoving Link a bit.

When Link didn't move, Donovan walked away, hoping the embarrassment of standing there like an idiot would get him moving. Donovan sank onto the bench and watched as Link remained frozen.

"Come on," Donovan said.

Finally, Link moved, wandering for five minutes before he balled his fists and determinedly headed towards a pair of girls taking selfies by the Reflecting Pool.

For the next twenty minutes, Donovan watched as Link approached girls and talked for barely a minute before practically fleeing. Each time he looked at Donovan as if wanting to give up but Donovan shook his head and pointed to another group.

"Excuse me," a feminine voice said.

Donovan looked up and found a pair of girls smiling down at him. From their features, Donovan guessed they were sisters. One was closer to his age, probably seventeen while the other looked younger, possibly fifteen.

"I was wondering if you could point us in the direction of the American History museum?" the older girl asked.

They were both pretty with soft faces and bright eyes.

"It's two blocks that way on the right," Donovan said pointing. "You won't be able to miss it."

"Thanks," the older girl said. "We got turned around. Are you here with your school?" She gestured to Donovan's uniform.

"No. I skipped class," Donovan said.

The girl smiled, the action enhancing her attractiveness. "Playing hooky, huh?" She glanced at her sister. "Feel like walking two strangers to the museum? We've already lost our way twice, would hate to make it a third time."

Donovan felt his face warm with surprise and opened his mouth to say no but a thought struck him.

"Would you be willing to do me a favor?" he asked. "In exchange, I'll walk you to the museum."

The girl eyed him curiously. "What's the favor?"

Donovan found Link and pointed him out to the girl.

"Can you go ask my friend there for directions and then ask him to escort you both to the museum? I'm trying to help him build up his confidence when talking to girls. You're both pretty and it would really boost his confidence if you approached him."

At the compliment, the girls perked up.

"Give us a second," the older girl said. She tugged her sister a few steps away and they had a whispered conversation. They returned and Donovan could see the resolve. "Okay, we will but that means you both have to walk around the museum with us. Deal?"

Donovan didn't have to think about it, this would give Link time to find footing with keeping up a casual conversation and a place where topics were numerous.

"Deal," he said.

"Okay then. I'm Ariel and this is my sister, Claire."

"It's nice to meet you, I'm Donovan and my friend over there is Link."

"Link," Claire said. "I like that name."

The two girls headed off and Donovan pulled out his phone.

Donovan: Call me in half an hour yelling at me about skipping class.

Brock: You skipped class? Are you serious?

Donovan: Save it for the phone call. Be loud enough to be overheard.

Brock: Okay.

Donovan pocketed his phone and looked up in time to see Link headed towards him with Ariel and Claire alongside him. Donovan fought a smile at how elated Link looked at having succeeded in his mission.

"This is my friend Donovan," Link said, motioning to Donovan.

Donovan stood and waved. "Hi."

"I'm Ariel and this is my sister, Claire," Ariel said with a hint of an amused smile. "Your friend Link said you both would be up for being our guides to the American History museum."

Link held Donovan's gaze as if afraid he'd somehow decline the offer. Donovan nodded but didn't smile, he didn't need this turning into something that would only be complicated later on.

"Sounds good," Donovan said.

He took the spot next to Link and away from the girls. As they began to walk, he elbowed Link in the ribs.

"So!" Link said, startled. "Where...where are you both from?"

"Georgia," Ariel said. "We're here with our parents. They wanted to take a nap and trusted us to go out on our own. Hard to be nervous in a place with so many people always around. Then we got lost and found you."

Link grinned. "Lucky me."

At that, Donovan turned his face away, his smile too strong to contain. As they walked, Donovan gently guided Link into talking more until Donovan saw Link's shoulders relax and his steps become less hesitant.

By the time they reached the museum, Claire seemed genuinely taken by Link's boyishness while Ariel kept throwing Donovan appreciative glances. Glances Donovan tried not to react to but found a little difficult with how pretty she was.

When his phone rang, he inwardly sighed. He pulled out his phone and sent Link a nervous glance.

"What's up?" Link asked.

"I have to take this," Donovan said.

He took a single step away from the group and answered the phone.

"You skipped class!" Brock roared on the other end. Donovan winced and drew the phone away from his ear, aware of Ariel and Claire exchanging a look. "Do you know how this will affect your permeant record?! I don't know where you are, but you need to come home right now! This is inexcusable."

Donovan winced again and dropped his gaze, feigning embarrassment.

"I'm sorry," he said, quietly.

"You will be sorry. If you aren't home in twenty minutes you know what the consequences will be."

"Yes, sir," Donovan said meekly.

Brock hung up and Donovan lowered his phone, looking at the screen. Slowly, he lifted his head and met Ariel's eyes before looking away.

"Huh, we have to go," he said.

"Will you be okay?" Ariel asked, knotting her fingers. Clearly, Brock had done too good of a job.

"Yeah, but I'll be grounded for a long time and my phone will most likely be taken away."

This would conveniently mean Donovan would have an excuse not to answer any attempts Ariel might have of trying to contact him.

"Okay. Well, thanks for being our guides. Good luck with your dad," Ariel said.

Donovan nodded and took a step away, a silent command for Link to follow.

"It was nice meeting you," Link said to Claire.

She beamed and nodded. "Same."

Link waved as he joined Donovan and the two left the girls behind. As they headed towards the entrance, Donovan sent off a message.

Donovan: Thanks. You should have been an actor.

Brock: You owe me an explanation.

Donovan: I'll call you later.

Brock: Good. But you should know you are grounded. I'm very disappointed in you.

Donovan rolled his eyes and slipped his phone into his pocket. Only when they were back out in the sunlight did Link dare to speak.

"You seriously had Brock call and yell at you?" he asked, grinning.

"I didn't want them to get attached," Donovan said.

Link burst out laughing. "He scared me for a second before I realized who it was." He stopped and stared at Donovan, his smile frozen. "When did you have time to tell Brock to call, you were never on your phone."

Donovan hesitated, scrambling for an answer. But Link came to the conclusion before Donovan could form one.

"The girls approached you first, didn't they? Then you sent them to me," he said.

Donovan rubbed the back of his neck feeling bad.

"Thanks," Link said.

"You're not mad?" Donovan asked.

Link shook his head and started walking again. "No. It helped. I feel like I didn't do too bad with them."

"Not at all. I was impressed."

Link bounced along, smiling. Donovan knew that it might not last when they returned to school and the usual way of things but for that moment his friend was happy. That's all that mattered.

Everyday

Donovan followed Link into their math classroom and nearly collided with him when Link stopped abruptly.

"Woah," Link breathed out.

Donovan started to ask what Link was talking about but held in his question as he looked to the front of the room. Standing next to their teacher was one of the most beautiful girls Donovan had seen before. He knew she didn't go to their school, he'd have noticed her before. Besides, she looked to be about twenty. A college student then. But why come here?

Someone nudged Donovan and he in turned prodded Link to keep moving, though he wasn't alone in his stunned state. Every boy that entered the classroom froze for a second or two upon noticing the girl.

Donovan took his seat in the back row, directly behind Link.

"Who do you think she is?" Link asked, keeping his gaze on the girl though angling towards Donovan.

"College student here to shadow Mr. Henley," Donovan guessed.

The bell rang and Mr. Henley hushed the murmuring students.

"Class, I want to introduce Rosie. She will be my student teacher for the next month. She's in her second year of college and plans to be a teacher someday. I hope you will all be welcoming to her."

From the way every boy perked up at this news, Donovan had no doubt she would be welcomed. But they were all idiots to think that they had a chance. They were all juniors in high school and she was in college. Only Donovan was technically the same age as her. But it wasn't like that mattered either.

Rosie said hello to everyone then headed to the back of the room as Mr. Henley began the lesson. He had to clear his throat three times before every head turned back towards him. Rosie took a chair at a narrow desk at Donovan's left. Link craned his neck back but Donovan kicked his chair to stop him. Rosie chuckled softly.

As Mr. Henley dove into the lesson, Donovan tugged out a book from his backpack and flipped it open, slouching in his chair to get comfortable. It was an hour-long lesson that day. He barely read two paragraphs when a low, silky voice spoke.

"You should really pay attention," Rosie said.

Donovan looked at her and was struck by the unique color of her eyes.

"Why?" he whispered back.

Rosie smiled a teasing smile which gave her an attractive devious look.

"I see," she said. "You sit in the back, don't pay attention. You're going for the hot and broody type, right?"

Donovan didn't think anything about him would say 'hot and broody' type. He didn't talk but that was about it.

"Not at all," Donovan said causally.

His simple response seemed to pique Rosie's curiosity. She rested her head on her fist, eyeing him.

"So then you're the type that doesn't care about grades, thinks school is overrated. You get by but only so you don't have to repeat a grade."

Donovan had to admit it was amusing that she was trying to figure him out. The edge of his lips lifted slightly.

"I feel the need to tell you that I have one of the highest GPAs in the school," he said.

Rosie straightened. "Really?"

"Really."

"But how can you when you're reading during class."

Donovan motioned to Mr. Henley with his still open book.

"Because I finished the homework for this lesson last night."

"How?"

"It's this thing called a textbook and it contains all the knowledge in the universe."

Rosie shook her head though she was smiling.

"Okay, Mr. Universe, then you wouldn't mind me grading your homework now and seeing what you got."

In answer, Donovan dug out his math assignment and handed it over. As Rosie sat back and went through the homework, Donovan went back to reading. He reached the next chapter by the time Rosie gave a quiet cough.

"Let me guess," he said. "Perfect score?"

Rosie held up the paper, revealing a 100 marked on it.

"It seems you do have the right to read your book," Rosie said. "I stand corrected."

"Thank you."

Donovan held out his hand for his homework and Rosie placed it in his palm. For a second, Donovan met her eyes and thought about how different this interaction would have played out if they were in a class together, if she knew they were the same age, if they were both in college. Would he ask her out? Where would they go on a date? What normal college conversations would they share?

He placed his paper on the desk and returned to his book. It didn't matter, from her perspective he was a junior, a baby compared to the guys she talked with in college. He didn't look at her the rest of the class and when the bell rang he left without a backward glance.

***

The coffee shop hummed around Donovan and Link as they sat at their corner table. Link worked his way through their math homework, Donovan giving him help every so often.

"Do you think she'd date a younger man?" Link asked unexpectedly.

Donovan tried not to laugh. Younger man? Link still looked like he was a fourteen-year-old somedays.

"Not really," Donovan said. "Not when she looks like she does. She could get anyone. Why get a high schooler?"

Link made a disappointed face. "True."

"I would probably be too much for her anyway," Link said. "I mean I am too attractive for people to handle."

Donovan laughed. "True."

The coffee shop door opened and a group of college students entered, all talking over each other. Donovan eyed them and spotted Rosie in their midst. When she caught his eye, she smiled and cut away from her friends. Link stared up at her, his mouth open.

"It's Mr. Universe," she said.

Donovan kicked Link under the table, knowing he'd face endless hours agonizing over how stupid he looked later on. Link started and snapped his mouth closed. A guy almost as good-looking as Rosie strode over to their table and claimed the spot beside her.

"Hey, Rosie," he said. "These friends of yours?"

From the way he eyed their homework and their school uniforms, Donovan knew he was being condescending, even if his tone managed to keep it hidden.

"Drake, this is the boy genius I was telling you about," Rosie said.

Boy genius. Yeah, his brothers could never hear about that name or he'd never be called anything else. At least their use of it would feel less humiliating than Rosie's use of it.

"Right," Drake said. "She told me about you. A bright student. I'm sure you'll go far in high school with that brain of yours."

Donovan stared at Drake and said nothing. There was no defense against a guy like this. Any response would be ammunition.

"No response," Drake said. "And Rosie spoke so highly of you."

"Drake," Rosie said.

"I'm just messing with you," Drake said, smiling.

Donovan continued to stare at him which started to unnerve Drake.

"Have fun with your homework," Drake said. "I'm going to go order."

"Don't mind him," Rosie said. "He's always like that."

Always a condescending jerk, Donovan never would have guessed that one.

"Well I'll see you in math," Rosie said. "This month should be fun."

Yeah, she was alone in that feeling.

"Guys are mean in college like they are in high school," Link said. "That's unsurprising and disappointing." He sighed. "You ever wish could you hit guys like that."

Donovan watched Drake as he made a joke and everyone around him laughed. He thought about all the guys who had managed to piss Donovan off over the years or who picked on Link. He thought of the years ahead of him where he'd have to continue to deal with them and not react. He crossed his arms and let out a breath.

"Yeah, every day."

High School Days Together

After The Attack

Link paced the length of the classroom and spun around to make the journey back, nerves carrying him from one end to the next. Carter sat on top of a table, her feet propped on a stool, watching Link's progress. Donovan rested against the table beside her, his arm touching her. Breathing out, Link ran a nervous hand through his hair. His mind was a frantic mess and he couldn't seem to gain control of it.

The classroom was empty except for the three occupants. Outside the closed door, the muted sounds of students could be heard. No one tried to enter the classroom. If they had they would have found the door locked. The minutes ticked on and no one said anything. The wait felt like it had lasted an eternity when there came a knock. Carter and Donovan looked to Link, who stared at the door. What waited for him was something he didn't know whether he wanted or not.

"You sure about this?" Carter asked.

Link nodded, but he knew they would see it wasn't the full truth. Rising, Donovan went over to the door and flipped the lock. When he opened the door, Mason was on the other side, shadowed by Smith.

The two newcomers walked in and Donovan engaged the lock again. Silence settled over the room as Donovan took up his position next to Carter. Link stood frozen near the table, eyes glued on his half brother. In turn, Mason seemed unable to look at Link. All his bluster and posturing were nowhere to be seen.

"Why did you want to see Link?" Carter asked, getting bored of the quiet.

Mason stuffed his hands into his pockets and finally made eye contact with the boy who appeared to be his opposite. Mason was blonde, built and bold. In comparison, Link looked like a little kid still trying to grow into his teenage body.

"I don't know," Mason said. "I guess I wanted to see you now that... I know. And...talk."

Link nodded, his gaze dropping like he was the one to blame for what he was.

"Talking is fine," Carter said. She leaned forward, eyes boring into Mason. "But if you say anything at all mean I will attack you so hard and so fast it will take both Smith and Donovan to stop me from killing you. Got it?"

Link held back a smile, drawing strength from her loyalty. Mason nodded but didn't seem scared. His whole demeanor was subdued and he looked uncertain. Link wondered if he had ever been uncertain in his entire life.

"Did you really not know?" he blurted out.

Cautious, Mason rubbed the back of his neck. "I wasn't sure, but..." he dropped his hand. "I saw you together with my dad and wondered. You look a lot like him."

Link crossed his arms, building a shield.

"Yeah, I know," he said.

Mason raised a finger to Link's hair. "But you don't have his hair color."

"It's dyed."

"Oh." A stretch of silence. "The glasses?"

Link took them off and laid them on the table. "Fake."

"Makes sense."

The two boys stood regarding each other as if truly seeing what the other was to them. The boy who was known by everyone, talked about and loved for being part of The Family. And the boy who lived in the shadows, seen by few and truly known by even fewer.

"Did you always know?" Mason asked.

"No, I found out six years ago."

"That must have sucked."

The sympathy was so startling that it caught Link by surprise.

"Yeah, it did," he said. "I hated him for a long time."

As if knowing that feeling, Mason chuckled.

"You're not the only son to feel that."

The binding word of 'son' seemed to crack another layer of tension that hung between the two brothers.

"Why do you hate him?" Link asked, curious.

Mason leaned back on the closest table, crossing his arms. The posture was relaxed like he had found common ground.

"There are too many reasons," he said. "He became President. He cheated on my mom. His job comes before me."

Link shuffled his foot, staring at the ground. Though he only saw his father once a month, the relationship they had built was a solid one. A connection that had come from Link dealing with his pain and accepting.

"At least you see him more than I do," Link said.

"What delusion are you under?" Mason said. "I'm lucky if I see him once a week."

"I barely see him once a month, even that doesn't happen sometimes."

Mason looked away, holding in his thoughts. The room filled with a new sort of tension, one built from trying to decide who had it worse.

"I thought...," Mason started. "I thought I was the target." The statement cracked the wall between them. "I'm the face everyone knows. I thought whatever was happening would be about me. I had no reason not to believe it." Mason broke his gaze with the wall and locked eyes with Link. "Then you were mentioned and I was so confused...then relieved."

"Were you scared?" Link asked, wanting to reaffirm that person before him wasn't 'Wonder Boy'.

"I was terrified."

Link smiled and Mason's mouth curled upward. Before the smile could settle, Mason's face turned serious.

"I'm sorry it was you," he said. "Doesn't seem fair to me."

"Nothing ever is."

Something like acceptance passed between the two brothers. For the first time, it felt like they didn't have to be fighting against each other, but beside each other.

The bell rang ending lunch and ending the meeting. Mason rose and took a step towards the door but stopped. For a moment he hesitated, debating something. Link felt the same apprehension, but fought it and extended his hand. Mason paused then took it.

"I always wanted a brother," he said.

"Me too," Link said. "I guess we both got our wish."

A Special Sort of Problem

"I have the subject in sight," Carter said. "He's on the move."

Shadows hid her as she rested against a back wall. Her eyes scanned the chaotic scene before her. The room thrummed with voices and pulsating music. Lights flashed and colors changed, distracting any unfocused person. But Carter was not thrown by any of it.

"Do you think he will make the play?" she asked.

"His previous MO gives me confidence he will," Donovan said. "But we should be at the ready if anything changes."

Carter switched her gaze to the other occupants of the packed room. The world seemed to be in constant motion as groups broke apart and reformed in different places.

"I have a group of seven hostiles, ten o'clock," she said. "What is your read on the situation?"

Donovan followed her directions and studied the group of guys huddled in one corner, their backs towards the mayhem.

"I don't sense any threat but we'll keep them in sight."

"Roger that." An approaching form caught Carter's attention. "Heads up, we have activity at 12 o'clock. She's made you. Do you need back up?"

Donovan's mouth twitched. "Do you want to give me back up?"

"I say my involvement is the fastest course of action to neutralizing the threat."

"Then by all means I accept back up."

Carter turned to Donovan, wrapped one arm around his neck and kissed him.

Knowing what had been coming, Donovan reacted right away, holding her close, his hands on her waist. For a second the world stopped and Carter couldn't seem to remember why she had started kissing him, but knew she didn't want to stop.

The girl in the high heels and sparkly dress halted in her steps. With an awkward shuffle, she spun away. Reality returning to her, Carter smiled up at Donovan.

"Threat neutralized."

"I never suspected military tactics would come in handy for Prom."

"I never suspected I would come to Prom."

Donovan gave her a teasing look. "Didn't think anyone would ask you?"

"No, I saw no reason to come. I can't dance."

Crossing his arms, Donovan leaned his shoulder against the wall.

"Interesting, I would have thought, based on your mobility and physique, it wouldn't be that much of a challenge for you."

"Taking down a 200 pound man is a far easier task than moving seductively to a rhythm."

The edge of Donovan's mouth curled. "Who said anything about being seductive?"

"The scene I have been watching for the past forty minutes."

Donovan looked over as if he hadn't been aware of the way the girls, in varying lengths of dresses, had been dancing. The dance floor was crammed with students all moving in ways Carter didn't have a clue how to mimic. Off to the side Link and Maddy danced together. To her surprise, Link looked more capable than she had imagined he would be.

"You don't have to dance like that," Donovan said.

Unable to look at him, she asked, "Would you like it if I did?"

He reached out and took one of her hands. The contact sent a surge of warmth through Carter. She met his steady gaze.

"No. I like you right here. Right next to me."

Carter smiled. The look quickly slipped into something teasing. "Good, 'cause I had no intention of humiliating myself."

"Also, your father would shoot me on sight," Donovan said.

He glanced across the room. Steve was dressed in a black suit and surveying the scene with an impassive expression.

"He never did strike me as the chaperone type of father," he said.

"No, but when he heard I was going with you he quickly signed up."

"He still doesn't trust me."

"Trust is something you earn. And you're getting close. It just takes time."

"Good thing I'm not going anywhere."

He smiled at her then looked back to the mass of dancers, reassuring himself Link was safe. With his attention elsewhere, Carter let her eyes linger on him. The way his dress shirt and slacks fit him perfectly. It was hard not to admire the build of his arms and torso. When her gaze rose from his chest to his face, she found him looking at her, a smirk spreading across his lips. She struggled to control her expression, but his eyes only brightened with a teasing look at her embarrassment.

"Thanks," he said, making her scowl in annoyance. "You should know the thoughts are mutual."

Unlike her, his gaze never left her face, as if the intelligence he saw there was all he needed to find her attractive. She tried to fight the grin creeping to her mouth, but it eventually won out.

"I have to say your outfit looks far more comfortable than mine," she said.

She looked down at her simple v-neck black dress.

"Maggie picked it out," she said, lifting one edge of the thigh length skirt. "I only said yes because the other option had sequins. It could have been worse. What do you think?"

Donovan took this as an invitation to let himself admire the way the dress followed the curve of her body. Carter returned his smirk when he met her gaze again, satisfied with the look in his eyes.

"You are the perfect combination of beautiful and dangerous."

She winked. "Good answer."

Donovan's attention jumped away as Carter's father left his post and moved towards one of the exits.

"Where is he going?"

"Checking the perimeter, is my guess. Make sure no students have snuck away to do things they shouldn't be."

"For their sakes, I hope they aren't. I can't imagine your father being very lenient with them."

"No, but it will tough them up to do twenty push ups in formal attire."

Donovan chuckled at the image. The music switched tempos and the groups of grinding students scattered into pairs, arms falling around necks and wrapping around waists. Carter noticed as

Maddy instantly rested her head on Link's shoulders and he rested his cheek on her hair. For some reason, she couldn't look away, watching as the couple was lost in their own world.

"I would say a thorough perimeter check takes about half an hour, wouldn't you agree?" Donovan asked.

Carter frowned in puzzlement at the question but nodded. "Roughly that, yes."

"Good."

He took her hand and pulled her onto the dance floor.

"What are you doing?" she asked.

"Dancing with you."

"I remember telling you that I can't dance."

"Fine." He pulled her close to him, one arm holding her waist while the other held her hand close to his chest. "We will not dance, we will merely sway in time to the music. Sound doable to you?"

Since Carter's body was already responding to Donovan's lead, she had no choice but to accept.

"Is this the part where you surprise me by telling me you're actually a phenomenal dancer?"

He laughed, the sound vibrating through Carter's chest. "I can assemble a Remington 700 rifle more easily than I can dance. No, I thought since this is your Prom you should have at least one dance."

"Are you assuming that if I didn't dance at least once I would be crushed for the remainder of my life?"

"No. But I figured it might be a memory you would want to share one day with your daughter. If she ever turned out differently than you."

"You mean she would be a normal teenage girl?"

"It's a possibility."

"One I have never given much thought to." Donovan was silent and she studied his calm expression. "Have you given it much thought?"

In answer, he merely pulled her closer and said nothing. A smile tugged at Carter's lips as she turned over the implications of his silence.

The smile froze when a masked figure emerged from a dim hallway.

The blood in Carter's veins turned cold as the figure was followed by six others. All of them were masked and fit. They wore tuxes as if they were trying blend in.

Carter's hand tightened around Donovan's and he instantly stopped moving.

"Hallway. Six o'clock."

As if continuing to dance, Donovan rotated them.

"I counted seven hostiles," she said, her voice calm though her heart was pounding. "I think they are concealing guns beneath their jackets."

"It's too dark to tell, but I think you're right. We can't bring attention to them or we will cause a panic." Donovan's words came quickly but his voice was even, as if keeping it that way could control the situation. "They haven't made a move to anyone specific yet, so we have time. We split up." His arm reflexively tightened around her as if he hated the thought of leaving her. "We'll take them from either side. I'll take the right."

"Okay."

Donovan kissed her deeply and was gone, cutting through the crowd.

Carter carved her way through the dense mass as the music switched to something upbeat. Couples let out cheers as they loosened their holds on each other.

Slipping into the shadows, Carter used the cover to creep along the wall. The group of masked guys had divided and four of them were heading her way. The music pounded against Carter's ears and spiked her heartbeat. Every cell in her body was shot with adrenaline.

The group was so focused on the dancing mob of students, that they didn't notice Carter's presence.

Before they knew what was happening, she was attacking. She slammed her fist into one attacker's face, breaking his nose, and kicked another in the stomach, winding him. The attackers staggered back in shock while she turned to the other two guys. She laid one out with a fast 1-2 sequence to the face and stomach. Spinning around, she clipped the final guy with the heel of her shoe, sending him crumpling to the ground.

The battle was over so quickly that no one noticed what had happened. A second later, Donovan found her with all her opponents moaning on the ground around her. She met his gaze.

"You take care of your men?" she asked.

He gave her a nod and raised a handgun.

"I got their weapons as well."

He pointed it at one of the moaning bodies. Before Carter could stop him he fired.

"Donovan!" The exclamation was ripped from her.

But nothing happened. On the floor the guy twitched at the cold water that soaked his shirt.

"All of them are water guns," Donovan said.

Carter knelt down and pulled off the guy's mask. Lucas was scowling back at her.

"What did you do to me?" he asked, still trying to regain his breath.

"Are you behind this prank?" she asked.

"Owens, you can be a real b-"

Carter punched him, knocking him out.

When she stood up, Donovan was smiling at her.

"What?"

He shrugged. "Nothing, except there's something amusing but completely normal about you surrounded by beaten guys."

She smiled and waved her hands to the helpless pranksters.

"So, do you think this is one of those Prom memories you were talking about?"

"Definitely. Our daughter will love it."

Before Carter could process his choice of words, the door opened and her father walked in. He eyed the scene and then pointed to them.

"That's it," he said. "I'm banning you from the training courses for a month."

Coming To Terms

Link thought he was going to throw up. Whether it was because of nerves or excitement, he didn't know. He stood at the bathroom mirror, gripping the edges of the sink willing his breakfast to stay down. As he thought he wasn't going to be able to hold on to it, someone knocked on the door.

"Link, are you ready to go?" Donovan asked.

Link let out a slow breath, forcing nausea away.

"Yeah," he said.

Combing his hair one last time, he left the bathroom. Donovan inspected him as he walked into the living room. The slight narrowing of his eyes told Link that he must still look a little ill.

"I'm fine," he said.

Thankfully, Donovan didn't point out the lie, merely nodded and led him to the door. All through the car ride, Link bounced his leg and stared out the window. Donovan might have said something to him on and off but Link didn't hear it. When they pulled up to the front of a lavish hotel, Link swallowed hard and wiped his sweaty palms on his jeans.

After handing off the car to a valet, they ignored the front desk and walked directly to the elevators, taking it to the very top. In a hallway between two penthouse suites, two large men talked with each other, holding a phone. They wore plain clothes and appeared to be sharing videos, but Link knew exactly who they were and what they were doing: Secret Service agents with a camera directed at the elevator.

Donovan nodded to them. After a quick pat-down and the confiscation of their phones, one of the agents opened the door to one of the suites. A small foyer was circled with three sets of doors and held a second set of Secret Service agents.

"Do you want me there?" Donovan asked.

Link shook his head, he knew this meeting was already going to be hard enough, he wanted privacy.

"I'll be here," Donovan said, then joined the two agents.

Wiping his hands again, Link crossed the foyer and opened the door to the living room. As he entered, his father, in plain clothes, spun away from the wall of one-sided glass windows. His father broke into a wide happy grin and hurried over to Link. Link accepted his father's hug without hesitation. No matter how many times his mother hugged him, it wasn't the same.

His father was still smiling when he pulled back and placed his hands on Link's shoulders, surveying him.

"I think you've gotten taller." His smile softened into something gentle. It was a look Link knew well, like his father was seeing the gap of time between meetings. He hugged Link again.

"Okay, tell me how you've been," his father said, leading him to a couch. "You're still dating Maddy, right? How's that going?"

All of Link's nerves were forgotten in the presence of his father, all he felt was happiness at getting to see him, talk to him.

"Good, really good. I have pictures of her but they're on my phone. Honestly, I don't know why she's still with me."

His father squeezed Link's shoulder affectionately. "I do. Because you are a smart, amazing young man."

Link ducked his head, embarrassed and gratified all at once. "Thanks. So...uh...how is Mason?" he said, needing to change topics before he got too uncomfortable with the praise.

Sighing, his father drew back.

"Mason hasn't been talking to me since the attack. I've tried to talk to him but he either walks away or tells me...well he's very colorful in what actions I should take. Have you two talked?"

Link nodded. "Yeah, a week ago we finally met in an empty classroom. But that was it. Do you know why he wanted today-"

The door to the living burst open and Mason strode in cutting Link off. Instantly, all the reasons Link felt like throwing up earlier came crashing back.

"Great," Mason said. "We already started the family reunion, this is fantastic."

He dropped into a chair, one leg dangling over the edge. Instantly the easy atmosphere of before evaporated. Their father straightened and Link pressed his hands down his jeans.

"I say we start with stories," Mason said, in a breezy manner. "We could always go with the classic of how my father had an affair with your mother."

"Mason," President Douglas said in warning, but Mason didn't care.

"Or we could go with the story of where you, Mr. President...wait sorry we're all family here, I can call you father. Where you father, lied to both me and Link for our entire lives."

Beneath the mocking tone, Link saw the anger simmering in Mason. Anger over the lies and betrayal.

"Mason," Douglas said in a low, calming tone.

Mason leaped to his feet and jabbed a finger at his father. "Don't! Don't play the politician with me! I'm so sick of your crap! This entire time you knew I had a brother and you never told me. This entire time you've known you're a terrible human being but convinced the country you're not."

Link wanted to hide behind the couch. Mason's fury felt like a physical force barreling into him, even though he knew he wasn't the target. Beside him, his father took all the anger in without a response. Though he knew Mason couldn't see it, Link saw the regret in his father's eyes, the pain that he hid.

"Are you done?" President Douglas asked.

"NO!" Mason snapped. "You are a scumbag and I hate you." He flicked a hand towards Link. "And I hate your mother too since this wasn't one-sided."

Link blinked surprised at the admission though didn't deny it. How could he when he'd been mad at his mother as well?

"We can talk this over," Douglas said.

Mason barked out a sharp mocking laugh. "You'd love that. The smooth talker wants to talk it over. Guess what, I don't want to hear it! Your word means nothing to me! You hear that, nothing!" He spun towards Link. "And you, I don't understand how you can stand to be around him after all he's done to you! You didn't even know about him until six years ago, but now you're best friends? How pathetic are you!"

Douglas jumped to his feet. "Don't you dare take your anger out on Link."

"Oh look at you acting like the caring father, who knew you had it in you."

"I've always cared, Mason."

"Liar. You've never cared because if you did you wouldn't constantly be lying to my mom!"

Mason stormed out of the living room and into one of the bedrooms, slamming the door shut. The silence that followed rang with the thud of the door and the last words. Douglas released a breath and dragged his hand down his face. Despite wanting to walk out to Donovan and leave, Link rose and crossed to the bedroom door.

"It might be best to let him be," Douglas said.

Link paused. "No, cause he's hurting and I think that's the last thing he needs. I would know."

When Link slipped inside the bedroom, he found Mason sitting on the edge of the bed, his back to Link, his head in his hands.

"Go away," Mason said, his voice choked. "I thought I made it clear that I hate you, Mr. President."

"I don't plan on being President," Link said. "I hate politics."

Mason straightened but didn't turn around, instead he wiped his face.

Slowly, Link joined Mason, pretending to not see that he had been crying.

"I don't know how my mom has stayed with him, he is such an a-"

"People are strange. They do weird things for people they love."

Mason grunted. "She's an idiot for loving him. Then again she doesn't know so I guess I can't fault her."

Link didn't say anything. They sat there for a long while saying nothing.

"How are you okay with this?" Mason finally asked.

"Because I lived most of my life without a dad and I wanted one."

"And so he waltzed into your life and you were all 'hey I have a dad now, this is great! Yay me'?"

Link snorted. "No, I hated him. The first time we met I almost punched him."

"What?"

"Yeah, but a Secret Service agent stopped me. I even think it was Carter's father."

Mason shook his head, almost smiling. "I've wanted to hit him so many times." He sighed. "You're really calm about this. I don't like you for that."

For some reason, Link found himself liking Mason more and more for his blunt honesty. At least here was one person who wouldn't lie to him.

"You forget," Link said. "That I've had years to come to terms with all of this."

"So you're saying that I should come to terms with all this?"

Link shrugged. "I don't know. You're different than me, you might not want to. But if you hear him out then at least you can decide with all the facts."

Mason stood abruptly. "Fine, let's get this over with."

Startled by the sudden decision, it took Link a second to follow Mason back to the living room. Like a petulant child, Mason sank into a chair, glaring at his father. Link hovered in the doorway, unsure where he wanted to sit. Finally, he decided to take the second armchair so they all sat separately.

"Alright," Mason said. "I'm going to ask you questions and you're going to tell me the truth. As impossible as that sounds to you as a politician, I'm sure you'll manage it."

Douglas dipped his head. "Go ahead."

"Why?" Mason asked. "Why did you cheat on my mom?"

Douglas clasped his hands together. "It was the biggest mistake of my life."

Despite knowing that it wasn't a statement against himself, Link felt the sting of the words. He dropped his eyes, hating that besides the title of 'bastard', he had 'mistake' as well.

"Link," his father said. "Look at me, son." Link lifted his gaze to see his father staring at him with intense eyes. "That does not mean I regret having you in my life, you hear that? You are the one good thing to come of my mistake."

Link nodded, but still felt the weight of who he was. His father waited for Link to speak but when he didn't, he went on.

"I knew Monica from college," Douglas said. "We were working on a case together right before I became a senator. We'd been working together for months. The day we won the case we celebrated and got drunk..." He ran a hand through his hair.

"How long did the affair last?" Mason asked.

Link watched his father, he'd wanted to know this for a long time but never wanted to break what connection they'd created together.

"It was only that one night. We both woke up realizing how we'd messed up. From that point on we never worked together and broke all contact."

Mason grunted. "I see, it was the easiest way for my mom to never find out. Nice plan."

"Mason," Douglas said. "I told your mother what I did and asked her to do the unimaginable and forgive me."

"And she did?" Mason almost sneered.

"Yes, for some reason she did. Though it was a long road to her trusting me again."

"Yeah, and what did she think about you having another son?"

Douglas dropped his head. "She found out when I found out; when I talked of running for President and Link was about twelve."

Link felt like he'd been punched by the news. All those years when he was little, his father hadn't known he existed? All those years he had hated his father when he thought he'd known but never wanted to see him?

"You didn't know?" Link asked, barely breathing.

His father shook his head. "No. Your mother kept you a secret. She thought it was better that way. Only when she heard I planned to run for President did she get in contact with me. Both me and my wife. She told us both, wanting to be upfront." He swallowed like something was stuck in his throat. "I hated having to hear I had another son all those years and never knew."

He met Link's eyes. "I wanted to meet you right away but she said she'd have to break the news to you. I'm so sorry that I didn't know. I should have known."

Link didn't know what to say. Though he didn't blame his father for not knowing, he now hated his mother for never telling either of them. Part of him could see how it was better growing up not knowing that he was missing out on a different type of life. But the other part of him hurt for all the years he felt like there was a father out there who'd left him. Hadn't wanted him at all.

Mason swore. "How screwed up can this get?"

Link wanted to laugh and cry all at once.

"Look," his father said, glancing between Mason and Link. "Neither of you ever have to forgive me, what I did was selfish and hurtful on so many levels. I've failed you both. But I still want to ask for your forgiveness. And I need you to know that I love you both and I'm so grateful I can have you in my life." He focused on Mason. "However that looks."

The sincerity and conviction in his voice seemed to steal the last traces of anger from the room. Mason stood.

"I need to leave," he said.

Douglas nodded. "I understand."

As Mason headed for the room, Link went after him.

"Hey," Link said. He paused suddenly unsure how to proceed. He'd forgiven his father years ago, but it had taken years. He didn't know if Mason ever would, but he didn't want him to feel alone. "Uh...if you, I don't know...want to...yeah, I'm here."

Mason scuffed his shoe on the ground, frowning and looking unlike the hostile boy that had entered the room earlier.

"Thanks," he said. "I guess I can't really hate him."

"Why?"

Mason met Link's eyes. "Cause I'm starting to like having you as a brother."

Distraction

Carter read the paragraph again for the twentieth time. On the other side of the couch, Donovan shifted and ran his hand through his hair. This was ridiculous! She completely forgot what she'd just read. Again!

Pinning her eyes to the textbook, Carter forced all her energy into reading. Nothing would distract her this time. This time she would read and understand and be able to write her essay.

She read the paragraph. There. Done. She read it and understood. She moved on to the next paragraph. Donovan stretched and placed his hands on top of his head. An action that irritatingly accented his toned arms.

That's it! Carter couldn't do this anymore. There were only two weeks left of school. She needed to write this essay to maintain her perfect grade in English. To be able to write the essay she needed to be able to finish reading the page. But she couldn't stay focused on reading. There was only one solution.

Carter raised her head as Donovan looked over at her. They spoke at the same time.

"Do you want something to drink?"

"We need to break up."

Donovan stared at her for a long second then stood.

"All right," he said, casually. "Do you still want something to drink?"

He made his way to the kitchen, Carter gaping at him. What?

"Did you not hear me?" she asked. "I said we need to break up."

Donovan retrieved two glasses of water and walked back to Carter, setting one on the coffee table before her.

"Okay," he said, settling back on the couch. "Why are we breaking up?"

"Because you're too distracting. And I seem to have lost all control of my thoughts. You move, I look over. You shift, I forget what I've read. You breathe, I want to kiss you. I can't do this."

Donovan nodded thoughtfully and sipped his water.

"That makes sense," he said.

"Why are you so calm about this?"

Donovan leaned back and Carter hated him for how comfortable he looked in her living room. For how much she liked that he looked so comfortable.

"I'm calm," Donovan said. "Because one: I get what you mean. Two: my mom said this would likely be a common reaction."

Carter stared at him. "Let's start with the first part of that. You get what I mean?"

Donovan laughed. "Carter, you understand I want to kiss you constantly, right? Among other things. And I've been on the same equation for the last ten minutes because you scrunch up your face and I find it insanely cute."

Color flooded Carter's cheeks and she wasn't sure she liked this response either. When had she started blushing? This was out of hand.

"What about what your mother said? You talk to her about me?"

This time Donovan stared at her like it was a trick question.

"Of course," he said. "You're my girlfriend. I talk to her a lot about you."

"But it sounded like you analyze me."

Donovan hesitated as if knowing he was entering dangerous waters.

"We do." Carter crossed her arms, needing a physical barrier. But Donovan reached out and placed his hand over her arms. "You understand you're one of the most complex people I know. Of course I'm going to ask my mom for help because I want to understand you."

Carter let down her barrier. He wanted to understand her. That felt too strange. And the sincerity in his voice made Carter want to attach herself to him. And that terrified her. Kissing was one thing, but more... That was a level of vulnerability and trust Carter did not have in her. Not right then. And maybe not for a long time.

But there was a part of her body that wanted that even when her emotions and mind didn't. That was another aspect that scared her, that she didn't feel in control of herself.

"What has your mom said then?" Carter asked, wondering if his mom could understand something in her that she didn't.

"She said that you'd most likely react to our relationship like you did with our friendship. You'd push me away to see if I'd go."

Carter didn't know how his mom could be so spot-on in her analysis.

"Did she say anything else?" she asked.

"Yeah, to go slow."

"And you accept her advice?"

"She's my mom, of course I do. She's smart and has a lot more life experience than me."

Carter let out a quiet breath. Something about knowing he'd accept advice about taking it slow made her feel safe. They'd only been together a little over a month and she didn't want to lose him. But knew she wasn't willing to give up more than she wanted to keep him.

"So that's why you hold back on kissing me as much as you want?"

Donovan smiled. "Yeah, I don't want to lose you."

Hearing her words echoed by him made Carter smile.

"Then I guess I should take back my declaration that we should break up."

Donovan let out a dramatic breath. "Good, you had me freaking out there for a second."

Laughing, Carter shoved his shoulder. Donovan smiled at her and she held his gaze. The urge to kiss him and keep kissing him returned, slamming into her like a semi-truck. Donovan glanced down at her lips and swallowed, clearly feeling the same thing.

"I have to finish my homework," he said.

Carter nodded but found her body struggling to move back to her side of the couch. Donovan didn't move at all and the air felt electrified between them.

"I need to finish my essay," Carter said.

"You do."

"I really need to move."

"I really want to kiss you."

That broke Carter. She pulled Donovan towards her and his lips met hers. The familiarity of him flooded every inch of Carter until it felt like there was too much space between them. She needed more of him.

The need battled with Carter's logical side, the one telling her exactly where this path would lead as her emotions screamed at her to pull back, it was too soon, too fast. Not ready! Build a wall, take cover behind it. The chaos overwhelmed Carter and she broke away, breathing hard like she'd sprinted a mile.

She hovered before Donovan, trapped in what her body wanted but her emotions and mind didn't.

Donovan opened his mouth to say something but the apartment door opened. Captain walked in and froze. Instantly, Carter knew how this looked to her father. She quickly backed away but there was no erasing that image. Instead of seeming angry, her father appeared completely calm, which was more foreboding.

"Donovan," Captain said. "I think it's time to leave."

Donovan hurriedly gathered up his things looking like a teenage boy instead of a grown adult. As Donovan stepped outside, Captain followed, closing the door behind him.

Carter collapsed back on the couch. She knew she should worry for Donovan, but all she could think of was how conflicting it felt to be her right then. She'd never faced this before and it unnerved her. How did you control your body when it didn't want to listen?

When Captain walked back inside, Carter looked at him.

"What did you threaten him with this time?" she asked.

Captain merely smiled and stepped out of his shoes and took off his suit jacket.

"I didn't threaten him."

"Somehow I just don't believe you," Carter said.

"I didn't. I simply asked him if he was ready to have the weight and responsibility of being a father because there are no guarantees in this life."

Carter flushed. "It wasn't as bad as you're thinking."

Captain claimed the opposite side of the couch, resting his arm on the back of it.

"No, I could see that, but I also know where moments like that go."

Carter fidgeted, wanting to find a black hole and jump into it. She thought of Donovan and how he talked to his mom. Captain was always there for her.

But this?

This felt so different. Embarrassing. Humiliating.

"Sarge," Captain said. "You've always been smart, level-headed, and I trust you. But right now, I'm going to lay down some ground rules."

He paused as if expecting Carter to roll her eyes but she remained still.

"Your room is off-limits. His room is off-limits. His car is used for getting from point A to point B. There is no between, no hanging out in his car. If you're on a couch, leave room between yourselves. And be home before one. My father used to say nothing good happens after midnight."

Carter listened. Though there were a lot of restrictions, they made her feel loved.

She didn't know how to handle all of this. Having a boyfriend was uncharted territory. Feeling like she didn't have any control over herself was confusing and terrifying.

But she wasn't alone. Her father, someone she loved and who loved her was helping her navigate this unknown. In the moment, she felt completely looked after.

"I know this might come off as harsh or overbearing," Captain said. "But the best thing I've ever experienced is having you. I want you to have that experience too, but when you're ready for it."

Even though Carter knew it would be an avenue they'd never gone down before, she found she didn't want to talk about this with anyone else. Who else did she trust as much as him? Maggie came close.

"Captain..." Carter reminded herself she'd lived through learning about periods with Captain. This could not be worse. "I'm not sure what to do. I don't feel like I'm in control of myself anymore. I kiss him and..."

When Captain started to smile, Carter curled her legs up and buried her face in her hands.

"I can't. This is too embarrassing."

Her father laughed and jostled one of her knees.

"I might be your old man, but I'll tell you a secret: hormones have been the same since back in my day. In the Dark Ages."

Carter raised her head. "Wait, you weren't around when dinosaurs roamed the earth?"

"A little before my time. But it was the same then. I'm going to tell you something, you're not abnormal. Right now you're going to be all over the map. It's new, exciting. But over time you'll learn to get used to it and control it."

"Yes, but how do I do that now?"

Carter didn't want to feel like she somehow had to be on guard around Donovan. Like she had to worry about touching his hand in case it made her go crazy. She'd been distracted by him stretching for crying out loud!

"With practice," Captain said. "Sticking to my restrictions with help avoid situations you don't want. But if you feel like being physical," Carter winced at how embarrassing that sounded. "Then be physical. Go channel your energy into boxing. Go paintballing together. Go to the gun range. Go for a run. Take what you're feeling physically and point it in a different direction."

Carter had to smile at that. It was a philosophy she knew already worked. When she was sad or angry, Captain had told her to take it out on her punching bag. When she'd struggled with homework or school, he'd taught her to assemble a gun, helping her put her emotions into something else.

Carter felt relieved. This was a plan she could follow.

"Thanks, Captain."

He nodded but looked at her with kind, sad eyes.

"I thought for a moment there that you might never meet someone then I could keep you with me always."

Carter hugged him. "You'll always have me."

"Yeah, but now you have a boyfriend and I feel out of control about it all."

Carter laughed. "Don't worry, me having a boyfriend is just as shocking and scary to me as it is to you."

Taking A Chance

The elevator doors opened but Carter didn't step out. Instead, she stood frozen with indecision. When the doors started closing again, she stuck out her hand and halted them. Shaking her head at herself, she walked out. The hallway seemed to stretch on, growing as she stared at it. She balled her hands and strode forward, stopping at a door.

For a long moment, she simply stared at the gold number hanging on it. Her thoughts were a current of annoyance and concern, the annoyance heavily berating the concern. But still, she didn't leave. Letting out a breath, she knocked. She inwardly cursed herself for even being there.

When no movement came from the other side, she spun on her heel ready to walk away, but the tug of concern stopped her. Grounding her teeth, she knocked once more. A single second ticked off in her head and she decided she had waited long enough.

But as she went to leave, she heard the faint shuffle of footsteps. She faced the door, already forming excuses and blasé comments about her presence there.

When Donovan opened the door, there were three things Carter instantly took in.

The first was the fact that he was shirtless. This was the first time she had ever seen him in such a state and she hated how the sight of his muscular torso affected her thoughts.

The second was the fact that he seemed to be sweating. Which this set her mind in a riot of directions.

The third was the fact that he looked awful. His eyes were red as well as the tip of his nose and his hair was an utter mess.

"Carter," Donovan said, her name coming out in a sharp rasp.

She blinked, taking everything in.

"I hadn't heard from you in a few days, I wanted to check-in."

Donovan opened his mouth to respond but snapped it shut. He staggered away from the door and to the bathroom. A second later, Carter heard him throwing up.

Unsure if he would even want her there but unable to leave, she followed him. He was seated on the floor, his head resting on his arm that sat on the rim of the toilet. He breathed heavily, his eyes closed.

Carter grabbed a hand towel from a rack, soaked it in water, rung it out, and crouched beside him. Closer, she could see how his skin was pale.

"Here," she said.

He pried his eyes open and accepted the towel, wiping his mouth.

"Can you stand up?" she asked.

"In...a...minute..."

The words seemed to take everything from him.

"Okay."

They sat there in silence for a long while until Donovan raised his head and looked at her. It was as if he were registering that she was there for the first time.

"Hey," she said, hurting at the worn-out look on his face. "Let me help you stand up."

She wrapped his arm around her neck and slid her hand around his waist. His skin was hot and clammy. They rose, Donovan leaning on her. They made a slow progression back to Donovan's room.

It was the first time Carter had ever seen it. There was a wall of windows with a desk and a leather armchair beneath it. The view was of more apartment buildings. On another wall was a line of bookshelves all packed with more books than Carter knew was in her own house. Donavan's bed was a tangle of forest green sheets. On the bedside table was a Kleenex box and a trash can next to it, piled high with used tissues.

She helped him onto the mattress and he tucked his feet under the blankets while Carter pulled the rest around him. He closed his eyes, all his energy spent.

"You don't have to be here," he said.

"Yes, let me leave you while you die."

The edge of Donovan's lips curled.

"It's just a bad flu. I've taken care of myself before."

Something about the fact that Donovan had already gone through a similar situation like this all on his own made Carter sad. Any time she had gotten sick Captain had taken care of her or Maggie had. She remembered the way they would sit by her bed and watch over her.

"Now you have me," she said.

Taking the trash can, Carter moved back to the living room. For the most part that laid untouched, except for a few blankets neatly folded on the end of the couch. The kitchen, however, was in need of care, the sink stacked with dirty dishes. Carter emptied the trash can into a larger one and returned it to the side of Donovan's bed.

"What do you need?" she asked.

He shook his head, offering nothing. Carter went back to the kitchen and called Maggie as she began to clean.

"Hey, hon," Maggie answered.

"Donovan has the flu, what should I do to help him?"

"Aww, that poor boy."

Carter fought a smile, knowing Donovan would hate being called that.

"What are his symptoms?"

"He's hot and sweaty, but cold at the same time. He threw up and I think his nose is stuffy, I don't know."

Plates clattered as Carter loaded them into the dishwasher.

"Sounds like a bad bug," Maggie said. "Okay, keep him warm and that should help break his fever. A cold washcloth on his forehead should help. If he can keep liquids down then make sure he keeps drinking water and if he's up for it broth."

"Got it. Thanks."

"Do you need me to come over and help?"

Carter smiled at the offer. "If it gets worse then yes."

"Okay, just let me know."

"Will do."

Carter pocketed her phone and went searching through Donovan's cupboards. When she found his water glasses, she took one down and filled it. She gave his fridge a cursory glance and was surprised to find that there was a container of broth already there. Making note of it, she took the water back to him.

He opened his eyes as she entered and seemed confused as if surprised she was still there.

"Do you think you can drink?" she asked.

He nodded. Perched on the edge of the bed, Carter helped him drink. He got half of the glass emptied, before sinking back onto the pillow. Carter set the glass aside and got a damp washcloth from the bathroom. She folded it and placed it on Donovan's burning forehead. The coolness of it seemed to ease him. She then dragged the armchair over to the side of his bed and sank down. She watched his face, sighing when the wrinkled lines of pain smoothed.

"Do you want to watch something?" she asked.

It was usually the remedy that her father used for her sickness, a way to take her mind off it all. Donovan shook his head.

"I don't watch TV," he said.

"What?"

"I usually read."

Carter blinked, trying to wrap her head around the fact that she had never known this about Donovan. They had been dating for a month and this bit of information had never come up. It explained the wall of books.

"Seriously?" she asked.

He nodded, eyes still closed.

"I was homeschooled, remember? Half of my life was reading. We didn't even own a TV. My entertainment was books and causing trouble with my brothers."

Carter smiled, pieces of his life taking more defined form in her mind.

"What other secrets have you been keeping from me?" she asked.

Donovan laughed but halfway through it turned into a harsh cough and Carter's smile fell away.

"Never mind," she said. "Don't talk."

He nodded to this and Carter offered him more water, helping clear his throat. When she was back in her seat, he spoke.

"Talk to me," he said.

At the statement, Carter found her mind going blank. They had had countless conversations before but this was something she wasn't sure she knew how to do. She could navigate any argument or even throw insults but a one-sided conversation was unnatural. Still, as she stared at Donovan she found that there wasn't anything she could deny him.

"I think I decided what I want to do," she said. "That might sound weird since the majority of the time I always know what I want to do, but this...well, it's an idea I didn't think about before. Even though now that I've thought about it it seems stupid for not having seen it before." Carter winced at her ramblings. "I sound like an idiot."

Donovan smiled. It was weak but it managed to make her feel relieved.

"What have you decided?" he asked.

"I'm going to join the FBI after college."

At this, Donovan opened his eyes. She raised an eyebrow.

"What do you think?" she asked.

She took in a breath and held it, for some reason knowing that his opinion held the biggest weight.

"I think it's a good fit."

She released the breath.

"It's also good to know I'll have a partner."

She grinned. "You should know I didn't decide to join cause you've mentioned that's where you planned to end up. I'm not some crazy girlfriend who blindly follows her boyfriend, okay?"

Donovan's eyelids got heavy and closed. "I wouldn't dream of it, cause I know my girlfriend isn't crazy."

Carter slid down in the chair, hating how much she loved hearing the title on his lips.

The rest of the day slid by with Carter helping Donovan drink water and eventually broth. He was able to keep it down, but the fever still hung on.

Somewhere through the day, he fell asleep, but Carter didn't leave. She remained in the chair beside his bed. Eventually, her own tiredness got to her and pulled her into dreams.

A couple of hours later, she was roused by the shutting of a door and the sound of footsteps. When she opened her eyes, Brock was in the doorway, looking at her. She shot up, her cramped muscles instantly protesting.

"I didn't mean to wake you," he said.

Carter shook her head like it didn't matter and turned to Donovan. He was still sound asleep. Gently, she removed the cloth from his forehead and found that his fever had broken. She let out a sigh of relief and stood. Brock backed out of the room and Carter followed.

"His fever is gone so that's good," she said.

Brock nodded, but said nothing, watching her. Self-conscious, she set the cloth on the kitchen counter.

"Are you here to watch over him?"

Brock nodded again. "I've been sleeping on the couch. He was supposed to call me if he needed anything."

Carter shrugged at this. "I hadn't heard from him so I stopped by to make sure he was okay."

"Then thanks."

She retrieved her bag and took a step towards the door.

"I should head home. If he needs me tomorrow, just call."

"Will do."

Carter had the door open when Brock called out.

"You're a good girlfriend."

She laughed. "I don't know about that but I seem to be the only one he has at the moment so he's stuck with me."

Even after the door shut behind Carter, Brock stood there. Eventually, he walked back into Donovan's room. The messy sheets had been neatened and the stray tissues had been cleaned up.

As he rounded the bed, he found Donovan was waking up. Brock stretched out a hand and laid it on his little brother's forehead. Carter was right, the fever was gone. Relieved, he took a seat in the chair beside the bed. Donovan twisted his head as if searching.

"Did Carter leave?" he asked.

Brock nodded. "How long was she here?"

"Most of the day."

Donovan ran a hand over his face. "She had the pleasure of watching me throw up."

"It takes a dedicated person to stick around after something like that."

Donovan turned onto his side under the blankets.

"I know," he said, his eyes drooping as his lips lifted.

Watching the emotions on Donovan's face, Brock crossed his arms.

"You gonna marry her?" he asked.

Donovan sank deeper into the pillow, sleep already reaching for him again. Before it could completely grab hold, he replied: "Probably."

Graduation

Steam curled around the floor of the bathroom and slipped through the crack under the door. Link grabbed a towel and wiped away the remaining fog from the mirror. Resting his hands on the sink he stared at his reflection.

After today everything would change. He felt like he was standing on the edge of a cliff, looking down at an abyss of unknown. The last six years he had learned how to deal with the world from the safety of a school. Now he wasn't sure what the future would look like. There was college but it wasn't the same and he couldn't help feeling like he was falling without knowing where he would land.

Forcing the thoughts aside, he grabbed a comb and ran it through his damp hair. Without thinking about it, he parted it on one side and swept it over to the other. He froze, realizing what he had done. It was how his father wore his hair.

He snapped himself out of his daze and corrected his hair, erasing the tie to his parentage. He got dressed, trying not to think about his father but thinking all the same. He left the bathroom. In the living room, he found Donovan stretched out on the couch, his head resting on the back, a coffee mug balancing on the armrest. He wore a dark blue button-down and slacks. There wasn't a wrinkle in sight even though he was slouched, his ankles crossed.

A part of Link was annoyed that no matter what Donovan did he looked good and was at ease. The future wasn't terrifying to

Donovan, it was something he would take by storm cause that was just who he was. Link did not share the same confidence. He wondered if that level of confidence was embodied in a person or whether it could be learned.

Knowing there was no point in dwelling on it, Link approached Donovan and nudged his foot with his shoe. Blinking, Donovan raised his head and took a sip of his coffee.

"Why are you so tired?" Link asked.

Leaning forward, Donovan rubbed his eyes.

"Late night. That's all."

Though Link knew he missed a lot of things that Donovan and Carter usually saw, he wasn't dense enough to miss this one. When Donovan said 'late night', Link knew that it meant Donovan had been up talking to Carter on the phone. Sometimes he thought they were worse than Maddy and him. Knowing Donovan though, Link wasn't going to mention this knowing it would be denied.

"Are you ready to go?" he asked, instead. "It's a big day!"

Donovan drained the rest of the cup's contents.

"For you," he said. "You forget I've already graduated high school. My ceremony was a handshake from my father, a hug from my mom and a piece of paper. I'm guessing it's the best graduation there ever was."

"Okay, we all can't be you, but let's get moving cause I still want that slip of paper."

Giving a tired smile, Donovan stood up and dropped the coffee cup off in the sink. As they were making their way towards the door, Link's mother hurried out of her room still in a dressing robe though her makeup was done.

"Wait!" she said. "You can't leave without saying goodbye."

"You're coming to graduation, right?" Link asked.

His mother cupped his face. "Of course. I just wanted to say something first." An affectionate smile overtook her face. "I am so proud of you."

Link flushed under the weight of her admiration.

"It's only high school, mom. It's not like I won Nobel."

"I'm not talking about you graduating, I'm talking about watching you grow up and deal with life and how amazingly you've handled everything that has come your way. When you could have hated me or your father for these past years, you didn't. You forgave us and I'm so so happy that you are my son."

A lump formed in Link's throat and he felt himself on the verge of doing something embarrassing, like crying. His mother hugged him. When she pulled back, she smiled and gave his cheek a quick kiss.

"I'll see you at the graduation," she said.

Link nodded, not trusting himself to speak. When he turned to Donovan, Donovan raised an eyebrow.

"Don't expect me to get mushy on you, I'm here cause I get paid to be."

Link laughed, grateful that Donovan had said exactly the right thing to stop Link from getting too sentimental. Clapping a hand on Link's shoulder, Donovan directed them to the door.

"Let's go get you that slip of paper," he said.

***

The lobby to the auditorium was already filling with students when they arrived. The chaos seemed doubled with everyone wearing the same blue hats and robes, though most hadn't closed them and perfectly picked out outfits were displayed.

Before Link could try to figure out where to go in the mayhem, Donovan guided him over to the far side of the place. His choice in destination was obvious when Link saw Carter leaning against the wall, her eyes closed and her head resting back. Her robe hung open showing that she had gone with a pair of jeans and a t-shirt for the great occasion.

"Late night?" Link asked.

Grinning, Carter opened her eyes, her gaze darting from Link to Donovan in a telltale way. As if confirming her look, Donovan crossed his arms and leaned one shoulder on the wall, so he stood perpendicular to her, a small smile hidden in the corner of his mouth.

"You could say that," she said.

Fighting back a smirk, Link changed the subject to her outfit.

"I see you went all out for this grand ceremony," he said.

Carter spread her arms out, the robe framing her slim body.

"What can I say, I dressed with the level of care I feel for this day."

"Ready to be done with high school, then?" Link asked.

"If my birthday had been just a little bit earlier I would have already been graduated, so yes. I'm ready to be done." She looked at Donovan. "Though you had to go through high school twice so I think you have it worse than me."

This led to a conversation about the annoyance of high school and ate away the time that they had to wait. A man with a megaphone ordered everyone to take their seats and a horde of blue robes began to shuffle into the auditorium. The trio was divided and Link walked along his designated row, plopping into his red cushioned chair. The minutes ticked on as family members filled in the rest of the seats. Phones were brought out and conversations with neighbors were initiated as the wait continued.

When it felt like a year had passed the principal walked onto the stage just as a few straggling students slipped into their seats. Principal Withers talked about the future and the world beyond. Link was listening intently when a small commotion next to him ensued. He looked over and found that Mason was talking to the boy beside Link.

After a few whispered words, the two exchanged seats. Mason sank into the spot beside Link and gave him a nod. Confused, Link turned to the other side, almost wondering if Mason had been directing the nod to someone else.

"Hey," Mason said.

Link frowned. "Hi?"

The principal was replaced by the valedictorian and Link wondered if the greeting was the end of his interaction with Mason, but Mason planted on elbow on the armrest between them, bringing himself closer to Link, though he didn't look at him.

"I thought I would give you a heads up," he said, speaking to the head in front of him.

"About?"

There was a breath, then Mason went on, his voice quieter than before so only Link could hear it.

"My...our...um dad might be stopping by," he said. "I figured I should give you a warning."

The news shocked Link and he found himself floundering, wondering what he would do, but realized in such public place there was nothing he could do.

"Okay. Uh...thanks."

Mason nodded. "Yeah."

The speech from the girl at the podium rushed back as they fell silent. Link fidgeted and glanced at Mason, who hadn't moved back to his original seat.

"Where are you going to college?" Mason asked, the question stilted.

"Georgetown along with Donovan and Carter," Link answered.

Shaking his head, Mason dragged a hand through his hair. "That chick is terrifying."

Link let out a breathy chuckle. After a beat, he forced his own question out. "Uh, what about you?"

"UCLA."

"Cool."

"Yeah."

Both boys fell silent again. Then Mason spoke up.

"What are you planning on studying?" he asked.

"Law. My mom has a firm and I've kinda been drawn to it. What about you?"

The girl on stage waved her hands, clearly enthralled with her speech.

"Computer science," Mason said.

Link's eyebrows shot up. "Really?"

Mason gave a careless shrug as if the knowledge that he wasn't just a pretty face wasn't a big deal. "I have a thing for coding."

"That's cool."

The student on the other side of Link leaned forward and glared at the two boys.

"Are you seriously talking during our graduation?" she hissed.

"Are you seriously listening to this speech?" Mason asked. He gestured to the girl on stage. "This is the worst speech ever. Who uses utensils as a metaphor?"

Lacking any good response, the girl settled back into her seat, crossing her arms. Mason relaxed, seeming more at ease.

"You still dating the Maddy girl?" Mason asked.

Link nodded. "You still with Valerie?"

Mason made a face. "Nah, that chick was way too clingy. She was planning on taking me to her beach house for a month this summer."

"That doesn't sound too bad-"

"With her parents."

"Oh."

"Yeah."

The valedictorian was replaced by a renowned author who started talking about the importance of being true to oneself. Link barely listened, Mason, pulling him in with a question.

"What are your plans for this summer?"

Link shrugged, summing up all he had thought about for the coming months.

"Well..." Link looked over, his curiosity piqued with the hesitation in Mason's tone. "You know my family doesn't leave for

Camp David until after the Fourth of July, so we could," he shrugged, "I don't know, hang out or something. If you wanted to."

"Really?"

Mason shrugged again as if it could underplay the weight of the offer. Link went along, giving a casual nod.

"Yeah, that could be cool," he said.

"Yeah?" Mason asked, raising one eyebrow.

"Yeah."

Mason nodded and leaned back in his seat. "Cool."

A hesitate smile curled one edge of Link's lips.

The speeches ended, names were called and lines of students crossed the stage accepting diplomas and handshakes. Cheers echoed from different sections as family members encouraged their own.

Following his group, Link was halfway to the stage when a hand nudged him. He glanced around and found Mason jerking his head to the back of the auditorium. Link tried to find what he was motioning to but stopped when he almost tripped. When he stepped up to Principal Wither's and accepted his diploma with a handshake, he looked once more to the back of the room.

Standing in the shadows flanked by two men in black suits, was his father looking at Link and wearing a proud smile. Link returned the look, feeling a sense of warmth. As he returned to his seat the future didn't seem as terrifying as it did before. Though it was unknown he wasn't alone. Besides Carter and Donovan, he had - however strange it might be - a brother and even though it wasn't perfect, a father as well.

No, the future didn't look too bad at all.

Finding Solutions

The day was warm contradicting what the calendar said. The late afternoon sun was sighing and soaking up the last of its glory before it dimmed for the autumn.

Donovan cut the car's engine and climbed out, feeling as heat encased him. The metal staircase clanged as he jogged up it. Link was secure in his room talking to Maddy and that meant that Donovan was free for at least six hours.

Though he had been at Carter's place countless times since they had started dating, Donovan still felt a nervous pulse. He knocked. From beyond the door, he heard the thumping beat of a bass that was too loud. He knocked again, but still no answer. He gave the knob a tentative twist and found it unlocked.

The full force of the music hit him as he stepped inside.

"Carter?" he asked, cautious to enter further without full permission.

There was no answer. Determined to still see her, Donovan made his way to her bedroom where the source of the noise was coming from. He rapped his knuckles on the door, but with the volume of the music, he guessed the chance of her hearing was pretty slim. Taking out his phone, he called her, but she didn't pick up.

After a minute debate, where his hand made treks through his hair, he reached for the doorknob. Hoping he wasn't going to regret his next move, he opened the door.

What waited for him on the other side made him freeze.

Carter was dressed in workout clothes and beating the punching bag. With a spin, she kicked the taut leather, making the bag swing. Before the bag had drifted back to her, she dropped to the ground and did a round of fifteen push-ups, then flipped onto her back and did a rep of thirty crunches. She had barely finished when she jumped back to her feet and attacked the punching bag again.

The ferocity and speed in which she performed the routine startled Donovan. It was more than a want to get her heart racing, it was as if she were trying to outrun something.

"Carter!" he said, over the thundering bass.

When she didn't respond, he crossed the door and shut off her music. At the silence, she spun on him, her face lined in irritation.

"What?" she snapped.

Donovan raised his eyebrows, surprised at the bite.

"I wanted to see you," he said.

Carter blew furiously at a strand of hair that had fallen into her face.

"Well, I don't want to see you. So stop being a clingy boyfriend and leave me alone."

Donovan frowned, the words striking something in his chest. Staring at her, he ran a hand through his hair again, disheveling it even further. Carter turned back to the punching bag and gave it a savage kick. Knowing a threat when he saw it, he left.

At the top of the stairs, he paused, confusion clouding his mind. He was halfway to his car when a thought hit him. Checking his phone, the wrinkle of puzzlement cleared. Passing his car, he sent out a message.

"Sir, I want confirmation on a bit of information. Carter is doing a routine of push-ups, crunches and attack maneuvers. Is this what I think it is?"

Donovan had stepped into the convenient store down the block when he got the reply.

"Affirmative."

Nodding to himself, Donovan bought all that he needed then headed back to Carter's apartment. When he entered this time, the music had remained off but the sound of her landing blows to the punching bag could still be heard. Grabbing a pair of spoons and settling the shopping bag on the coffee table, Donovan kicked off his shoes and sank down onto the couch. After a quick search, he found what he was looking for.

The tv screen began to play a movie that opened with an establishing shot of a high school gym and a class picture day.

By the time the main character had said her name was Jenna for the third time, Carter had appeared. Seeing Donovan on her couch, eating ice cream and watching a movie, she scowled.

"What are you doing?" she said.

Donovan gestured to the screen with his spoon.

"I'm watching 13 Going On 30, want to join?"

Carter eyed the tv and the collection of ice cream cartons like they would attack her at any moment.

"You know how I feel about romance movies," she said, her fists clenched.

"I do, but I figured you could make an exception for me."

An internal battle seemed to rage in Carter's head, as she stood stock still. Donovan watched the movie and acted as if he weren't half watching her, seeing if she would run or attack. Finally making a decision, she grabbed a spoon and carton then sat down beside him.

Donavon let out a breath, feeling a strange sense of accomplishment. Carter jabbed her ice cream. Minutes passed, as Carter's ice cream took a beating.

"You haven't actually ever seen this movie have you?" she asked.

Donovan debated over the two answers but decided from the less aggressive scowl and the tone of her voice that the truth wouldn't bring him bodily harm.

"No, but it was ranked as number three most-watched romance movie when girls are..."

Instead of finishing that sentence, he ate some ice cream.

"How did you know?" she asked.

"Last month you almost bit off my head when I startled you. The month before that you nearly broke my finger when I tried to hug you. Each instance was note-worthy enough I marked it in my calendar. I also got confirmation from your father."

He shrugged as if it wasn't a big deal. Without warning, Carter kissed him.

The shock of it kept him from reacting. By the time his brain kicked back into gear, Carter jerked away. Her face was a mix of desire and frustration. Letting out a breath of annoyance, she slammed her ice cream on the coffee table and stood.

"I hate this. I hate this so much!" She walked a few paces, clutching her hair. "I don't feel like myself. It's like some demon has taken over my body." Donovan rose and moved closer to her. "I want to cry and hit things for no reason. Now you're part of my life and you're seeing me being a complete mess and I hate you for it."

Donovan placed his hands on her shoulders, stilling her.

"Hey," he said. "I get that this is just how it is. And I want you, mess or no mess."

Carter threw his hands off.

"Like that!" She said. "You're being really nice and cute! Will you please stop doing that. It's really annoying and I want to punch you for being so freaking calm all the time! I wish you would stop being perfect for one second."

Feeling like he was getting whiplash, but determined to stick it out, he spread his arms out.

"Fine, I'll stop being nice. Sometimes I think your hair is too messy. It pisses me off that one day you might actually beat me in a fight. Though you hate them, I wish you would wear dresses sometimes cause you would look amazing. I also wish you would wear heels cause I know they would make your legs look extremely hot. There? Is that better?"

Carter's eyebrows inched together. "You think my hair is too messy?"

Donovan rubbed his face, having the feeling he was never going to win.

"Do you really?" she asked.

Knowing that whatever he would say next could end up with them broken up or his arm broken, he went with the next best option, he kissed her.

The frantic, tangled mess that was Carter's emotions seemed to still. She melted into his hold like he was the eye of the storm.

When they broke apart, she rested her forehead on his chest.

"I really hate being a girl sometimes," she said.

He kissed the top of her head. "Yes, but I like you as a girl and wouldn't change a thing."

Carter gripped his shirt. "You're doing that nice thing again."

"Okay, I'll stop." He paused. "You want to watch 13 Going On 30 and eat ice cream."

"If I say yes, does that make me weak?"

"If I said yes, you could break my wrist, so I think that answers your question."

Raising her head, Carter smiled at him. Kissing the tip of her nose, he led her back to the couch. They sat, Carter curled up beside Donovan.

They transitioned from one movie to the next as the ice cream diminished. Eventually, the work out from before got the best of Carter and she fell asleep beside him, a pillow tucked under her head. Having no place he would rather be, Donovan rested a hand on her waist as his other hand played with her hair.

They were towards the end of their third movie when the front door opened. Donovan tensed with panic, while Carter slept on.

Steve walked in and stopped at the sight of his daughter sleeping next to Donovan. In reaction to the line that cut into Steve's brow, Donovan raised his hands.

"Please don't shoot me," he said.

There was a tense moment where Steve held Donovan's gaze. When it slipped down to Carter, Donovan let out a breath.

"You made it through the day," Steve said, hanging up his suit jacket and dropping the keys into their bowl. "I'll give you credit for that. Any more ice cream left?"

Donovan nodded, daring to relax. Grabbing one of the remaining cartons, Steve took a spot by Carter's feet.

"This is one of our favorites," Steve said, to the tv screen.

Donovan focused on the movie as if forgetting what he had been watching for the last hour and a half.

"Notting Hill? Really?"

Steve nodded. "The push-ups, crunches and attack routine was my way of helping her cope. Romance movies were Maggie's way of helping her cope. So I got used to watching them with her." He looked down at his daughter. "It's good to remind her that it's okay to be a girl once in a while."

"You can stop talking about me now," Carter mumbled.

Steve chuckled and nudged Carter's leg. "It's your favorite part, Sarge."

Carter shifted to get a better view. On the screen Julia Roberts stood in the bookstore, staring at Hugh Grant. Instead of watching the movie, Donovan watched Carter. A smile tugged at the corner of his lips as he saw her mouth the words.

"I"m just a girl. Standing in front of a boy. Asking him to love her."

Donovan's smile grew because the answer to that question was so simple. It was always yes.

The Twelfth Date

Donovan parked the Mercedes outside of Carter's apartment and climbed out. The early evening air felt pleasant despite the heat of the day. As he ascended the stairs, he straightened his shirt and rolled his shoulders. Each time he approached her front door he felt this knot of anxiety in his stomach. But once he saw her, that all went away. He knocked and the door opened.

It wasn't Carter on the other side but Steve.

Donovan tried to make his posture even more formal but it was difficult since he was already rigid.

"Hello, sir," Donovan said.

He wished that seeing Steve in casual jeans and a t-shirt would make him less intimidating but it wasn't true. He figured nothing would change facts: he was Carter's father, former Navy SEAL, currently Secret Service.

"Come in," Steve said.

Donovan walked into the living, trying not to look around for Carter.

"Have a seat," Steve said. "Carter is running late with Maggie. Do you want something to drink?"

Donovan nodded since his throat felt suddenly dry. No Carter and alone with her father. Even after going through three different courses to prove he could watch out for Carter, in front of Steve he felt like some reckless teenager here to steal his daughter. Not the twenty-two-year-old he was.

Steve handed Donovan a glass of water and Donovan drank it, reminding himself to slow down so he didn't choke and spit up all over Steve. In contrast, Steve looked completely at ease sipping his water.

"Donovan," Steve said. "This will be your twelfth date."

"Yes, sir."

Steve nodded, regarding Donovan with solemn eyes. Slowly, he set his glass down on the coffee table. Donovan wanted to bolt for the door and make his apologies to Carter later. But he held firm. It was more threats, he could handle that. He'd grown up with three older brothers after all.

But what Steve said startled him.

"Did you know I was a year younger than you are now when Carter was born?"

Seeing the strong, capable man in front of him, Donovan found it hard to picture Steve that young. And with a newborn.

Steve smiled softly, leaning over, arms resting on his knees, hands clasped. "I was twenty-one when I first held Carter. I thought at first that my love for her would come over time." He shook his head. "It was instant. The moment I saw her I knew I would kill to protect this precious baby girl." He locked eyes with Donovan, his gaze serious. "A love like that only grows with time. So imagine how I feel about her now, if back then I was willing to kill for her?"

Donovan swallowed but his throat was dry again.

"I'm telling you this because I was your age once. I know that it's easy when you're young and first getting close to someone to say a lot of things. Make a lot of promises." He held Donovan's gaze. "Do not make my daughter promises you can't keep. Is that clear?"

Donovan swallowed again. "Of course, sir."

Steve eased back, his smile calm. "Good."

The door to the apartment opened and Donovan almost sagged with relief but knew Steve would notice so held himself together. Carter rushed in but stopped at seeing them. She threw one hand behind her making Donovan notice the shopping bags she was attempting to hide.

"How long have you been here?" she asked Donovan.

"Few minutes."

"Captain, you didn't kill him," she said, beaming at her father. "I'm proud of you. I'll be ready in a second."

She darted into the hall and Donovan heard the door to her room close.

"She went shopping with Maggie," Donovan said.

"Yes."

"Of her own free will?"

Steve nodded slowly as if making sure Donovan understood the significance of that. He did.

"Like I said, do not make my daughter promises you can't keep."

Donovan didn't know what to say. He wasn't someone likely to make shallow promises. But he also thought about all the things he did want to say to Carter. How he was seriously falling for her. How he didn't like to think about a future in which she wasn't a part of it in some small way, even if she decided she didn't want to be with him.

Instead of seeing Carter as the girl he loved, he saw her as a girl who was loved by a protective father.

He couldn't admit all the things he wanted to. Steve was right, Donovan couldn't say things that couldn't be unsaid, Carter deserved more than that. She deserved actions more than words. Words were easy, actions would say it all.

So he would wait. He would show her over and over again that he chose her. That she was the girl who he wanted by his side always. That now or in five, ten years it didn't matter, he would feel the same way.

When she emerged from her room in a maroon top - that blended perfectly with her skin tone -, a pair of loose cotton shorts, and her hair free of a ponytail, he was hit again with how much she meant to him.

As long as she wanted him around, he would be there.

"You ready to go?" she asked.

Donovan stood. "Yes."

He shook Steve's hand and nodded, letting Steve know that he understood it all. Steve smiled in return. Carter opened the door.

"Don't wait up, Captain," Carter said.

Steve snorted. "Funny one. I'll be right here when you get back."

"You need a life," Carter said.

"I told you, you are my life."

Carter grinned and took Donovan's hand. Somehow the action meant more to him than before, as if his promise to himself meant everything he did with Carter held more weight.

"So," she said, as they headed to his car. "You said you wanted to show me all your favorite places in DC, is that still the plan?"

"It is."

They drove off and traveled in silence. For the first time, Donovan wasn't worried about doing things right but things wrong. Utterly aware of how he could mess up this perfect thing.

"Captain's threat really got to you this time, didn't it?" Carter said.

"What makes you say that?" Donovan asked.

"Because you have a nervous bunny energy about you."

"Did you call me a bunny?"

Carter smiled. "Yes, a nervous bunny."

"I'm not nervous."

"You sure? Because I get the feeling that you're stressing over there in silence."

"I'm not."

"Sure," Carter said mockingly.

She turned her head away, watching the passing scenery. Donovan didn't say anything, realizing that he was stressing. Hearing Steve talk about how precious Carter was made him see her as that even more than before. It made him aware of how he could lose her.

"You're not going to hurt me," Carter said to the window. "I trust you."

The girl with trust issues trusted him.

"What if I do?"

She looked at him. "Then you'll be dead and I'll move on."

Donovan smiled at that and Carter relaxed. "Thank you. I thought you were going to be Mr. Intense from here on out and then I would be the one hurting you."

"Like you could hurt me?" he said.

"There are more ways to hurt than physical. I should know."

Though the comment was made lightly, Donovan still understood the depth behind it. And again he feared he would somehow make that list of people who'd left a scar on her.

Carter hit his shoulder. "Snap out of it. I'm allowed to make morbid jokes." She shook her head. "I'm talking to Captain when I get home. He has to stop threatening you. It's ruining my date."

"Sorry."

"Don't say sorry, be Donovan again. You know, that obnoxious know-it-all that I've felt like punching on multiple occasions."

"And have tried but failed to."

"That's mean."

Donovan sent her a wicked grin and she laughed.

He pulled the car up to the curb outside a used book store and they both got out. When Donovan rounded the car, he hesitated, eying Carter.

"Am I supposed to make mention of how you look good in your new clothes or do you not want me to draw attention to the fact that you went shopping at all?"

Carter threw up her hands. "I have no idea. I felt like I kept wearing the same thing on our dates and wanted something new. But now I don't know if I should feel better that I have new clothes and I don't know if I want your approval or not? And if I do, does that make me less me?"

"I don't know. I bought this shirt and wondered if you'd like it, does that make me less me?"

Carter leaned back, taking in the dark blue shirt. "No, because that shirt just makes you look better."

"And those clothes make you more attractive to me."

"I guess I'm happy I got them then. Now, why this place?"

Donovan took Carter's hand and led her into the bookstore. It smelled like a second home to him. The cost of new books added up when he'd first started buying them online when he arrived in DC. That's when he'd found this place and made a trip to it once a month, sometimes twice.

"Hey, Donovan," Doug, the cashier, said.

"Hi, Doug."

Donovan guided Carter into an aisle and she stared at him.

"The cashier knows you?" she said.

"Yeah, I might come here...often."

Laughing, she just shook her head.

"Since I'd already finished high school by the time I went back to Middle School with Link, I needed something to distract me from the boring teaching. Books became that thing."

Donovan took her all over, showing her his favorite genres. When he found a series he loved, he pulled out the first book and started talking about it. Carter rested her shoulder against a bookcase and looked up at him, never interrupting.

There was something in the way she watched him that made him feel loved, though he couldn't explain why. She was simply looking at him, listening to him. But it wasn't the same as her other looks.

Once finished, he checked his watch, realizing he'd been talking for almost half an hour.

"We should keep moving," Donovan said, slightly embarrassed he'd talked so long about one series. "There's more to see and we don't want to miss it."

The next stop was a Mexican food place. When Donovan pushed open the door, the aroma of spices welcomed them. This was another home to him. Books for his mind, food for his stomach.

"Smells good," Carter commented.

"Growing up near San Diego I lived with Mexican food being a staple in my life. When I moved here I missed the food almost as much as I missed my family." He drew her to the counter. "You can imagine my happiness when I found this place. It's the closest you can get to authentic this far from the border.

After they ordered, he talked about how this was where he took Brock when he got his job at the FBI. And where he visited with his brothers whenever they came to town.

When Carter finished eating, she admitted that it was one of the best meals she'd ever had.

After that, Donovan took her to an ice cream place that added crushed-up candy bars to the ice cream while customers watched. With their desserts, Donovan held her out of the shop and towards the Mall. They arrived as the sun set. Sitting on the steps of the Lincoln Memorial, they ate their ice cream and watched the sky as it blended pastel colors together.

"Does this place have any special connection?" Carter asked, stealing some of Donovan's ice cream. "Or are we here for the sunset?"

It took a moment for Donovan to answer since he was enthralled with her action of stealing his ice cream. It was so simple but something about it made him content. Like this was something they'd always done and would always do.

He cleared his throat. "This was the first place you met James. Also, this was the first place I talked to Brock about you."

"Oh? And what did you say about me?"

Donovan thought about how he'd gone on some monologue about her and then his thoughts had run away from him. Both were too revealing and he focused on scooping his ice cream.

"I think I said something about finding you interesting or something like that."

"Okay," Carter said, skeptically.

She sent him a smile that said she didn't quite believe him. He didn't mind. Having her know him well enough to know that he wasn't admitting everything made him feel like they shared a special connection.

Finished with their ice cream, they tossed their trash and Donovan took Carter's hand again. He walked through the city, talking about in the first year how he'd run every street, charting a new path each morning. He'd wanted to know the layout and by the end of the year, he did. Eventually, their journey ended back at the car and a short drive later, they idled before Link and Donovan's apartment. Donovan didn't move from the driver's seat.

"I still remember my father dropping me off here," he said. Carter stared up at the building. "I thought about how weird the city sounded. I grew up with the loud rumble of trucks, distant gunfire, helicopters overhead. It felt strange. Foreign."

Carter looked at him, her gaze intent.

"And you were only sixteen."

She touched his face, an awed glint in her eyes.

"Donovan Keller, you are unlike any guy I have ever met."

He grinned. "I should hope so, it means you can't easily replace me."

Carter kissed him and when she pulled back there was a quiet certainty in her eyes. It said everything, that he was irreplaceable, he was hers.

"So is this the end of memory lane?" she asked.

It took a second for Donovan to pull his thoughts together, she seemed to have that effect on him.

"No, there's one more stop."

They drove away, neither speaking, neither feeling the need to.

When Donovan pulled into the lane to Carter's home and stopped before her house, she frowned in puzzlement.

"You said there was one more stop," she said. "This is just you dropping me off."

"It is."

Donovan got out of the car and Carter followed. When he took a spot against the hood, Carter joined him. He tilted his head back, absorbing the night sky. He didn't understand why but the patch of sky looked better in this one spot. Maybe it was for the simple reason that it was the one patch Carter would always look up at. He focused on her.

"I've dropped you off here a lot of times," Donovan said. "But the time that sticks out the most is after that party we went to for Maddy. The one where Link fell asleep in the back of the car. Do you remember what you told me?"

Teasingly, Carter cocked her head to one side.

"I believe I told you I wasn't impressed by how much you benched."

Donovan nodded. He knew there were so many promises he wouldn't be able to give her. But he wanted to share a promise he'd made to himself.

"Yes, and you told me I would have to find some other way to impress you," he said. "As you walked away I told myself I would."

Carter laughed. "Is that why you're always flexing your muscles when I look over and wear a tight shirt?"

"Has it been working?"

Carter ran her fingers through his hair, her laughter fading. "No. Because you impressed me in so many other ways." Her hand came to rest on the back of his neck and he never wanted her to remove it. "You impressed me by protecting Link and by going through the million and one hoops my father has made you jump through just to date me."

She shook her head in wonder.

"There are so many days I don't understand why I'm worth the effort. Yet here we are."

Donovan felt his emotions building inside his chest ready to explode into words. But he held them in. Actions above words.

"Here we are," he said.

He kissed her, sliding his arms around her waist. When they eventually broke apart, Carter let out a sigh.

"I would say come in and we could watch something," she said. "But the living room curtain is twitching and somehow having Captain hovering nearby us just doesn't seem super romantic."

"You might be onto something there."

Carter kissed him briefly once more then headed to the stairs. Donovan watched her as she climbed and he never wanted to look away. As she slipped inside, she sent him one final smile. He made a promise to Steve that he wouldn't make promises to Carter. But that didn't mean he couldn't make a promise to himself.

So as he stood there a second longer, he whispered the words that echoed in his chest.

"I love you, Carter Owens. And one day, if you'll have me, I'm going to marry you."

When Carter Wasn't Herself

The sliding glass doors parted and Donovan glanced up. A teenager with a bleeding arm walked in, trailed by a nervous looking parent. Having given up on finding distraction in the muted TV screen hanging off the wall in the emergency room lobby, Donovan focused on the two newcomers. The mother talked with the nurse behind the desk. After a quiet back and forth, she accepted paperwork and led her son to a section of chairs.

Dismissing the teenager, having assessed the injury was from a biking accident, Donovan went back to staring at the double doors leading to the rest of the hospital. His heel bounced against the tile floor, his bottled-up energy needing some form of displacement. When the doors opened, he stood. A male in his late forties wearing a white lab coat over slacks and a button-down shirt stepped out.

"Doctor Andrews," Donovan said, approaching the man.

"You're the one who brought in Ms. Owens?" the man asked.

"Yes, sir. How is she?"

The doctor wrapped his hands around the stethoscope that hung about his neck.

"She's fine, it wasn't a break, but a bad sprain," he said. "She said she got it during training?"

Donovan nodded, trying not to think about the incompetent trainer who had attacked when he should have simply been demonstrating. The small intake of breath Carter had given and the pain that shocked her features was like a stab to Donovan's heart. It had taken all of his self-control to walk Carter away and not break the trainer's arm.

"Well," the doctor continued. "Her arm will be fine. It was a bad sprain so I gave her some morphine for the pain. I'll take you to her and then you're free to take her home."

The doctor pushed through the swinging doors, Donovan right behind. The corridor beyond was lined with beds with machines acting as bookends on either side and divided with thin pale blue curtains. Some sections were concealed while others showed grimacing patients being looked over by nurses and others asleep, escaping the pain.

"Here you are," Doctor Andrews said, motioning to one open section. "Make sure to drop off the release form on your way out."

"Thank you," Donovan said.

The doctor left and Donovan stepped towards the hospital bed. Carter was sitting up, wearing a paper gown, her arm wrapped up and hanging in a sling. When she focused on him, he saw the obvious effects of the drug. The intensity that always burned in her eyes had been numbed. She was still his Carter, but without the sharp edges.

"How are you feeling?" Donovan asked, stopping by the side.

"Grand," she said, with a lopsided smile.

A piece of Donovan's worry evaporated with the response and happy look.

"Ready to get out of here?" he asked.

A little wobbly, Carter placed a hand on his chest, grinning even more.

"I will go anywhere with you," she said.

Fighting his amusement, Donovan took her hand and helped her out of the bed.

"You should get dressed first," he said. "I'll be outside."

Scoffing, Carter waved her hand, the look floppy like she was swatting away a fly.

"Just turn around."

Hesitating, Donovan closed the curtain and kept his back to her. After two muttered curses, Donovan wondered if he should offer help, but didn't want to take advantage of the drugged moment. A third curse came and Donovan opened his mouth. Before he could speak, he felt a tap on his arm. Turning, he found Carter fully dressed and holding up her damaged arm.

"I need you," she said.

The statement was so simple but Donovan couldn't have ever imagined it freely coming out of Carter's mouth. Taking the sling, he eased her bandaged wrist into it. As he went to clasp it around her neck, she leaned into him, resting her head against his chest.

"Why do you always smell so good?" she asked, her eyes closed.

The closeness of her made Donovan falter, but he regained his composure and finished the task.

"You're all set."

Uncertain, Carter righted herself and stared up at Donovan.

"Hi," she said.

Donovan wanted to laugh. It was as if she were someone completely different. When she looked at him, her mind was quiet, she wasn't trying to solve the world. She wasn't trying to solve him.

"Hi," he said.

He moved the curtain aside, but Carter poked his arm, stalling him.

"Hmm?"

"I want your jacket," she said.

"You cold?"

She shook her head and teetered with the motion. Instantly, Donovan reached out and steadied her.

"How come you want my jacket?" he asked.

She squinted at him, the look asking if he were stupid.

"Cause it smells like you."

Shaking his head in wonderment, Donovan removed his jacket and draped it over Carter's shoulders. Snatching the release forms from the edge of the bed, they headed out.

A soft brush of skin startled Donovan and he glanced down. Carter's brow was scrunched up in concentration as she tried to connect her hand with his. Part of him wanted to watch as she worked to take his hand but decided to take pity on her and offered it up.

Sighing, Carter slipped hers through his and held onto it tightly. It was like he was her anchor in a storm and she was never going to let go. He was fine with that.

"Since your father is away, Maggie wanted to take you home, but something happened at the deli and she couldn't come."

"I'm glad it was you."

Carter stumbled to the side but course corrected, leaning against Donovan instead. After two failed attempts, she managed to rest her head on his shoulder. Donovan stared down at her. She seemed to fit so perfectly there, yet this occurrence was rare.

They dropped off the forms and Donovan led Carter out to the parking lot. He opened the passenger side door for her and guided her in. When he climbed into the driver's seat, he found Carter struggling to work the seat belt.

"Stupid thing," she groaned.

Donovan reached over and clicked it in. Relieved, Carter sank back against the seat, smiling at him.

"My hero," she said.

Donovan chuckled. "I've definitely been working way too hard then."

They pulled out and eased into the late afternoon traffic. When he glanced over at Carter, she had curled up on the seat and was gazing at him.

"Is it ever annoying being so good looking?" she asked.

Donovan fought a smile at the comment.

"There it is," Carter breathed out, gently touching the corner of his mouth where the smile was hidden. "That's my favorite smile. It's the one that says you find me amusing. Or you don't want to show how much you like me."

Donovan's eyes cut to her. "I didn't realize I had a smile for that."

Carter gave a sleepy nod. "You do. You have a lot of smiles. Thirty-seven to be exact."

Donovan chuckled, glancing at her again. She looked at home beside him in the passenger seat, like she never wanted to be anywhere else but his side.

"You have six different ones just for Link," she said.

"Really?"

"Yup. For when he's sad. When he needs someone like a big brother. When you want to help him not feel alone. You have so many smiles. Like you have so many thoughts and I will never know them all." Carter blinked at him. "I know you so well and then there are times you look at me and I can never fully understand what's going through your mind."

She closed her eyes and nestled deeper into the seat.

"I see you interact with others and know what's on your mind, but you look at me...and I don't know anything." Her voice was soft, unaware she was talking out loud anymore. "Maybe I just get lost in you. You have such pretty eyes and at the same time, they are so much more. It's like...you see everything. You see everything in me. I'm not a mystery to you, I'm...I don't know."

Donovan wanted to speak, to admit everything she was to him, but he also knew that this moment would be erased from her memory. These truths she was sharing weren't meant for him. These were the thoughts he was always trying to read when he looked at her. Now he knew them and now he loved her more for them because she was just as taken with him as he was with her.

"You're my everything, Carter," he whispered.

Beside him, Carter let out a happy sigh. Donovan looked at her and found a tiny smile dotting her lips. The rest of the drive passed in silence, Donovan stealing glances at his sleepy companion. When they pulled up to the apartment, Carter stirred. She blinked at the fading light and her home. Donovan got out and rounded the car, opening her door by the time she had gotten her seat belt undone.

"Need help?" he asked.

Carter gave a drowsy nod. When Donovan leaned forward to assist her out, she wrapped her good arm around his neck. Smiling, he scooped her up and nudged the door closed with his foot.

"I take it you can't walk then," he said.

Carter shook her head. "I like your arms."

As he walked to the stairs, her head fell against his shoulder. He felt her warm breath on his neck and for a second his thoughts collapsed. Shaking himself, he climbed the stairs and got them into the apartment.

When the lights flicked on, he found the living room had been recently cleaned and the touches of Steve's seriousness about Maggie popping up in small ways: The pillows on the couch and the throw blanket draped across the back, the potted plant in the kitchen and newly framed photos hanging on the wall, covering the empty faded spots that had been there.

"You want to go to sleep?" Donovan asked.

Carter shook her head.

"A movie then?"

A nod. He laid her down on the couch. After kicking off her shoes, she curled up, head resting on one of the new pillows. Donovan took the blanket off the back and put it over her. Grabbing the remote, he then flipped on the TV and found something that had at least one explosion and a car chase. When he turned back to Carter, she was staring up at him.

"You want me to call Maggie?" he asked, not wanting to leave but uncertain.

"Stay," she whispered.

"Okay."

He took a spot on the couch. For a while they watched the movie, neither talking, but both thinking of each other. Halfway through, Carter sat up.

Before Donovan could ask if she needed anything, she crossed the couch and curled up beside him, dragging the blanket with her. Donovan reached for it and pulled it around her as she rested her head against his shoulder. Instinctively, he wrapped his arms around her, cocooning her.

The suddenness of it all surprised Donovan but he said nothing. Right then his life felt perfect. Every moment of feeling trapped or frustrated over the last seven years didn't seem to matter. If it had lead to this one instance, it was all worth it.

Carter sighed, relaxing against him.

"In case you were wondering," she said, her breath warm as it fell over his bare arms. "You're my everything."

He smiled, yes it was all worth it

College Years

Meeting The Family

A tight coil of nerves formed in Carter's stomach as the Marine at the guard house waved them through the gates, offering Donovan a cheery welcome home. As the car drove through, Carter tensed. Even as the torrent in her mind picked up, she could still sense the change in Donovan. Though nothing shifted in his demeanor a sort of lightness came over him. The passivity of his face softened. He was home.

Carter tried to let his ease be enough to reassure her, but it didn't. As they headed further onto the base, she wasn't aware of their surroundings, too focused on their destination. By the time they stopped outside a one-story house with a fresh coat of tan paint and a trim front yard, she was gripping the center console. Her knuckles were white but she couldn't bring herself to let go.

As Donovan drew out the keys, he looked over at her. Carter felt his gaze but couldn't tear her eyes away from the house. Donovan's house. His true home. Donovan rested his hand on hers, gently prying her fingers off. Even when he laced his hand with hers, she didn't look away.

"Carter," he said, his voice coaxing her to met his gaze.

Forcibly, she ripped her attention away from the brown front door.

It was only then she saw his transformation. He was smiling at her. A smile that was offered up without any true cause. He looked younger, the weight of responsibility always weighing on him left outside the gates. Even his blue eyes had a brightness to them like he was simply a college kid coming home for Thanksgiving.

"I can't cook," Carter blurted out.

The laugh that this comment received was untroubled and somehow different than any laugh he had given. It spoke of the boy Donovan had been in this place. Someone who tackled his brothers because they annoyed him. Someone who joked around with men twice his age and never felt the difference. Someone who knew exactly who he was and what he was going to do when he grew up. It was a laugh that soothed a fraction of her nerves.

"You don't have to cook," Donovan said. "My mom will and she doesn't expect you to. Come on, they're going to love you."

Releasing her hand, Donovan climbed out. After a slow breath, Carter did as well. It was warm despite the season. The California sun watched over the world, unobscured by clouds. Around her, the smell of dirt, machine oil, and a dry heat layered the air. The low rumble of tires undercut by gunfire filled her ears. Even far from the main training area, the ground thrummed with energy. All these pieces seemed to fit into the puzzle of Donovan, defining him even more.

Taking her hand, he guided Carter up the front path and to the house. When he opened the door, they were swept up into the scent of Thanksgiving. A long hallway stretched out in front of them, doorways lining it.

"Mom, dad?" Donovan called out.

Carter knew those terms but hearing them from Donovan felt strange. He was a bachelor, a man that had been on his own since he was sixteen. But he was still someone's son. They stepped into a living room and Carter was struck by it. It was neat, a dark blue couch butted up against a white wall with a light gray carpet beneath.

But that was not what she noticed, instead it was the signs that this house had held four boys. There were marks in the wall from fights that had gotten out of hand. A spot in the carpet that looked like someone had burned a hole in it. Fraying edges on the couch that told of roughhousing boys who had clambered over it too many times.

This was Donovan's childhood. This was the part of him that she had been slowly teasing out of him. Now she saw so much and felt like she knew him better than before. His early life hadn't been easy, but these markings were signs that he had been young and wild once.

As they entered the living room a man in his fifties rose from the couch. His gray hair was military short, his face hard with earned lines and though he wore a button-down shirt and slacks it was all with the air of a uniform.

A door at the end of the room swung open and Donovan's mother stepped out. She was in every aspect a contrast to her husband. A soft face with caring blue eyes sat atop of a rounded figure. Before Donovan could say anything, his mother rushed forward and hugged him.

"My boy is home," she said.

Donovan had to bend down to hug her and even then still managed to look like a little kid for a brief second. When he shook his father's hand, that boy was tucked away.

"Donovan," his father said.

"Sir."

Donovan stepped back and gestured Carter forward, placing a hand on her lower back. The feel of it was a comfort as her nerves had doubled.

"Mom, dad. I want you to meet my girlfriend, Carter Owens."

Eleanor closed the distance first, taking Carter's hand and resting her other on top.

"It is such a pleasure to meet you," she said.

"The pleasure is mine," Carter said.

Up close she could see that past the caring blue eyes was a keen intelligence underneath. An intelligence that Donovan had inherited and one that Carter felt could pick her apart layer by layer until it saw the core of who she was. But Eleanor's smile was welcoming and Carter let herself relax. When she shook Ted's hand, it was callused and as strong as a rod of iron.

"I'm happy you're here," he said.

"As am I."

Ted offered up a smile. It was a look that didn't come quickly and Carter could see that this gesture was rare for him, as if smiles were only meant for easing the spirits of a dying man.

"Ted," Eleanor said. "Why don't you and Donovan catch up and I'll show Carter around."

Beyond the swinging door was a dining room and off that was a kitchen, the smell of cooking food doubling.

"I'm not great in the kitchen," Carter said. "But I would be happy to set the table or do dishes."

The offer had been a suggestion of Maggie's when Carter had confided her lack of culinary skills and that she would have nothing to give. Eleanor's smile widened in appreciation but she shook her head.

"You're our guest, you don't have to do anything. Come, I'll show you Donovan's room."

They cut across the hallway into one of the bedrooms. Sunlight illuminated the two different single beds pushed to opposite sides, a desk that sat in the middle and odd assortment of posters and framed photos.

Without having to be told, Carter knew which side was Donovan's. Though both beds held the same military neat corners, the one on the left had a more rigid tidiness to it. The items on the bedside table were all set into straight lines and even the old pair of shoes beneath the mattress were perfectly positioned side by side.

Carter walked over and settled onto the bed, peering around the room. It was easy to see how in such a small space Donovan would butt heads with his brother. Eleanor sat down at the desk chair, resting her head on her fist. The casualness of her posture seemed at odds with the air of Marine strictness Carter could sense around her.

"He was so young when he left," she said, eyes traveling around the room.

The comment brought Carter's focus on her.

"How did you feel about him leaving?" she asked.

A sad smile played around the corners of Eleanor's mouth. The lines around her eyes seemed to deepen with a loss that hadn't healed.

"I didn't want him to go. He was only sixteen. I was worried about how being on his own and with such a big responsibility would affect him. Effect his spirit. He was such a wild and adventurous kid that I knew having to grow up so fast would steal some of that away. But even after we had talked it over in the month before he left, he still wanted to go."

The sadness faded from her smile as her eyes took on a distant look, memories taking hold.

"None of his brothers or even his father knew, but he called me every day for a year. Even if I was busy making dinner he would just ask me to put the phone on speaker so he could hear me moving about. I helped him as he adjusted. Those first few months were the hardest.

"More than being on his own it was the shock of what he really had to face. Link was struggling to come to terms with his situation and wanted nothing to do with Donovan. I believe that was the hardest part. The other part was going from being taken seriously by grown men to being surrounded by boys that still laughed at fart jokes."

Carter knew all these facts from having Donovan tell her, but somehow in his old room and hearing it from his mother, the reality of all he had gone through hit her. More than ever her respect for him grew.

"I could feel him losing himself in that year," Eleanor continued. "It wasn't until he told me of his thoughts of quitting that we came up with the idea of college classes. He needed something that reminded him of who he was and his true age. It helped and Link eventually accepted Donovan. But for a long time, I didn't know if he was going to be able to get through it." She smiled, the look speaking of her pride in her son and his strength and determination. "But he did."

"I'm glad he did," Carter said.

Eleanor's eyes cleared, coming back from the past.

"I am too," she said, her eyes twinkling with affection.

The front door opened and the call of male voices rose, crushing the quiet of the house.

"It appears my sons have arrived," Eleanor said.

Despite how she had felt meeting Donovan's parents, Carter didn't have the same apprehension about his brothers. Already she had met two of them and her nerves weren't in the same state of agitation.

When they walked back into the living room it was to find Donovan getting roughly pulled into bone-crushing hugs. A comment was made that Carter missed and Donovan shoved James. That was all it took, the two went at each other like they were still boys. They crashed into the couch, James punched Donovan's side as he retaliated with a kick to the shin. Eleanor cleared her throat and even with the grunts and shouts, it was heard like a sixth sense.

Clint grabbed James, hauling him off Donovan and Brock gave Donovan a hand up. Next, to each other, the brother's looked like copies of one another with small aspects changed. Donovan was the smallest in size by far, the years of having to look like a teenager keeping him from developing as his brothers had.

"I believe you have someone to meet," Eleanor said, eyeing her sons.

More than their father's commanding voice, their mother had the power to still the jostling bunch. Donovan stepped over to Carter, his smile wide with something wild and mischievous. As he turned back to his brothers, he took Carter's hand in his, giving it a reassuring squeeze.

"You already know James." In response to this, James gave Carter a teasing wink. "And you briefly met Brock." The oldest and the one beside James with a more square jaw nodded. "That one is Clint." The second oldest had his father's strong, sloped nose. He gave her a quick smile. "Guys this is Carter Owens."

Instead of offering up the usual forms of greetings they jumped straight in.

"You're really the one that beat Donny in a race," Clint said, head cocked like he didn't believe it.

James spread his arms out. "Makes sense to me, Donovan is the slowest."

Carter raised an eyebrow at him. "Are you saying that I wouldn't be able to beat you?"

The guys fell into a round of laughter. Donovan looked at Carter, but she wasn't offended.

"Carter, please," James said. "I understand that you might be able to win against this sorry excuse but against us? Well, that's another issue."

"So you wouldn't mind proving that?" she asked.

All three guys raised their eyebrows in surprise, looking back and forth between each other.

"Now?" Clint asked.

"Sure. Unless you want time to prepare," Carter said.

James cracked his knuckles, a wicked grin spreading over his lips.

"You planning on running in that?" he asked, nodding to her outfit.

"Nope," she said, crossing her arms. "I got my bag in the car and workout clothes in there."

Brock nudged Clint's shoulder, glancing between his brothers.

"All right let's do this."

As the guys went off to change into their own clothes, Donovan turned to Carter.

"You sure about this? Cause you don't have to do this," he said.

"I'll be fine. I promised you once that I would beat them, didn't I?"

Donovan smiled but there was a hesitancy in his eyes. Before he could question her again, she held out her hand for the keys and he placed them in her palm.

After she had retrieved her duffle bag and was about to step back into the house, the door opened and Ted stepped out.

"Carter," he said. "I want you to understand that you don't need to do this if you don't want to."

Carter smiled at him. "Sir, I see how even though they joke and mock Donovan, that they are protective of him. They want someone good enough for him. I can't cook, I'm only in my first semester of college and I'm not a leggy blonde that can stun men with my looks. I'm an eighteen-year-old girl who can assemble a gun under a minute and run your sons into the ground. They are Marines, what they understand are competition and victory. So to win their respect yes, I have to do this."

He gave her another one of his stored away smiles.

"You're a smart girl."

"I was raised by a Navy SEAL."

Ted gave a rough chuckle. "I would suggest not telling them that."

***

As Carter was pulling her hair back into a ponytail, a knock came on the bathroom door. She opened it and went back to tying her hair. Donovan rested on the door frame.

"You ready?" he asked.

Carter would never admit this to Donovan, but two months ago, the day after Donovan had made an off-handed comment about Carter eventually meeting his family, she had started training at five in the morning. Even though he had always promised her that his family would love her there had been a seed of doubt that she would fail. That somehow if she didn't earn their approval she would lose Donovan's. And so she had done everything in her power to never let that happen. She was going to win this race because she planned on never losing him.

She cupped his face and kissed him.

"Always," she said.

Outside, Ted and Eleanor climbed into the cab of a black truck as their sons clambered into the back. When Carter sat down on the ridged floor, Donovan took the spot beside her. Dirt rose in clouds around them as they drove off, Carter's hair dancing in the wind.

As they bumped along, the brothers shared stories of their time riding in the back of the truck. Like when Clint had gotten drunk and tried to surf as they drove, nearly falling out of the back. Or how Brock had done a drive-by with paintball guns with Donovan acting as a sharpshooter. With the stories came Donovan's laugh contagious and filled with a part of him she had never seen before. It was a part that she loved seeing.

They stopped at a training area that held a track and football field. Everyone scrambled out and stopped on the track. As Carter stretched, Donovan offered whispered advice, telling her the weakness of his brothers, how Clint liked to sprint at the beginning but always lost wind towards the end. How Brock was a steady runner and if she got out in front of him after he found his stride, she couldn't lose. James was a wild card and would pull a burst of energy at the end.

By the time Carter was warmed up, she had a game plan.

"Are we doing a mile?" she asked.

The trio glanced at each other and then nodded. As they lined up, Carter could see Donovan's unease. It struck her then that he wanted them to like her just as much as she did. More than ever she wasn't going to let him down or let him go.

Ted held a stopwatch as Donovan held a starter's pistol.

"On your mark," Donovan shouted.

Around her, the energy of his brothers morphed into an intense focus that blinded them to everything else.

"Get set."

Carter felt her heart thudding in her chest and adrenaline coursing through her. The heat, the pressure of the race and the world faded away. This one moment was all that mattered right now.

The crack of the gun ripped through the air and she took off like a comet. Her feet pounded against the track, her legs pumping harder, shooting her forward. As Donovan had said, Clint sprinted forward. Carter let him, focusing on Brock instead. The moment he found his rhythm, Carter increased her speed and cut ahead of him.

As they entered their final lap, Clint had lost a bit of his steam and Carter passed him, leaving only James beside her. She waited, sensing his mounting energy as they rounded their last curve. Just as he was about to surge forward, Carter beat him to it, pulling from her reserve of strength and charging forward.

The suddenness of it was enough to surprise James for a fraction of a second. It was all the time Carter needed, taking the lead and cutting across the finish line a half a second before him.

As Carter raced to a stop, she became aware of Donovan shouting with excitement as he ran to her and scooped her up into a hug. He spun her around, careless of how sweaty she was. When he set her down, he kissed her, his face beaming with pride.

"My girl," he said.

His brothers crowded around them, jostling Donovan and offering Carter congratulatory high fives. She accepted them with a tired smile. As they ambled their way back to Eleanor and Ted, James and Brock nudged and pushed at Donovan, asking him how he managed to get her. Still trying to gather her breath, Carter barely noticed as Clint sidled up to her.

"Welcome to the family," he said.

She gave a weak laugh. "You understand we've only been dating for a couple of months and aren't even engaged, right?"

Clint gave an uncaring shrug.

"Yes, but that's on you now." Carter gave him a puzzled look. Clint pointed to where Donovan was putting James into a headlock. "I saw my brother's face when you crossed the finish line. The position is yours whenever he finally admits it and you finally accept it."

Carter smiled, feeling her fear melt away.

Part Two

"James, if you eat another marshmallow you will have all the dishes," Donovan's mother said.

Donovan grinned, his back to the kitchen as he continued to peel potatoes. He won. The last count James had was 28 marshmallows while Donovan's count was 32.

"And Donovan," his mother said. "Don't for a second think I didn't notice you stealing marshmallows as well."

Donovan put on his best innocent face. "Mom, I wouldn't do that."

Carter snorted and his mother shook her head, leaning close to Carter. "He always thinks because he's the baby boy that I won't punish him."

Despite the embarrassing title, Donovan smiled, enjoying the sight of his mother and Carter connecting. Though he knew everyone in his family would like her, he'd been nervous. His family meant the world to him and now Carter did. He hadn't been sure what he would do if those two worlds clashed.

"She likes to think she's tough," Donovan said. "But my status has been a source of escape for a lot of troubles."

"Fine," his mother said. "Maybe I'll make up for my lack of punishment now, you can do the dishes all by yourself."

Brock, Clint, and James all burst out laughing. Donovan wrapped his arm around his mother's shoulders, always surprised to find he was taller than her.

"Mom," he said, gently. "You wouldn't want me to miss out on time with you and my girlfriend, would you? The two most important women in my life."

His mother rolled her eyes, though Donovan knew he'd won. Carter shook her head, a disbelieving smile in the corner of her mouth. When he locked eyes with her, she crossed her arms.

"Don't think for one second that those little teasing games are going to work on me. 'Cause I promise you, they won't."

Donovan grinned and kissed Carter on the cheek, eliciting an eye roll and a suppressed smile.

"Of course I would never dream they'd work on you," he said, even as he saw her soften.

"Can someone make him stop, I don't feel like throwing up my marshmallows all over these potatoes," James said.

Donovan smacked the back of James's head as he returned to his own pile of potatoes. In return, James kicked Donovan in the butt. Before they could break out into an all-out brawl in the kitchen, their mother cleared her throat. They both settled back into their tasks.

"Okay," Eleanor said. "Carter do you know how to handle a knife?"

"I can hit a target dead center at fifty yards with one," she said.

Donovan knew he was in love with this girl.

"And here I was completely baffled why my son was dating you," Eleanor teased. "How about cutting up vegetables?"

"Show me what to do and I can do it."

"I'll show her," Donovan volunteered.

His mother gave him a knowing smile but nodded acceptance anyway. Grabbing a load of peeled potatoes, Donovan carried them over to Carter.

"If you think that you can use this as a ploy to wrap your arms around me to show me how cutting is done, I will stab you," she said.

Donovan grinned and slipped a knife from the holder. "That only works with sports. Here this is how you hold the knife."

As Donovan instructed Carter what to do, he silently savored it all. Having her standing next to him in the house he grew up in. Hearing his brothers talk behind him and seeing Carter smile at their comments. Laughing when she threw a quip back at them.

She fit into his family like a missing puzzle piece.

When all the prep work for the Thanksgiving dinner was completed, Donovan looked to his brothers and they all grinned.

"Okay, what are you all thinking?" Carter said. "Because I know you're all sharing the same thought."

"How do you feel about football?" Brock asked.

Carter crossed her arms. "I've watched it with my dad but that's about it."

"You up for a game?" Clint asked.

She shrugged. "Tell me what to do and I'll do it."

With a cheer, James ran to grab the football, Clint called up a few cadets still on the base, and Donovan led Carter out of the house with Brock. Though November the sun still offered rays of warmth.

"You ready to lose," James asked as he came racing out of the house with Clint.

"Not likely," Donovan said shoving James, who hit the dirt.

As James moved to kick at Donovan, Donovan took off running, his brothers chasing after him. Before he could think of looking back for Carter, she sprinted past him.

"Come on soldier," she said. "Let's see what you got."

Laughing, Donovan picked up his pace and darted after her. The group arrived at the beach, sweating and laughing as they tried to outdistance each other. Donovan stopped at the water's edge, panting and hands on his knees.

"I declare myself the winner," he said.

For that statement, he got hit by Clint and Carter and staggered, falling into the sand.

"Fat chance," Carter said. "Brock beat you by a mile."

"No! I won," James said.

The argument felt like home to Donovan. All his life he'd grown up getting into fights over the smallest things. None of it ever mattered but to him, this was family, pointless debates, and conversations that ended with someone getting tackled. It felt good to be home.

Their argument eventually died as a group of Marines arrived and called out.

"Are we going to play?" Cadet Addison asked.

"Yeah, I'm team captain," Brock announced.

"I'm second," Gomez said.

"Who's this?" Williams asked, eying Carter.

Donovan stepped closer to her, smiling but wanting to make it clear that she was not to be harassed.

"This is Carter, my girlfriend," he said.

All the men nodded, still taking Carter in. For her part, she stared back, making it clear she didn't feel intimidated in the least.

"Are we going to play?" she asked. "Or are you going to continue to stare at me like you haven't seen a girl before?"

"It's not that," Gomez said. "It's that Donovan could get one that's so attractive."

As everyone laughed, Donovan grinned good-naturedly. All the taunts in the world couldn't dampen his mood that day.

"Let's play," Brock said.

At the end of the pick, Donovan ended up on a team opposite Carter. To his surprise, when they lined up for the first play, she took the spot before him.

"I see, my brothers are trying to put us against each other," he said.

"Naturally," she said. "They said all I had to do was smile at you and you'd forget what you were supposed to be doing."

Donovan shook his head. "Not going to happen. My family runs on competition, I'm not giving up this game for anyone, not even you."

"We'll see about that," Carter said smirking.

And Donovan had to hand it to Brock and James, it was a good ploy, he did love her smile. When the ball was hiked, Carter raced past Donovan. As he caught up to her, she snatched the ball from the air and he grabbed her by the waist, lifting her off the ground.

"Does this count as a tackle for you or do you want me to drop you on the sand?" he asked.

"Carter!" James said. "What happened to smiling at Donovan!"

"Didn't work!" Donovan called back, letting go of Carter.

She scowled and headed back to her team, Donovan trailing behind.

With passing play, Donovan watched as Carter got more determined and more frustrated, her competitive side coming out in the face of him and his brothers. But despite her best efforts, he still always had the upper hand with his height and speed.

When they faced each other for the last play her team could make for the goal line, Carter narrowed her eyes at Donovan.

"You are going down," she said.

He couldn't help it, he grinned. "Is that what's been happening? And all this time I thought we were winning."

She glared which only managed to make him more amused.

"You're cute when you're determined."

"And you're unattractive when you're cocky."

Before Donovan could retort, Brock hiked the ball and Carter ran. Donovan sprinted after her, watching as she twisted and caught the ball. Donovan reached for her, snagging her waist. But inside of lifting her off the ground, he felt as she planted her feet, bent forward, and flipped him onto the sand. Shocked, he just laid there as she took off towards the end zone. None of his teammates even tried to follow her. They were all too busy laughing.

Carter returned to Donovan as he pushed himself.

"Told you I would take you down."

Brock and James circled Carter, draping their arms across her shoulders.

"MVP right here!" James shouted.

Donovan stood and brushed himself off as Clint called out that it was time to head back to the house. As they left, the cadets called out congrats to Carter for the well-executed maneuver and taunted

Donovan for being taken down so easily. Donovan barely heard it, hurrying up to take the spot by Carter's side, slipping his hand into hers.

As they neared the house, Donovan looked to James and knew they were thinking the same thing. They both broke into a run, Brock, and Clint hot on their heels.

"I call dibs on the shower!" Donovan called.

James slammed Donovan into the doorway and Clint knocked Brock to the side. All four of them crashed into the front hall, shoving each other out of the way.

"What are you doing?" their mother shouted.

All four brothers stilled and Carter sauntered into the house, wearing an amused expression.

"We have a guest," Eleanor said. "Carter, you can take the first shower."

Carter waved this away. "It's okay, I promised Ted I would help set the table. I'm fine waiting."

With that admission, the battle started up again. Clint made it into the bathroom first and shut the door in Donovan's face.

"Remember we're taking a photo," their mother called out to Clint. "Dress nice. Oh and Carter don't worry, whatever you have will be fine. But this is the one day my boys are required to look nice."

"Mom, I wear a suit to work every day," Brock said.

"Yes, but somehow when you're here, you dress like a surfer."

There was no arguing with that. As they all moved back into the kitchen to help with the last bit of the meal, Donovan kept an ear out for Carter. Occasionally, he'd peek through the archway into the dining room.

Each time, Carter circled the table behind his father, putting out place settings while listening to Ted. Donovan smiled, knowing his father to be the silent type and knowing that if he was talking this much, it meant he was making an effort to welcome Carter.

Eventually, Donovan's turn to take a shower came. When he opened the door to head back to his room, Carter was waiting outside with a towel. Donovan smiled, it seemed to be an instant reaction while at home. Or maybe it was simply because he loved seeing Carter inside his family's house.

"How are you doing?" he asked, running his towel over his hair.

"I really like your dad," she said.

"He was talking, that means he likes you too."

Carter smiled but there was something hidden in her eyes. Donovan cupped her face.

"Hey, what's going on in that mind of yours?"

She paused, peering down the hallway to where the chatter of Donovan's family could be heard.

"Is it my brothers? 'Cause I know they can be overwhelming and loud and obnoxious."

"It is your brothers-"

"I can tell them to take a step back."

"Donovan, it's a good thing. You all love and bug each other so much. It merely makes me wish that I'd had siblings."

Donovan nodded. Part of him wanted to tell her that this family would be hers when they got married.

But he didn't say it.

She was it for him, he didn't want anyone else. But he was also aware that they'd only been dating for a few months and didn't want to frighten her away.

At Prom, he'd made a comment about their daughter, but Carter hadn't replied and he'd worried he'd crossed a line. And so he'd kept his thoughts to himself, knowing that when the time was right he would ask and he prayed she'd say yes.

"I'm happy that I get to share them with you now," Donovan said. "Any longer than these couple of days though you would regret wanting siblings."

She laughed. "Maybe."

Slipping around him, she headed into the bathroom.

The aroma of Thanksgiving filled the house as Donovan and his brothers helped carry dishes out onto the table. With everything finished, they all stood around joking back and forth as they waited for Carter. They were all laughing when she entered the room. Instantly, the laughter died.

Carter stood just inside the doorway wearing a simple, short-sleeved dress. She'd let her hair fall loose over her shoulders. With all eyes on her, she fidgeted.

"Maggie thought you might dress up for Thanksgiving," she said. "She suggested I bring something just in case."

Donovan's mother crossed the room and wrapped her arm around Carter's shoulders.

"You look wonderful," she said.

And she did. All Donovan could do was stand there staring, struck by the lengths she'd gone to fit in with his family. This was Carter after all, she hated dresses. Yet for him, she'd done this. And he knew without a doubt he was going to marry her.

"Dude," James whispered to him. "What in the world did you do to deserve this girl?"

Donovan said the only thing that he could in that moment. "I have no idea."

College Party

"Why are we doing this again?" Carter asked, looking away from her reflection to Donovan.

He sat on the edge of the bathtub/shower, bent over his knees, hands clasped together. His gaze roamed around the cramped bathroom like even after five months of being together the space would reveal something new about her. At her question, his eyes landed on her.

"Because Link and Maddy decided that college parties are something that should be experienced at least once."

Shaking her head, Carter went back to combing her hair into a ponytail.

"It's still stupid," she said.

"You don't have to go," Donovan said.

"What? Let you go alone and get mauled by drunk college girls, I don't think so."

Donovan chuckled but said nothing.

"Can you hand me a hair tie, it's in the top drawer."

Donovan leaned forward and pulled the mentioned drawer open, rummaging through it. After handing Carter what she wanted, he lifted out a switchblade.

"Why is there a switchblade in your bathroom drawer?" he asked, amused.

Carter shrugged and tied her hair back. "Always good to have weapons stashed where they are easy to reach in an emergency."

Shaking his head, Donovan replaced the knife. The front door open and a second later Carter's father appeared in the doorway. Donovan stood as if he had been doing something more incriminating other than sitting.

"Where are you two off to?" he asked.

Carter rolled her eyes. "The idiotic tradition formally known as a college party."

Her father chuckled. "Did you know your mother and I met at a college party."

Surprised, Carter stared at her father's reflection. "I didn't know that."

He nodded, a strange distant look in his eyes. Carter spun around, but before she could press him for more information, his gaze focused and narrowed on her t-shirt. It was black with the Marines logo on the front. At her father's obvious displeasure, she grinned.

"Breathe, Captain," she said. "And remember you both fight for the same thing: life, liberty, the American way, and me."

As she slipped passed him, she patted his shoulder.

"I'm going to get my shoes. Donovan don't die before I get back. Also, remember there's a switchblade in the bathroom drawer."

As Carter tugged on her shoes, she heard the murmur of voices and figured it meant at least Donovan wasn't being strangled. When she walked back out, it was to find her father with his hand on Donovan's shoulder.

"....her safe," he was saying.

Noticing Carter, her father dropped his hand and nodded to them.

"Try to avoid as much stupid as you can," he said.

"It's a college party, I'm pretty sure that request is impossible."

"Still."

Her father hugged her and kissed the top of her head. "Stay safe, Sarge."

"Will do, Captain."

The pair left, picking up Link and Maddy before driving to the edge of Georgetown University campus. The house they stopped at looked like a manor from the 19th century, two-story redbrick with columns in the front, but what was going on within was anything but. Music blared from inside and managed to rattle even the windows of the cars parked on the curb. Strobe lights cut into the night like a lighthouse on drugs.

Carter climbed out of the car and stared up at the fraternity house, already hating everything about it. Sensing everything that was speeding through her mind, Donovan rounded the car and took her hand. Maddy bounced once as if gearing herself up for what was to come.

"We have to do it at least once, right?" she said, looking at Link.

He had the appearance of a man about to face hell, but when Maddy grinned at him, he relaxed.

"Yeah, at least once," he said.

Bracing herself, Carter stepped forward leading the group into the fray. The moment they walked inside, the air seemed to try and choke them. It was hot and reeked of alcohol and pot. The mass of bodies pressed in on all sides and the pounding bass slammed against Carter's eardrums. The front room was packed with bodies grinding against each other, the flashing lights distorting the scene into a jagged motion.

To Carter's relief that further back they went, the less crowded it was and she was able to inhale without it being someone's exhale. The back rooms were filled with games that were made all the more amusing when the players were drunk. There was a kitchen crammed with bottles and kegs that never seemed to lack for attention. Beyond this were a set of doors that stood open, revealing a deck and backyard beyond.

Before the group could decide what form of idiocy to get involved with first, someone staggered and ran into Maddy, upending their drink over her. Link shoved the guy off as Maddy scrunched her face up in annoyance.

"Carter, help me find a bathroom," she said, holding the shirt out from her skin.

Carter directed them down a hallway, knocking on doors and hoping that when she opened each one she wouldn't regret it. Most were locked and they were about to retrace their steps when a door further up opened and Carter caught a flash of tile. Maddy let out a breath as she slipped into the bathroom.

"Promise you won't leave," Maddy said.

With a nod from Carter, she closed the door. Carter leaned against the wall, acting as sentry. The noise still thrummed against her but it was growing more bearable with each minute. Around her couples had found the seclusion of the hallway a good place to try and suck each other's faces off.

One couple made a stumbling progression towards a bedroom door and slipped inside, their mouths never once breaking contact. The display twisted Carter's stomach as her father's earlier comment resurfaced. Her mind raced across time to a similar scene that might have involved her parents. The vividness of the occurrence gripped Carter, blinding her to the rest of her surroundings.

It was for that reason she didn't notice the guy who had been watching her and finally made his approach.

She snapped back when she felt a hand land on her waist and smelled the wave of alcohol on his breath.

"All alone with no one to be with," he said as if he knew she was desperate for company.

His hand lowered to her butt. Carter's annoyance flared and she grabbed his hand. This seemed to only spark something in his eyes.

"Are you an athlete?" she asked.

His lips curled. "No. Why? Want to play a game?"

"No, just checking."

She deftly broke his pinky finger. Crying out, the guy dropped to one knee holding his wrist. When his gaze rose to meet Carter's once again, she merely stared back.

"Still want to play that game?" she asked.

Holding his hand tenderly against his chest, the guy backed away. Part of Carter almost wished he hadn't gone, for with his absence her mind was able to revert to its last train of thought, one that had her crossing her arms, her fists clenched. Years of beliefs about her parents and how she came to be were thrown into question, history fracturing.

The bathroom door opened and Maddy stepped out.

"Well, it was never my favorite shirt so I guess it's okay," she said.

"Good," Carter said, trying to control her thoughts but only barely managing.

Back in the heart of the party, Carter found herself spinning, everything about it pounding against what she was thinking and all that she had thought as a little kid. When Maddy spotted Link, Carter let her go and pushed herself to the backdoor, needing to breathe something other than the fumes of beer and weed.

The deck was less full, but still, Carter had to move to the furthest edge before she could find a piece of available railing. She leaned against it, and closed her eyes, trying to forget the chatter and too loud laughter around her.

Even with all that she knew about her parents and how she had been a surprise, part of her had thought they had been together before it happened. But given her current setting and the look in her father's eyes she wondered if she was the product of a drunken one night stand that lasted longer than both of them imagined.

Carter buried her face in her hands, hating how childish she felt. Though her mother was no longer part of the picture she still wanted to believe some of her had been born out of love and not intoxicated stupidity.

Someone bumped into her and she straightened, knowing that this was not the place to lose herself. As she turned around, she found herself dreading returning to the party. But to get to Donovan it's what she needed to do. Shoving her emotions down, she made her way back inside. Though she wouldn't have thought it possible, the music had grown in intensity and was trying to deafen her.

She moved through the rooms, trying to find a sign of Donovan or even Link and Maddy. When she spotted the couple dancing, she knew Donovan would be somewhere in the vicinity. She spun around, searching every face.

What she found instead froze all thought and overwhelming emotions.

Pinned against a wall was Donovan with some girl's mouth attached to his and her hands under his shirt.

Carter elbowed her way to the pair. Despite the lithe muscles that told of the girl spending a majority of her time in some sport, Carter managed to yank her off. She stumbled back in surprise.

"Touch him again and I'll break you," she said.

The girl was taller than Carter and the top she wore showed that even her body had an advantage on Carter's but that changed nothing.

"Maybe he doesn't want you, he seemed pretty happy with me."

Angrier than she should have been, Carter jabbed the girl's throat. The girl clenched her neck, choking on her words. Carter turned to Donovan and found him crouched on the floor, palms pressed against his eyes. The vulnerability of his posture startled Carter and she touched his shoulder.

"Donovan," she said.

He raised his head and she knew something was wrong, there was an unfocused look in his eyes. Carter spun around.

"What did you do?" she yelled at the girl.

Still unable to speak, the girl only smirked.

"Donovan," Carter said, gaining his attention again.

This time his eyes managed to meet hers. In a breath a moment of clarity hit him. Grabbing the closest container - that happened to be what looked like a random empty ice bucket - he stuck his fingers into his mouth and threw up. Uncaring about anyone else, Carter snatched someone's discarded jacket and handed it to Donovan. He used it to wipe his mouth, then tossed it away.

"Your drink?" she asked.

He crouched back against the wall, shaking his head, but instantly stopped, putting his head in his hands. "It was in her mouth."

The words were slightly out of focus. Carter reined in her desire to punch the girl unconscious.

"How are you feeling?" she asked.

The question took a while for Donovan to gather his scrambled thoughts.

Carter knew she had only been gone for less than twenty minutes so depending on the drug it wouldn't have had time to take full effect. She hoped that he had thrown up the majority of it and that he could avoid the worst of the side effects.

"Dizzy," he said carefully as if working to control his mouth.

Carter let out a breath, knowing that murdering the girl would do nothing.

"Stay here," she said.

Finding Maddy and Link, Carter told them that they needed to leave. To her relief, the couple happily agreed, having satisfied their curiosity and ready to never return. Carter found Donovan in the same spot and lifted one arm over her shoulder.

"Just lean on me," she said.

He nodded but grimaced when the world tilted. Carter held onto his side, keeping him stable. With the help of Maddy and Link, they managed to find their way back to the car. The drive home was a quiet affair. By the time they arrived back at the apartment building, Donovan had drunk three bottles of water and eaten four power bars in the hopes of draining his body of the drug.

"Well, that was something," Maddy said as they paused at Link's door.

Smiling, Link tugged at her hand. "Want to come in and fall asleep to a movie like a couple of old people?"

She laughed and nodded. "Sounds like my kind of wild night."

With an assurance from Carter that she was fine with taking care of Donovan, the couple slipped into Link's apartment. Donovan's stability had mostly returned. To help it along, Carter did everything it said online to help stave off any more effects. When Donovan felt he could move about without any help, he went and took a shower, saying he needed to rid himself of the girl's perfume.

Hearing the patter of water on tile, Carter sank onto the couch. With the crisis averted, her mind flowed back into the path she had tried to break it from. But the thoughts that had risen up earlier gnawed at her, demanding attention and consideration. Exhausted with the night and all it had brought, Carter buried her face in her hands.

She remained that way until the water cut off and the door opened.

"Carter?" Donovan asked.

She lifted her head. His hair was damp and he wore sweatpants and a faded t-shirt.

"How are you feeling?" she asked.

"Better."

She stood and crossed to the kitchen.

"You hungry? I can make you something."

Donovan accepted the offer, settling onto one of the barstools. As Carter made a basic meal of eggs and toast, she watched him, looking for any signs that he still had side effects. In turn, he watched her too, the edges around his eyes softened with an unseen smile.

"Here you go," she said, sliding the plate over to him and leaning against the counter. "How did she get the jump on you?"

Donovan swallowed. "I'm not sure. She approached me at the drinks counter and I ignored her. Then I was making sure Link was fine and the next second I'm against the wall with someone's tongue jammed down my throat and her hands..." He shook his hand like he rather not remember that incident.

"I'm sorry," she said.

Donovan finished eating and pushed his plate away. Carter rose, knowing she needed to go home though she felt hesitant to see her father, fearing what truth she might learn. As she picked up her bag, Donovan reached for her hand. She paused, looking at him.

"You could stay," he said, his thumb making circles on her skin.

If it had been any other time, Carter knew she would be tempted, but with her mind buried so deeply in the past, all she could see were the repercussions and the disastrous endings. She took a breath, not knowing if what she was about to say would change everything, but knowing she needed to.

"Donovan," she said. "I think we should wait."

She held her breath, waiting for him to be annoyed with her. To comment on how he had been waiting for the last six years.

About how they had been together long enough. Asking her whether she truly did want him.

But all he said was one word. "Okay."

"Really?"

Donovan smiled at the disbelief in her voice.

"Does that mean you don't want to-" Carter didn't get to finish the question.

"Of course, but more than that I want you." He shrugged. "That makes it a non-issue."

Carter stepped forward and kissed him. "Thank you. Though part of me wonders if you still have the drug in your system and whether you will remember this later on. And whether the answer will be the same."

Donovan rested his forehead against hers then kissed her.

"Then ask me again later. It will be the same."

Carter ran a hand through his damp hair. "You going to be okay on your own?"

He nodded and stood. "I'm going to go sleep the rest of it off."

They kissed once more then Carter left.

The lights in the living room were still on as she climbed the stairs to her apartment. When she opened the door, her father looked up from the book he was reading - a pastime Maggie had been nudging him into. Seeing him, Carter froze in the doorway. Her father frowned in concern.

"What is it, Sarge? Are you okay?"

She nodded but found she couldn't move. Fearing the result but knowing she needed the answer she forced out the question that had been plaguing her.

"Am I the product of a college party one-night stand?" she asked, hating how pathetic she felt asking.

Her father's eyebrows shot up. "What? Carter, no." Her father crossed the room to stand in front of her, his hands on her shoulders. "Sarge, I met your mother at a college party and we started dating after that. It was months later that you came along."

Carter let out a shaky breath.

"Okay. I just thought..."

Her father smiled. "You were not a mistake, simply ahead of schedule."

A thought struck Carter. "Do you think she would have stayed if you had waited and had me later?"

Her father sighed the sound heavy with years of turning over that same question.

"I don't know, maybe." He squeezed her shoulders. "But it makes no difference 'cause I got you. Whether it had been later wouldn't have changed anything, I love you."

Carter hugged him. "I love you, Captain."

Christmas Presents

Christmas music played overhead, infusing the air with a cheery holiday spirit. Carter barely heard it in her concentration of the rack of men's sweaters. As she pulled out a dark blue sweater, a guy approached her.

From the corner of her eye, Carter could make out a defined build and good height. She glanced at him to find he was attractive and wore his good looks an air that said he knew it and used it to his advantage. He smiled at her and Carter jumped in before he could speak.

"Good," she said. "Take off your jacket."

He stared at her bemused as she held up the sweater to him. When he didn't do as she said, she raised her eyebrows.

"Jacket. Off."

More amused this time at her command, he did as she asked. He was the right size and Carter held the sweater closer to him, inspecting it.

"I'm Drake," he said.

"Not information I need," she said.

At this, the guy chuckled. Carter returned the sweater to the rack and tugged out a deep maroon one. When she held this one up to him, he tilted his head.

"I feel the need to tell you that I don't actually work here," he said.

"I'm well aware of that," Carter said. "What size are you in this type of sweater?"

"Medium." He paused. "You know I don't work here?"

"Of course, you're not wearing the button-down shirt and slacks of the other workers. It's not rocket science."

Drake gave her a long appraising look like he wasn't sure what to make of her, but curious enough to take the time to find out. Carter ignored this look. She wasn't going to give him that time. She returned to the blue sweater but got a darker shade.

"If you know I don't work here, why ask for my assistance?" he asked.

Carter let out a heavy sigh like he was the densest person she'd ever met. Facing him, she rested her elbow on the sweater rack.

"Because I knew you were going to attempt some sort of flirting or pickup line and I'm really not in the mood for it. Besides, I'm clearly buying a Christmas present and there's a 45% chance it's for a boyfriend and not a family member. Yet still, you approached me. Not really someone I would want to talk to if you knew this and still took the risk."

Drake stared at her and Carter raised the sweater in farewell.

"Thank you for your assistance. I'm sure my boyfriend will love the sweater."

Spinning on her heels, Carter left the still stunned Drake and headed to the checkout. Purchase complete, she left the store to find Donovan waiting for her, eyeing the mass of Christmas shoppers.

"How'd it go?" he asked.

"Good. Want to stop at Starbucks?"

Grinning, he took her hand. "I never pegged you for a peppermint hot chocolate addict."

"It's the embodiment of Christmas, don't judge me for my holiday spirit."

"No judgment here."

She kissed him. "Liar. You are judging me but that's okay. It does mean you're paying."

"Fair enough."

The interior of Starbucks was overflowing with shoppers eagerly seeking stimulate for another round at the stores. With their drinks in hand, Carter and Donovan managed to snag a table in the lounge area of the coffee shop.

"How'd your shopping go?" Carter asked.

"I'm pleased with my gift," Donovan said.

"See, I'm brilliant. Instead of stressing for weeks about what to get each other for our first Christmas, it was solved by allotting only one hour for the task and the results will be what they are. You can tell me I'm brilliant now."

"You're brilliant now."

Carter eyed him and his teasing grin.

"For the record, I've always been brilliant."

"I am well aware."

"Really? You're emphasis on the now implied otherwise."

Donovan's only response was a mocking grin. One Carter loved though she would die before admitting it.

Before they could dive into another topic, a girl passed by their table but paused, eyes landing on Donovan. The first thing Carter noticed about the girl was she was beautiful to the level of it being ridiculous. Who had eyes that interesting of a color? And her hair couldn't really be that lush?

To Carter's surprise, the girl didn't move on but continued to look at Donovan. From the intensity of the girl's gaze, Carter wondered if she was going to have to kiss Donovan to get this girl to back off.

"Donovan?" the girl said.

She knew him. She knew him?

"Donovan," the girl said, smiling, which made her more stunning. "It is you."

Carter looked to Donovan, wanting to see his reaction to this beautiful girl smiling at him. Also, she wanted to know why he hadn't ever mentioned dating Miss Universe.

But when Donovan stared back at the girl without a hint of recognition, Carter softened. Okay, maybe dated was the wrong word but this girl knew him.

The girl's smile faltered at Donovan's lack of easy response. Carter had to wonder if this was a first for her.

"Rosie," she said, pointing to herself. "I shadowed a class you were in about a two and a half years ago."

Donovan brightened. "Right. Now I remember. It's good to see you again."

His even tone and reserved manner made Carter want to grab his face and kiss him right there. But she managed to hold herself back.

"How have you been?" Rosie asked. "I always wondered what happened to the Boy Genius."

Carter snorted at this and Donovan winced.

"Rosie, this is my girlfriend Carter," he said.

Rosie smiled at Carter. "It's nice to meet you."

"Same. So you shadowed one of Donovan's classes?" Carter asked.

"Yup, I had no idea what to make of him. He read all through the class but got the highest grades. You're in college now, right?"

Donovan nodded.

"At Georgetown," Carter said, not above a little bragging about her boyfriend. "After next year, it's Quantico then the FBI."

"Really? But how can that be?"

"I took college courses during high school," Donovan said. Carter could see how Rosie wanted to ask more but Donovan kept talking. "What are you doing now?"

"Finishing my final year of college. I'm studying here before my shift."

Rosie paused as a guy joined her. Drake took in Donovan then his gaze landed on Carter. She sent him a wide smile. He looked like he wanted to run away.

"You ready to study?" Drake asked.

"Drake," Rosie said, gesturing to Donovan. "Do you remember Donovan, you met him once. He's the student I always told you about in the class I shadowed."

Drake looked Donovan over like he couldn't bother trying to remember. Donovan stood, his face completely calm. Something about the exchange told Carter Donovan remembered their interaction but it wasn't a pleasant one. Carter imagined it wouldn't be. Drake was the type of person who belittled others to make himself feel better.

"We'll let you get back to studying," Donovan said. "Carter."

He held out his hand and she accepted it.

"Oh," she said to Drake. "Thanks again for the help in the store. You'd make a great store assistant."

What could she say, she wasn't above belittling either.

They left, tossing out their coffee cups as they went. Donovan remained quiet as they wound their way through the mall.

"Drake one of those guys you felt like punching?" Carter asked.

"Yup."

"Want to tell me about it?"

He shrugged. "He talked down to me and that's on him. But honestly wasting breath on it now doesn't even seem worth it."

"And what about talking about you knowing the most beautiful girl on earth."

Donovan faced her, his eyes earnest.

"Carter," he said, softly. "You understand the most beautiful girl I've ever met is you, right?"

Carter laughed.

"I'm serious."

"That's sweet, but I have these things called eyes and I know what I saw."

Carter knew what she looked like. She ran enough that she didn't have the curves of most other girls. Maggie was helping her but she still struggled to make her hair look decent. She knew she had a pretty face. Her eyes and skin tone were an interesting combination. But...

Rosie was like someone who stopped the world where ever she went. All through high school Carter had been around girls with enough money to make themselves look flawless on a daily basis. Carter wasn't like that.

She'd come to terms with it.

"Come on, I want to see what you got me," she said before Donovan could say anything else.

She tugged him towards the exit. In the car, Donovan threw glances her way but she didn't acknowledge them. Finally, he spoke.

"I know you won't believe me when I say this," he said. "But being with you means that no other girl exists. It's only you."

"You're right, I don't believe you."

She smiled so the words didn't sound too honest.

"Carter, do you know why I think you're the most beautiful girl?"

"My eyes..."

He laughed. "Your everything. But more than that it's who you are. Each day the more I learn about you, the more beautiful you are to me. It's beyond how you look, it's everything that you are. Your heart. Your mind. Your soul. All of that makes you beautiful to me."

Carter didn't know how to answer. Those words made her feel special, set apart. But she was scared because it meant Donovan loved all of her. She didn't know if she was worth that.

Donovan reached out and took her hand, lacing his fingers with hers.

"Do you find me attractive simply because of how I look?" he asked.

"Of course. It's the only reason I'm with you."

Donovan shook her hand like he could knock down the wall of humor she put up between them.

"No," she admitted.

She found she loved his sharp intellect, caring heart, and compassionate soul. If she loved him for all those things...maybe she could trust he felt the same.

"I'm not sure I deserve to be the most beautiful girl to you."

Donovan shrugged. "Sucks, you are."

Carter laughed and Donovan grinned at her. Most beautiful girl. She still didn't believe him. But right then she decided to simply accept his words as a gift.

In Donovan's apartment, they both kicked off their shoes as Donovan flipped on the lights.

"Do want anything to eat? Drink?"

"Your apartment looks so bare," Carter said.

Donovan shrugged. "I'll decorate with my family at home in a couple of days, so I saw no reason to do anything here. Though compared to the Christmas explosion at your apartment I can see how it would look weird."

"Yeah, Maggie went all Santa's workshop on the place. And roped me into helping."

Donovan elbowed her playfully. "And you loved it."

Carter rolled her eyes. "I will neither confirm nor deny that statement...But it feels good to have it look so cheery. It used to look like back when... It's nice." Before Donovan could say anything, Carter clapped her hands. "Okay, I want to know what you got me."

More than that, Carter simply wanted to give him her gift. They sank onto Donovan's couch, facing each other with their shopping bags in between them. Donovan fidgeted.

"I feel I have to be honest with you," he said.

"Never! Don't you know the best relationships are built around constant lies?"

He grinned, which was the reason Carter joked as much as she did. She knew she'd never get tired of his smile.

"Before you came up with your one-hour for shopping idea," Donovan said. "I already figured out what I was going to get you."

"Really?"

Donovan nodded as he grimaced. "I'm sorry."

Carter laughed. "No, it's fine. I got you something as well. I came up with the hour shopping thing so you wouldn't feel pressured to get me an amazing gift."

Donovan looked at her with a soft glint in his eye, like he wasn't quite sure what he'd done to deserve her.

"You have to open my gift first in case you got me something a lot better," she said. "This way I won't feel miserable about my sad gift."

She nudged the shopping bag towards him.

"This one first."

Taking the bag, Donovan dug in and pulled out the dark blue sweater.

"Since we're being honest, I bought this mainly because it's really soft and it will mean hugging you is more enjoyable."

Donovan eyed her over the sweater. "Because hugging me now is pure torture?"

"Put it on."

"Okay but turn around."

Carter shot him a flat look. "I've seen you shirtless."

"Yes, once and I was throwing up at the time. It's not the same. We've decided to wait and I'm not going to tempt you. Besides, if this sweater makes you enjoy hugging me more we might already be getting into dangerous waters."

"Just put it on."

"Then turn around."

Holding up her hands in surrender, Carter scooted around on the couch cushion until her back was to Donovan.

"Okay, I'm decent again," Donovan said.

Carter flipped around and paused. Donovan held out his arms for her inspection. Decent? He was more than just decent in that sweater. She whistled appreciatively.

"I have amazing taste," she said. "And I was being honest, I am dating you for your good looks."

It wasn't true, but with the way the sweater fit him and brought out the blue in his eyes, Carter could imagine dating him purely for that reason. Good thing he also had a brain to go along with those looks or it never would have lasted.

"What's your other gift?" Donovan asked.

His question brought Carter out of her admiration of him. Grabbing her satchel, she pulled out a wrapped package. She handed it to him but felt nervous about his response. Donovan took the gift and shook it, even though it was solid and could only be one thing.

"I think I hear something rattling inside it."

Carter shoved his shoulder. "Shut up and open it."

Underneath the wrapping was a beautiful hardback version of The Scarlett Pimpernel. Carter gnawed on her lip as Donovan ran his hand over the novel. When he flipped open the front and began to read the inscription, she froze. Was it too stupid? Embarrassing?

It wasn't long but from the amount of time Donovan took to read it you'd think she'd written an essay instead of*: Donovan, did you know that when you read sometimes you get this tiny smile in the corner of your mouth. It's the same smile you have when talking about books. Who knew you were such a book nerd. - Your current girlfriend, Carter.*

Donovan lifted his eyes to her. Instead of saying anything, he leaned over and kissed her.

"Thank you," he said, his thumb brushing her cheek.

"Well, you mentioned how you related to it since you've had to hide who you are. And well...who doesn't love a hardback copy?"

Carter guessed readers did, it was something she looked up. The books in her house were all paperbacks: action, and mystery novels her father picked up for traveling.

"I love it," he said. "Though what is with this whole 'current girlfriend thing'?

"I don't want your future girlfriends to be jealous or whatever."

Donovan kissed her again, deeper this time. When he pulled away, he didn't say anything. He simply rose, found a pen, and made an adjustment to the inscription. He flipped the book around so Carter could read it. He'd crossed out current and written: always above it. Your always girlfriend.

Carter didn't have any words. No jokes. No witty comebacks. He looked at her with such certainty that she felt she didn't deserve it.

"Now my turn," Donovan said, settling down on the couch again. "I have to be honest."

"Again with the honesty, man this relationship isn't going to make it."

"Do you want your gift or not?"

Carter sealed her lips, trying to look repentant.

"I asked Maggie for ideas of what to get you in November because I actually was stressing about it. And so this is 90% her doing and about 10% mine."

Donovan set a shopping bag before her. "I merely picked it up today, so technically it still happened within the allotted hour."

Carter reached in and pulled what felt like a soft patted square book but what actually was a photo album. She stared at Donovan in utter disbelief and he looked as nervous as she imagined she had a few minutes ago.

Carter flipped it open and saw a photo of Captain holding her as a baby. Page after page showed Carter growing up.

"Like I said Maggie did most of it. She had pictures and the more recent ones are from Link and Maddy, apparently they've been taking pictures of us without either of us knowing."

Carter understood what he meant when she saw the last few pages were full of moments snapped between her and Donovan. The final page had two pictures, the family photo from Thanksgiving at Donovan's house and one of her, Captain, and Maggie.

"Since I did so little but still wanted it to feel like it was from me I wrote small notes beside the photos. Thoughts and...comments like how you were a chunky baby, things like that...um...Carter?"

Carter couldn't lift her head, if she did he would see the tears. So many good memories. There were so many. Sometimes looking back on the past all she saw was the hurt, but he'd found the happy memories she'd forgotten.

"At least tell me if you hate it and then I can get you something else."

Finally, she raised her head and Donovan looked like he was about to panic.

"I'm sorry, I didn't think that it would-"

Carter curled up beside him, wrapping her arm around him, the photo album pressed between them. She hid her face in his chest.

"Good thing this sweater makes me huggable, right?"

She laughed and he held onto her.

"Thank you," she whispered, the words feeling so small when what he'd given her was so big.

Donovan kissed her head. "Merry Christmas, Carter."

Fighting Back

Carter couldn't fight back her smile as she watched Donovan make his way across the quad to the coffee shop on the other side. The warm spring day spread sunlight over the freshly cut grass and encouraged students to sprawl out and soak up the rays.

"What are you smiling at?" Link asked looking up from his studying.

Carter planted her chin in her hand, still following Donovan's path. Eyes trailed after him and every so often a girl would pause to say hi.

"Last week I told Donovan that the shirt he is currently wearing is my favorite. He is now wearing it again and I asked him to get me some coffee so I could see how many other girls noticed that it brings out his eyes and talk to him."

Which the results were about as positive as Carter expected them to be, the shirt did look really good on him after all.

"Why?" Link asked. "You know it annoys him when girls approach him."

"I wanted to see whether he would talk with any of them."

Link frowned. His silence lasted long enough that Carter glanced over at him.

"What?" she asked.

"Carter, has it ever occurred to you that you have trust issues and a propensity to push people away?"

Carter went rigid, gaze locked on the glass windows where Donovan stood in line.

"Your girlfriend having fun in her psychology class, I take it."

"She says you make an interesting case study."

"You can tell her she can stop studying me."

"Does that mean she's wrong?"

Link titled his head trying to catch Carter's eye but she wouldn't meet his gaze. The once warm sunlight felt suddenly dull.

"I know I have trust issues," Carter said quietly. "Donovan's mother told me that exact same thing when we visited them for Easter."

"Really?"

Carter slowly nodded. "Yeah, I asked whether Donovan ever did sports when he was younger and if he ever quit." She swallowed remembering the way Eleanor stared at her like she cut through Carter with a single glance and saw her heart. "She told me that it was better if I were upfront and asked whether her son was likely to break up with me after a year of being in a relationship. She also pointed out that having trust issues was not uncommon for someone with my history."

"Oh, wow."

"Yeah."

Neither of them said anything for a beat, Carter playing over the interaction with Eleanor, feeling the embarrassment of being caught. Eleanor had also told her that Donovan was not the type of person to give up easily. Though it should have reassured Carter, it didn't, she knew exactly how much of a challenge she was.

"Do you want Donovan to break up with you?" Link asked.

The thought of Donovan severing ties with her felt like losing a limb. Each day she fell further and further in love with him and it scared her to her core. She'd asked him to wait and he'd agreed.

But would he wait as long as it took?

When she looked at him, she saw someone who held so much of who she was. She'd let him into her life in a way she never thought she'd have the courage to. She trusted him beyond words.

But fear told her it would be easier if he left now then later on when she couldn't imagine living a life without him.

He didn't complete her, but around him, she felt whole.

"No, I don't," she said.

"You should probably stop pushing him away then."

Carter laughed. The solution sounded so easy, but in practice felt impossible. She felt trapped in a tug-a-war with her present self and past self, both equally stubborn.

When she spotted Donovan heading back to her, she wondered if she'd ever stop loving the way he walked, the way the sunlight cast shadows on his face making it sharper. It felt terrifying to know that he cared for her because all she could think about is how that could all go away.

As if aligning with her thoughts, she noticed in the anger in his eyes.

He stopped before her, thrusting the coffee cup at her.

"If you want to break up with me have the guts to do it," he said almost growling in frustration. "If you don't understand how much I care for you now then maybe you should end this because I'm done with you putting me through stupid tests."

Grabbing his books, Donovan shoved them into his bag.

"Link let's go to class."

Scrambling, Link gathered up his stuff as well and followed Donovan, throwing Carter a startled, sympathetic glance. As they walked away, Carter felt like someone had shot her. They drew further away, but Carter could still see Donovan's anger in the way he walked, in the line of his shoulders, in the curl of his fists. She'd pushed him too far.

Every fear she had of losing him slammed into her as she watched it playing out, immobile while Donovan left her behind. Images of her mother walking out a door as her father just stood there flashed in her mind.

Carter blinked, her cheeks wet without her realizing why. Part of her knew she needed to go after him. He hadn't said he wanted to break up, but the weak, damaged part of herself sat like a stone on her, keeping her rooted to the grass. The part of her telling her that it might be better this way.

Without comprehending how it happened, her phone sat in her hand, pressed to her ear.

"Hello Carter darling, are you alright?"

The soft, gentle voice soothed and convicted Carter.

"I pushed your son too far," she said.

"Ah, why don't you tell me what happened?"

Through a tight throat, Carter gave a brief explanation.

"I see," Eleanor said. "You tested him. Carter, did you not realize that in return he was testing you?"

Carter palmed her cheeks, trying to get her eyes to stop sweating. "Why?"

"Because sweetie, he understands your past. He wants to see if you will let this be the end of you two, or if you will be the fighter he knows you to be and overcome the hurt you still carry with you."

Carter didn't feel like a fighter right then, she felt like a broken girl.

"I'm going to hang up," Eleanor said. "You know what you need to do. I hope you have the strength to do it."

The line went dead and Carter sat frozen, staring at the place where Donovan and Link had disappeared. When her phone beeped she glanced at it, wishing it to be Donovan, but it wasn't.

"He loves you, Carter, the question is do you love him?"

Behind Eleanor's message, Carter saw the picture of Donovan and her. Maddy had taken it without them knowing. They were grinning at each other like they had finished a long debate and were ready for another one.

Looking at the picture she knew there was only one answer to the question.

Hurriedly, Carter stowed away her notebooks and headed towards Donovan and Link's class. Part of her wanted to barge into the room and make some grand declaration, proving to Donovan that what she said was true, but she didn't. It would be a weak action. She knew sometimes it was easier to declare something before dozens of unknown people than humbling oneself before a single person.

She waited, feeling each minute stretch into hours until an eternity had passed by the time the door to the room opened. As students spilled out, Carter stood her ground, mentally gearing up. When Donovan exited with Link, he found her right away. But the anger that she'd hoped would be lessened was still there, his face a mask of hard lines. Link glanced between them and pulled out his phone.

"Oh, look at that Maddy is calling, I should answer," he said, shuffling off but keeping himself in view of Donovan.

Carter crossed her arms, needing the illusion of a shield even as she planned to lay herself bare.

"I have to say, I'm not sure why you're still with me, I'm pretty damaged," she said.

"Stop being self-deprecating. You know exactly why I'm still with you, you're simply choosing to not believe it."

Even though his words were kind, he didn't soften. She saw how he was pushing her as she pushed him. The only difference was his action came from needing to see where she stood while hers had come from being afraid.

"I'm sorry," she said, letting her arms fall to her side. "Sometimes it scares me how much I care for you, how much it hurts thinking about being without you and..."

She didn't finish the sentence, not sure she could.

"You think that you'll lose me, that somehow I will change my mind? So to be preemptive you're forcing me away. Do you hear how stupid that sounds?"

She did, there was no arguing with that.

Donovan stared at her, anger rolling off of him. "What have I done, Carter, to make you believe I'm leaving you? What actions have I shown that I'm someone who will easily give up? Because I think I've worked pretty hard to show you I'm here. Is that not enough?"

Something snapped inside Carter and she exploded.

"That's the problem, you've done everything and I don't feel like I deserve any of it! Over and over again I see how you prove I can trust you and I don't see how you could still want to be with me when it takes so much work! I'm not worth it, okay? I'm not worth it!"

Carter could feel herself on the edge of letting him go, of knowing that as much as she loved him there could be someone else who would love him more. Love him without asking so much, without having to be a burden on him. Love him without being afraid.

"You deserve better," she murmured.

"You are so stupid you know that!" Donovan said, irritated. "I don't want better, I want you! I'm fighting to keep you, why can't you fight to keep me?"

"Because like you said I'm stupid," she said, a single flicker of hope sparking.

"Yeah, you are, because if I wanted someone else I wouldn't have stayed with you past the first day we met at high school. You were a pain then like you are a pain now and never in my life have I met a girl who pisses me off more, challenges me more, puzzles me more, makes me laugh more than you. So who the hell else am I suppose to be with? Huh?!"

He shouted it like a challenge and Carter felt that fierce, determined side of her that her father had encouraged come raging forward, shoving her doubts, fears, insecurities to the side.

She grabbed the front of his shirt. "No one! And if you even think about leaving me, you better be ready for a fistfight, because the only way I'm letting you go is if you're as bloody and bruised as I would feel, you got that?"

Carter pulled him forward, crashing his mouth against hers. The tangled mess of her emotions still twisted inside her, but right then, right there she knew she couldn't let them get the best of her. Because the best of her was when she was with him.

When Donovan pulled away, he smiled. "It's about time."

Conflicted

Carter shoved her hands into her pockets, the bag hanging off her shoulder feeling heavier than usual. As she climbed the stairs to the apartment, she heard muffled laughter and paused outside the door.

The sound was familiar by now, Maggie's light laugh entwining with her father's deep one. There was a harmony to it that spoke of happiness. Carter reached for the door handle but stopped, hand hovering above it.

When more laughter echoed from inside, she turned away and headed back down the stairs, away from the apartment and the abundance of happiness. The lane was growing dim as the sun sank into the horizon.

Without thinking, Carter walked, her feet eventually taking her to the neighborhood playground. It was empty, the fading light and chilly night ushering children indoors. The gate whined as she pushed it open. Leaving her bag by the opening, she walked over the wood chip ground to the swing set, settling onto one.

Curling one leg up, she hugged it and pushed her foot against the carved out hole beneath her, making herself sway. Around her, the glow of windows cast patches of illumination on the old wooden play-set. Without touching it, Carter knew that it would creak and groan underfoot. Knew that if you run across its bridge too fast that it would shudder. The tremble adding a hint of excitement and adventure.

The evening was windless and so there were no whispers to fill the silence hanging about Carter. There were no voices to be tugged out of homes and sent floating on the breeze. There was nothing to offer comfort to the lone figure rocking back and forth on the swing.

As if having somehow knowing this, the gate creaked open.

But Carter didn't look back. Didn't take her eyes off the sight of childhood.

A shadow trailed forward and behind it was Donovan.

He took the swing beside hers and sat down, wrapping his hands around the chains.

For a while, neither of them said anything, as they were thrown back to a time where they were little kids and friendship was a tentative dance of being next to each other but not saying anything.

"What was the last thing you said to your parents?" Carter asked the night.

Donovan peered over at her, but she didn't meet his gaze.

"I told my mother that I'd call her later and that I loved her. My father I said that I would take his advice and would talk to him soon. Why?"

Carter didn't respond to his answer or give one of her own. She pushed against the ground again putting her back in a gentle swing.

"Did you know my mother used to take me to this playground?"

Donovan knew the question wasn't one that needed a reply and so gave none.

"She would stay on the ground and chase me about the structure as I would run away."

Carter could see so clearly the half-laughing smile of her mother's as she roared as if she were a dragon Carter had to flee from. It was all a game. All an act of playing with her daughter. Until it wasn't.

But it hadn't been Carter that fled for the last time.

"The last thing I told my mother was that if I ever wanted to talk to her again I would let her know and then I left."

"I remember," Donovan said.

Carter dropped her leg and curled her hands around the chains holding up the swing. "I walked away thinking that was it. It was all over. All in the past now. I could move on. But..."

"But that's not the end of the story."

Carter gripped the cold metal, imprinting the links into her palms. She stared at the wooden bridge, the one she darted across as a little kid, laughing at the pretend fear all the while knowing without a doubt that there was nothing to fear at all because the one that chased her, loved her. It was all pretend.

And now it wasn't. There was a chase going on in her mind and she didn't know where to run or what she was running from.

Carter swallowed hard, her throat tightening, her eyes stinging. She blinked, trying to push away her emotions. Trying to box up memories she didn't want to remember. Pressing her lips together, she stared at the ground needing to close it all off.

She heard the rattle of chains and a second later Donovan was crouching before her. When he gently cupped her face, she closed her eyes hating the traitorous tears that slipped out.

"What is it?" he asked, swiping at the tears with his thumb.

She shook her head, not knowing how she could say the words that sat heavy on her tongue, the emotions that weighed on her chest when they were things she hated.

"I'm right here."

"I can't."

Donovan pried Carter's hands away from the chains, holding them between his own. He said nothing and Carter almost wished he would demand to know her thoughts, give her a diversion away from what she felt.

But of course, he didn't, he remained there, a solid presence. A reminder that whatever she was facing, she wasn't alone.

When she finally raised her eyes to his, he was gazing back at her. Patient. Understanding.

"It's not going to make sense," she said.

"It's okay, you don't make sense half the time and I'm still here."

Carter laughed, the sound ragged from the tears. She took in a deep, shaky breath.

"I miss my mom."

Donovan held to his calm expression, leaving Carter room to go on.

"It sounds stupid. It doesn't make sense. She hasn't been part of my life for over five years. She left. She abandoned us. I shouldn't care. I shouldn't miss her. I shouldn't feel anything for her. Yet...I have moments of missing her."

Carter looked to the play-set. "I think the hardest part is that I have good memories. Even when so much of my life is filled with the great times with Captain, she is part of them and part of some that are just her and me."

Between Donovan's hands, Carter curled her fingers into fists, trying to keep herself together. "I wish there was nothing happy to remember. It makes it all the harder, because how do you come to terms with having good times with the person that created so many bad? How can I remember laughing with her when she is the reason I cried? How can there be any good when she left?"

Tears spilled over Carter's eyes as she looked at Donovan, lost, confused, and vulnerable. Instead of answering, he pulled her from the swing and into his arms. His warmth and steadiness comforted her and she buried her face in the crook of his neck. He held her close, letting her feel all that she did without judgment or comment.

When Carter felt herself drained of tears, she laid her cheek on his shoulder.

"I don't know what to do with it all," she said.

"It's not something that is likely to go away," Donovan said. "It's not a friend you once had and moved away. It's your mother. There will always be a connection between you no matter how many years are between you and your memories."

He cupped her cheek, making her meet his eyes.

"You have to learn to accept the good and the bad. You've found peace with the fact that she left. Now you need to find peace knowing that there were happy times. And it's okay to grieve those happy times because it means that her leaving still hurts."

Carter let out a breath, feeling the heaviness on her chest lifting.

"Just because she left doesn't negate the good memories. Nothing in life is black and white. She was never a completely awful mother and she was never a completely perfect one. She was a flawed mother and still is. That is something that will take time to accept. And missing her...that is simply what comes of not having a parent there, you're going to miss what once was. It's okay. What you feel is okay."

Carter didn't know what to say. Everything he said seemed to lighten the burden and the chains she felt weighing her. The hate she held over what she felt melted away. The tangled mess that was her at that moment didn't need to be sorted out, it could simply be and that was okay.

The gratitude she felt for him right then was overwhelming. The understanding and comfort he gave her felt completely undeserved. She wrapped her arms around his neck and hugged him, knowing she would never be able to tell him all that he meant to her.

"Thank you," she whispered.

He kissed her cheek right where her tears had fallen.

A Secret Discovered

Yawning, Carter rubbed her eyes and glanced at her phone screen. The time was just a little before midnight. Strewn across her bed were pages of notes and textbooks laying open. On her computer was an essay for her psych class.

The apartment around her was silent, the absence of her father creating the strange void. Carter snatched her phone and found the one person she wanted to help break the silence. The rings echoed in her ear as she waited, biting her thumbnail.

"Carter?"

Donovan's voice was thick with sleep and she couldn't help picturing him in his bed, shirtless.

"Did I wake you?" she asked, trying to shove away the image.

There was a rustle of sheets and in her mind's eye she saw him rolling onto his back and stretching an arm above his head.

"Are you alright?" Donovan asked, ignoring the fact that she had woken him up.

"Yeah, I'm fine. I just..." She curled her toes, twisting her lips to the side. "I just...ummm...had a question about..." She grimaced. "Psych class."

Donovan gave a deep, throaty chuckle. It was the sexiest sound Carter had ever heard.

"Carter, you understand if you want to call me just to hear my voice, you can. You don't need a reason."

Cheeks flaming, Carter buried her face in her hand. It had been the truth for her call but still, she felt stupid.

"I'm really not good at this girlfriend thing," she muttered.

That same sexy laugh rolled over the line.

"I don't care, as long as you're my girlfriend you can be terrible at it." The title pulled a smile from Carter. "So, do you want me to monologue for you so can fall asleep to my voice?"

Carter laughed. "I don't believe you're capable of monologuing."

"For you, I could figure something out."

A warmth that seemed to only appear when he talked that way spread throughout Carter. She sank back onto her pillows, cradling the phone to her ear.

"How about you just tell me about your day?" she said.

"That seems pointless since you were there for most of it or the only good parts of it, but sure, I'll tell you about my day."

The sleep in his voice drifted away as he talked. Most of what he said barely made an impression on Carter's tired brain but it didn't matter. What mattered was he was talking to her because despite having been woken up to do it, he cared for her. It was such a strange sensation that even after a year of officially dating, she couldn't wrap her mind around the truth of it.

"Are you asleep?" Donovan asked.

"No, I'm still here." Carter was curled up on her bed, facing the other side of the mattress, imagining Donovan laying beside her. Donovan yawned and she could hear as he shifted.

"Okay," he said, a sleepy note in his voice. "Now you talk."

"You sound like you're about to fall asleep again."

"Then I'll get the best night's sleep ever."

Smiling, Carter talked. She couldn't remember what she said, the words were meaningless but the affection behind them wasn't. When half an hour had passed, she heard the gentle tones of Donovan's heavy breathing.

"Night, Donovan," she whispered.

She hung up and slid off her bed, padding into the kitchen. The refrigerator light glared at her as she went searching for something to eat. She was about to settle for a bowl of cereal when the lock on the front door turned. Shutting the fridge, Carter sank into a crouch.

"I'm not sure why we're here," her father said. "I should have taken you home first."

Maggie let out a teasing laugh. "You've been a bit distracted tonight, I imagine your brain went on autopilot."

Carter shifted to her stomach and edged forward on the cold tile, peering around the corner of the kitchen counter. Outlined in the doorway was her father, his hand on Maggie's waist, while her hand rested on his cheek. From her light summery dress and his slacks and button down, they had clearly come from a nice dinner date. The thought of announcing her presence felt too awkward at that moment, so Carter remained hidden.

"There's a reason for that," Steve said.

As Maggie cocked her head, the corner of her mouth curled up in question. Carter's father ran a hand through his hair and moved his weight from one foot to the other. Carter's eyebrows shot up. Her father was...nervous.

"The thing is," he said, each word measured like he had practiced them. "The last time I told a woman that I loved her, it was my ex-wife, I was twenty and I said it too early, not understanding what those words really meant. When the divorce went through and I realized I was a free man I promised myself I wouldn't say those words until I was prepared to make the commitment they demanded."

Carter knew to her core that this was not a conversation her father would want her to overhear, but there was no way in hell she was going to stop listening. Steve cupped Maggie's face, smiling down at her. It was a look so full of admiration and affection, Carter felt herself grinning.

"Maggie," Steve said. When he sank down onto one knee before her, Maggie sucked in a breath and Carter had to cover her mouth to stop herself from gasping. "I love you and I never want to say these words to any other woman but you. Will you marry me?"

In the moonlight, Carter could see the glistening of tears on Maggie's cheeks.

"Yes, of course."

When Steve stood and began kissing Maggie, Carter buried her face in her hands. More than giving them privacy, it was the only way she could contain her happiness. Before that moment she had never understood why people jumped up and down screaming when they heard good news, but right then she understood. All she wanted to do was shout at the top of her lungs that her father was going to be happy.

Eventually, the pair broke apart and whispered something to each other.

"I'll see you tomorrow," Maggie said. "We'll tell Carter then."

"Tomorrow."

Maggie kissed him one last time.

"I love you," she said, then slipped out the door.

The smile Carter's father wore was one she had rarely seen since her mother left. It made him look ten years younger and almost boyish with happiness. Scooting away, Carter sat on the kitchen floor waiting for her father to head off to his room.

To her surprise, he made his way to the kitchen. When he flipped on the light and found Carter grinning up at him, he froze.

"You heard-"

"Every word," she said. "It's nice to know you're not as slow on the uptake as I thought you were, old man."

He father laughed, it was filled with amazement, happiness, and wonder.

"You approve then?" he said.

Carter pushed herself up. "I was the one telling you to marry that woman ages ago. It's you who took forever to get on board."

Still smiling a smile that Carter hoped would never go away, her father hugged her.

"I love you, Captain," she said. "And so does Maggie. It's good you can finally see it."

"I can." He kissed the top of her head. "I love you, Sarge."

Everything Changes

Carter sat on the edge of her bed, one leg tucked beneath her. Outside the late afternoon sun was bathing the world in a warm golden glow. Spring buds bloomed on trees and tossed their sweet scent into the air, to be swept up and carried off by the breeze. From her open window, Carter caught the flower fragrance.

Laying before her was a maroon dress that was cut to be flattering as well as flirty. Thoughts turning in slow circles, she played with the silky material. From beyond the door, she heard the even movements of her father. But there was something different to the usual rhythm of his footsteps. It was as if they had become even lighter than before. A knock echoed on her door.

"Carter?" he asked.

She murmured 'enter'. Somehow her father heard the response and opened the door. Leaning on the doorframe, he studied her. He was dressed in a dark suit, but one that was distinctively different from his Secret Service attire.

"Sarge?" he asked, his voice tinged with concern.

Unable to meet his gaze, she stared down at the dark fabric, rubbing it between her fingers.

"Everything is going to change," she said.

Her father walked over and sat on the bed, facing her.

"You understand that bringing Maggie into the family will change nothing about how I feel about you, right?"

Carter nodded but still didn't look up.

"Sarge," Steve said. "You're not losing me, we're gaining her."

Finally, Carter raised her head. "It's just been only us for so long."

Her father crossed his arms. "True, but if you look back, we've had Maggie for almost just as long." He smiled with a memory. "Who made sure that both of us were eating after your mother left? Guess who was the one that reminded me that you did need new clothes? Who do you think was the one who bought you pads when I wasn't man enough to do it myself?" Carter felt the beginnings of a smile appearing. "Who has been with us for so many years, making sure we didn't fall apart? Who do you think has wanted to step into the role of your mother since she saw you lose one?"

"She's always been part of this family, hasn't she?" Carter said.

Steve smiled, the look so full of affection and happiness Carter felt it wrapping her up in it.

"She has and now we get to make it permanent."

"I guess it's about time then."

Steve laughed and Carter grinned, knowing that if Maggie had this effect on her father then everything would be fine. Rising, her father leaned over and kissed the top of her head.

"Hurry and get dressed, we don't want to be late."

Carter slid off her bed. "I must like her cause I'm wearing a dress for her."

At the door, her father looked back, a teasing gleam in his blue eyes.

"Is it for her? Or is it that Marine you are determined to keep dating?"

Carter's embarrassed scowl was all the confession she was going to give. It was all Steve needed.

"That's what I thought," he said, closing the door.

Shaking her head as she tried to hide her smile, she turned back to the dress. She changed and took a moment before the mirror to criticize the length, tightness and overall appearance. When convinced she was mad for agreeing to the dress, she put on her shoes and headed out. Her father looked up from his phone when she entered the living room and beamed.

"You ready?" he asked, holding out his arm.

Nodding, Carter took it, hating that a part of her was still very aware that this was an end to her current way of life. It wouldn't be just the two of them again.

The drive to the courthouse was a quiet affair as Carter let all the moments they had shared like this fill the space. Waiting inside was Maggie, in a white dress that brushed her knees and her hair artfully piled on top of her head. The smile she wore though was truly the most beautiful thing about her. When she spotted them, instead of going to her future husband, she wrapped Carter up in her arms. She smelled like vanilla. Breaking away, she held Carter at arm's length, grinning.

"You are beautiful," she said. "I wasn't sure if you would wear the dress, but I'm glad you did."

Carter shrugged like it wasn't a big deal. "It is your day after all."

Tears building in Maggie's eyes, she shook her head, giving Carter's shoulders an affectionate squeeze.

"No, it's not, Hun. It's our day. Cause today I get to become part of your family."

Carter hugged Maggie, a rush of emotions overwhelming her.

"You've always been part of our family," she said.

Maggie held Carter like she was proud to simply know her.

"Now let's make it official," Carter said.

Smiling, Maggie nodded and took Steve's hand. After a few directions, they found themselves in a small room with a gray-haired man. As the man walked them through a short ceremony, Carter felt a tangle of happiness and something else she couldn't explain winding through her. When Steve leaned in and kissed Maggie, Carter clapped and cheered, making up for the lack of a crowd.

Smiling, the trio left the courthouse and drove a short distance to a hotel. When they entered the ballroom shouts of celebration and congratulations washed over them. Friends and distant family members all rushed to offer their form of well wishes. In the mass of people, Carter was separated from the pair. Taking the division as an excuse, she found an alcove to tuck herself into. Though her heart was bursting with joy, it still held a tug of sadness.

"It's okay," a familiar voice said.

Carter spun around and found Donovan looking at her. He was dressed in slacks and a button down. Each time she saw him, she wondered if somehow he had managed to get more attractive. He took a step forward but made no move to reach for her, letting her have space.

"What's okay?" she asked, though she had a feeling she knew.

"Being sad," he said.

She let out a strangled laugh. "But how can I be sad when I'm so happy for Captain?"

It was then he reached out and brushed a hand over her cheek.

"Because you're a complex person completely capable of feeling two emotions at once."

At the acceptance of her hidden grief, she swallowed trying to force back the bubble of tears in her throat.

"It's going to change," she said.

For a moment, she thought he would repeat what Captain had said, that it was really just the same as it had been before, they were simply getting Maggie.

"Yes, it is," he said.

Carter let out a teary laugh.

"But that doesn't mean it's going to be a bad thing," Donovan continued. "But yes, it will be different. It won't be just him and you anymore. It might be bumpy at first, but you will adjust. At times it might even be hard to accept Maggie being a bigger part of your life but that's natural. All changes take time."

Carter stared at him, trying to understand as this wonderful person had chosen to be part of her life despite the mess she was.

"How do you know all of this?" she asked, his words soothing her emotions.

Donovan leaned in like he was going to share a secret, his grin mischievous.

"I talked to my mom and asked her what to expect from a situation like this."

Laughing, Carter wrapped her arms around his neck and kissed him. In that moment she glimpsed a piece of how much he truly cared for her.

The crowd around Steve and Maggie had broken apart. Music flooded the ballroom and guests diverged to tables and chairs. Holding Maggie's hand, Steve led her out to the center of the dance floor and pulled her into his arms. The two swayed back and forth to the song, whispering to each other like young lovers. Carter held

Donovan's hand, watching them, letting herself feel it all, happiness, sadness...hope.

When the song shifted, other couples joined the pair, entering the happiness of the day. Donovan looked to Carter, a soft smile on his face.

"Since your father is otherwise occupied and less likely to kill me in front of a crowd of witnesses, do you want to dance?"

"You know neither of us knows how to dance, right?"

Donovan tugged her forward. "Then we will stand on the sidelines and I will have an excuse to simply hold you."

A flutter of warmth filled Carter's chest. Claiming a corner of the dance floor, Donovan slid his arm around Carter's waist and took her hand. She rested her other hand on his shoulder. Donovan rested his cheek on the side of her hair and she leaned into him.

At that moment Carter couldn't imagine a world where Donovan wasn't in her life. Looking back, her world had been duller without him. Just like her world would be dimmer without Maggie. And so Donovan was right, it wasn't going to be the same, it was going to be so much better.

Maddy Finds Out

Carter stepped off the elevator and found Donovan waiting in the hallway. He leaned on the opposite wall, his arms crossed, focus on the ground. There was a slope to his shoulders that told Carter so much.

"Hey," she said.

At her voice, Donovan roused himself and lifted his head.

"Worried?" she asked.

He let out a slow breath. "It's a big step and even though they've been serious for a while there's no determining how this will affect her or them."

Carter nodded, sliding her hands into her pockets. The discussion on this topic had spanned over weeks, every angled examined, every outcome analyzed but in the end, there was no way to know for certain how it would all play out.

"How is he doing?" she asked.

Donovan pushed himself off the wall and headed towards Link's apartment.

"You can ask him yourself."

Inside the mid-morning light cascaded through the windows in golden strands. The warm autumn tones softened the apartment and haloed Link as he rested against the back of an armchair, facing the windows. Everything about his posture spoke of calm, but Carter didn't buy it, from this point on everything would change.

When Carter settled onto the couch's armrest, one foot on the cushions, Link looked at her. His hazel eyes were where the heart of his emotions lay. It was like seeing a storm forming on the horizon. As he breathed out, he ran a hand through his hair.

"Do you think I'm making the right decision?" he asked.

Donovan took the seat beside Carter, his shoulder brushing her hip as he leaned forward.

"Do you love her?" Carter asked.

Link contemplated his hands. "I've loved her since our sixth date and three years later I only love her more." He raised his head. "I still wonder if it's a teenage infatuation." He chuckled softly. "But we're not teenagers anymore."

"Then I think you're making the right decision," Carter said.

Link didn't respond to this, his brows furrowed, a hint of sadness in his eyes as he stared out on the world.

"And if I lose her because of this?" he asked.

No answer would make the question any easier to handle, so both Carter and Donovan remained silent. Link nodded as if they had spoken and he was agreeing. For a long while, the trio held onto the quiet, feeling the weight of change that hung just around the corner. Right then they were who they always had been, their friendship tightly knit. But the next step in their story was one that could shift the whole dynamic.

A knock on the door broke the moment. Looking at Carter and Donovan, Link rose. Taking in a deep breath, he crossed to the door and pulled it open. Maddy beamed at him from the other side. Stepping forward, she kissed him.

"Hey, babe," she said.

Link tried for a smile but it didn't come. Noticing, Maddy's own smile sobered.

"What's up? Are you okay?"

Link waved her into the apartment. Frowning slightly, Maddy walked in, spotting Carter and Donovan for the first time.

"What's going on?" she asked, spinning back to Link.

"Sit down, I have something to tell you."

Maddy did as he suggested, tucking one black strand behind her ear.

"You're not about to tell me you're dying, right?" she asked, letting out a nervous laugh.

Link sat on the coffee table in front of her, shaking his head.

"No, I'm not dying."

"Good."

Link managed a fleeting smile at this response.

"Look," he said, setting aside his glasses and gathering his courage. "What I'm about to tell you will be overwhelming but I hope you can understand where I'm coming from."

Before Link could continue, Maddy leaned forward and cupped his cheek.

"Hey. I'm not going anywhere. You don't have to worry."

Link's shoulders dropped and he sighed.

"If you do, I wouldn't blame you," he said.

"How about you just give me a chance before jumping to the worst."

He nodded once. "I can do that."

Maddy leaned back in the chair, her gaze loving and open. Right then Carter could see how deep the girl's affection ran for

Link. She hoped it was strong enough to weather a lie that he had told her for years.

"I've never talked about my father," Link said. "And the reason is that it's a sensitive subject." He swallowed. "Besides being illegitimate...my father is former President Douglas."

The words hung in the air and the trio held their breath waiting for the explosion of questions and emotions.

"I know," Maddy said.

With those two words, all the air was sucked from the room. Link frowned and Carter and Donovan exchanged looks.

"Wait? You know?" Link rubbed his face, confusion muddling his brain. "How do you know? When did you find out? How did you find out?"

Maddy rested her head on her fist, completely at ease with the whole situation.

"It was about a year and a half ago," she said. "I was doing a project for poli-sci class. I spent about two hours watching speeches given by President Douglas. It was during the second hour that I realized he has this habit of talking out of only one side of his mouth like one corner is frozen." Maddy's eyes softened. "It's what you do." Reaching forward, she brushed a fingertip over the edge of his mouth as if it were her favorite spot to kiss. "From there I began to notice the connection between the two of you. You look a lot like him, you know."

Still stunned, Link could only bob his head in agreement.

"It was then I put two and two together. How you've never mentioned your father. If it was a bad divorce you would say so or if he were dead you would say that, but you never said either of those things. Figuring you might not know who he was I didn't push the subject. But once I knew all of that fell into place, I could see why you never spoke about him."

Carter smiled and looked at Donovan. He had his gaze trained on Maddy as if seeing her in a whole new light. Carter knew exactly how he felt. Though Carter had always liked Maddy, she now found herself respecting her.

Maddy pointed to Donovan. "Also explained your relationship. Bodyguard, right?"

Holding in a smile, Donovan dipped his head. Maddy focused on Carter, eyes narrowed.

"Second bodyguard or girlfriend to bodyguard?" she asked.

Carter shrugged. "A little of both."

When Maddy laughed, the sound tugged Link from his shock.

"Wait, you weren't mad that I hadn't told you?" Link asked.

Maddy shook her head but it held a past mix of emotions. "Oh, I was so pissed that you had kept something like this from me after dating for so long. I didn't talk to you for a week."

Link scrunched up his a face. "Yeah, I remember that I was really confused." He cocked his head. "What changed?"

"After I got past the initial anger I realized what it meant if your father acknowledged Mason as his son but not you. I realized that this wasn't a secret you share with a high school girlfriend or even a college girlfriend. It's a secret you share once you know that you can truly trust that person." The edge of her lips curled and she lifted one shoulder. "I figured I would keep your secret hoping one day I could be that person."

Link leaned forward and kissed her. When he pulled back, his eyes were intense and locked on her as if she were the only person alive. "Marry me."

She laughed. "Of course."

Grinning, Link kissed her again, pulling her into his arms. Knowing a cue to leave when they saw it, both Carter and Donovan slipped out of the apartment.

"Well," Carter said.

Donovan laughed. "Yeah."

They leaned against the wall, smiling at each other, soaking in the outcome neither of them could have foreseen.

Jealousy

"Your essays should be in my inbox by the end of Friday or I will not accept it," Professor White announced to the classroom. "That's all for today, you're dismissed."

The click of computers' closing and the shuffling of feet filled the auditorium. Carter rose and slid on her coat and stored away her laptop. As she made her way outside, a curly-haired guy with a splash of freckles across his nose approached her.

"Hey, Carter," Adam said. "I thought the points you brought up about the impactful years of one's life affecting their view of the world interesting. I was wondering if you wanted to get coffee and discuss it more?"

Carter surveyed the surrounding mass of people but didn't spot Donovan among the scarf and coated crowd.

"Sure," she said.

Adam smiled, the gesture accenting his natural good looks. The pair crossed the courtyard towards the small cafe. It was chilly, winter's breath icing the air. Though there was no snow yet, the ground was frozen and the grass crunched beneath boots. Adam hurried forward and pulled the door open, allowing Carter to slip into the warm, coffee-scented embrace of the cafe.

As the door swung shut behind the pair, across the quad, Donovan rounded the building. He scanned the collection of bundled figures, but couldn't spot Carter's face. When he ducked his head into the auditorium, he found it mostly empty, a single student left, lost in a discussion with the professor.

Biting down frustration, Donovan turned away, gazing out of the college grounds. His phone dinged, snatching his attention. He pulled it out. It was a single message: *Still alive.*

Donovan gripped his phone as he stared at Link's update. Though nothing in his face gave him away, inside he was starting to fracture. Years of being only one thing were coming to an end and he was struggling to know exactly what it would mean for him when the burden was lifted.

Eight years of his life had been dedicated to watching over someone else's. Before that, he had been a sixteen-year-old boy who hadn't known who he wanted to be. Part of Donovan feared that he would somehow revert to the unknowing state when the time came.

Pocketing his phone, Donovan went back to his search. There was one person who seemed to understand without being told and right then he needed that, cause he wasn't sure he understood himself. Before he could call Carter, a girl with a knitted cap pulled down over her pixie haircut, approached him.

"Hey, Donovan," she said. "I wanted to let you know that the study group is meeting at my place this Friday."

Donovan nodded, storing away the info.

"Courtney," Donovan said, stopping the girl from disappearing. "Have you seen, Carter?"

She pointed to the cafe across the way. "I saw her walk in with Adam."

Irritation stirred in Donovan's chest, but he managed to keep it from showing.

"Thanks."

He crossed the lawn and paused outside the door, peering in. In a back corner at a small table sat Adam and Carter. Adam's smile was on full display as he leaned on the table towards her.

Something snapped inside Donovan, all the emotions he had been fighting against converged into that one moment. Tearing open the door, he stormed inside. He gripped the front of Adam's shirt and slammed him against the wall.

"Stay away from my girlfriend, or I'll beat the hell out of you."

Power coursed though Donovan, fueling every cell. Adam cowered, his body shaking with terror as he nodded. The cafe was frozen with shock. Carter didn't move, rooted to her chair with surprise.

"I don't ever want to see you talking to her or even looking at her." Donovan shook Adam. "Do you understand me?"

Adam was paper-white and looked ready to piss himself in fear.

"I-I got it."

"Good, now get out of here."

Donovan threw him to the ground. Staring back with frightened eyes, Adam scrambled to the exit.

Donovan blinked and rubbed his eyes, dismissing the violent thoughts from his mind. He opened the door and strode into the cafe. It was almost stifling compared to the coldness outside.

As he drew towards the back table, he noticed more than he had from beyond the door. Though Adam was all smiles and eager energy, Carter sat back in her seat, arms crossed, creating a barrier between her and this flirty guy. Even though she wore a smile it was subdued, guarded. As he stopped before them, the pair glanced up.

"Donovan, hey," Adam said, his smile not containing the same brightness as it had a second ago.

Still feeling a chaos of frustration, Donovan gripped Adam's shirt and lifted him off his seat.

"Adam, I understand that you are attracted to my girlfriend," Donovan said, his voice almost soothing in its calmness. "I don't blame you, she's beautiful and smart. Right now though I want to talk to her alone and instead of throwing you through a window I'm simply going to ask you to leave. Is that alright with you?"

Adam blinked as if expecting a completely different speech.

"Uh...yeah. I can leave."

Donovan smiled. "Thanks, man. Also, study group changed and it will be at Courtney's house this Friday, in case you didn't know."

"Got it. Thanks."

Donovan let go and Adam dazedly brushed down the front of his shirt. He grabbed his coat from the back of his chair, still looking completely baffled.

"I'll see you both around," he said.

Carter nodded, trying to hide the fullness of her amusement. As he left, Donovan sank into his seat and rested his head in his hands. When Carter said nothing, Donovan twisted his neck to gaze at her.

"What?" he asked.

She leaned back in her chair. "Oh, I was simply waiting for you to tear your shirt, pound your chest, throw me over your shoulder and declare to the world that, 'you caveman, you strong, I yours, no man touch me'."

The edge of Donovan's lips curled at the exaggerated caveman voice.

"Compared to what I imagined doing to him, I say that was pretty tame," he said. He stole her drink and sipped it.

"You going to tell me what is going on?" she asked.

Donovan dragged a hand through his hair, staring at the table. The chaos he faced felt like trying to assemble a gun with parts missing and some pieces coming from a completely different weapon. He let out a slow breath. Carter shifted her chair over to his and rested a hand on the back of his neck. It was such a rare form of public affection from her that he closed his eyes, letting himself accept the gift.

"It's because in a month everything changes, isn't it?"

Donovan smiled and leaned back in the chair, staring at her. Her eyes were open, familiar and comforting. There was no judgment in them.

"I fear I won't know who I am."

She nodded, a hint of teasing sparking in her eyes. "So you decided to try on possessive boyfriend?"

"No, that was me frustrated that someone was stealing your time."

"Ah. Well, we can never have that, can we? I must always be yours."

Her mocking tone helped Donovan know she knew what he meant and that she knew her time was always her own.

"I'm sorry," he said. He crossed his arms. "It's been eight years and without a constant weight of protecting him...the world seems unknown."

Carter nodded. "I understand."

Though it was a simple thing, Donovan found himself comforted. She didn't try to reassure or fix anything, only confirmed that she would be there as he tried to make sense of his life. His phone dinged. Without looking, he knew what it was. Carter did too and stood, holding out her hand to him.

"Come on, you still have a month left and I will walk with you."

He took her hand, lacing his fingers through hers, never failing to enjoy the strength and warmth of it.

"On our way there you can growl at anyone who looks my way."

He laughed, a piece of his burden lightening. They threw away their trash and stepped out into the icy air. Whether for the warmth or comfort, they moved closer together.

"Donovan, until you find your new position remember that you still have one. You're my boyfriend."

He kissed her. "Now which one of us is being possessive?"

Three Little Words

Night had descended on the city, coating the sky in a thick velvet with a sprinkling of stars. The common room of Carter's dorm was silent. It was the silence that most weekends took on. It was the silence that came from an absence of occupants, most of them taking the freedom to share drinks and release the pressure of college workloads.

Carter was alone in the building, staring at a computer screen, books and notes were strewn about her. After her father got married, she decided to take a room on campus, wanting to give him space for his first year of marriage. The screen before her blurred and she rubbed her eyes. Exhaustion hung on her, making every action twice as hard and every thought slower. Though it was fairly early the idea of sleep came to her. Even as it did though, she refused it. For the past eight days sleep meant nightmares and images she could never banish.

She checked her phone but there was nothing to see as it had been for far too long. Though Donovan was just at Quantico training, she hadn't heard from him in eight days. Worry and fear crept along the ground, coming for her. Swallowing, she stood up, shoving back her chair. She needed desperately not to think, thinking of late had led her down avenues that she couldn't escape from.

Grabbing a pair of boxing gloves, she pulled them on. In the far corner, near a row of windows was a mannequin dummy. The addition of it had gotten a few curious and confused looks, but after seeing Carter attack it, her fellow dorm room peers had stayed quiet. Though she felt like she might fall to the floor, Carter slammed her fist into the rubber dummy, sending it quivering.

Eight days.

She forced the thought from her head. Spinning, she brought her leg up and kicked the mannequin's side, the thump breaking a piece of the silence. She spun back and landed three quick punches, hitting the face, ribs, and stomach.

Not a word.

Heart clenching, she threw herself into the next attack. She pounded away as if she could beat her emotions into submission. The storm in her thoughts threatened to consume her, fear battling worry. With each new bubble of speculation, her movements became more frantic, her arms flashing in rapid fire. The faceless dummy took each blow with an uncaring detachment that Carter wished she could punch away.

Eight days and not a single word.

She felt as if she were about to break into a million pieces. Her knuckles were raw but she didn't care. Blow after blow hit the mannequin, the force of it jarring her body. She clenched her teeth fighting the rise of emotions that was beginning to choke her.

The flicker of movement outside the window, on the path to the dorms, stopped her. Breathing hard, she walked over. What she saw made her heart pound faster. The relief of seeing Donovan strolling towards the building nearly did her in.

What stopped her from collapsing was the sight of a leggy girl right beside him, smiling up at him. For a breath, Carter let herself believe that it was the unwanted attention of some college student until Donovan smiled back.

All the emotions at seeing him, twisted and morphed into a knife that sliced through her. Anger and jealousy collided, clouding her mind. Clenching her fists, she backed away and returned to the mannequin. She attacked it with renewed vigor, though her body cried for sleep. She pummeled the unchanging face over and over again.

On the desk, her phone buzzed. Though she knew it was Donovan, she didn't answer it. Despite herself, she hated when the call ended and another didn't follow. Her mind was a tangled mess of exhaustion and hurt.

Even when the door to the building opened and Carter heard footsteps climbing the stairs, she didn't look around. She knew it was Donovan. She knew his tread like she knew the sound of his voice. The footsteps stopped, but she didn't, continuing to beat the dummy.

"Carter," Donovan said.

She said nothing, spinning around and kicking the mannequin's head.

"Carter," he repeated louder.

She still didn't look at him, pride keeping her from turning to him, letting him see for a second the pain that was drowning her.

"Who is she?" she asked, between blows.

"Are you serious?" Donovan asked, the disbelief clear in his voice.

Carter still didn't look at him.

"Carter, look at me," he said.

She didn't.

"Carter, you can't be serious about this," Donovan said, his patience fraying. "I haven't seen you in two months and couldn't talk to you for eight days and this is how you act? I've missed you. I thought you would have felt the same way."

Finally, Carter spun on him. Her emotions were a storm that was raging inside her. The fact that he didn't believe that she hadn't missed him every day, every hour, every minute, every second made her want to hit him.

Her sleep had been shot to hell because nightmares of him in danger had jolted her awake every couple hours. It was at the point she feared what terrors would come when she closed her eyes. But the first glimpse she catches of him is when he's smiling at someone else.

"Who is she?" she asked, glaring at him.

"You're being ridiculous, you know that! Do you seriously not trust me?"

Carter felt herself fracturing, her thoughts spinning and unable to land. Shaking his head in frustration, Donovan started rolling up the sleeve of his shirt.

"This is completely stupid." He moved to the next sleeve. When he was finished, he rolled his shoulders and raised his fists. Carter stared at him, emotions gripping her. "You want a fight, fine let's fight."

His eyes were determined and he looked ready to take a beating, but Carter didn't move. The turmoil inside her wouldn't end and she knew the source of it lay in the man in front of her. So before she could be submitted to more pain, she pulled away.

"No," she said, her voice deadly calm. "We're done, Donovan."

Shock hit him like she had landed the first blow. Without looking at him, she tore off her gloves, threw them to the couch, and headed for her room. She slammed the door behind her, but it was barely closed when Donovan opened it again, flicking it shut behind him. Anger spiking, Carter rounded on him all her emotions crashing to the surface.

"What do you want?" she snapped.

"I want you to talk to me," Donovan said, crossing his arms.

"I don't want to talk to you," she said, waving her arms around. Everything inside felt like it was breaking and she was breaking alongside it. "I don't want to hear anything you have to say." She shook her head, her heart betraying her as it beat for him and hurt because of him. "We never should have started this!"

Donovan's own emotions rose to the surface. Frustration radiated off of him as he balled his fists.

"Is that honestly what you believe?"

The broken sleep, nightmares and hours of fear and worry converged on Carter, sucking her under.

"Yes."

The lie singed her tongue but she didn't take it back. She couldn't, not when the reality of them hurt so much it might kill her.

Donovan ran a hand down his face, losing all his passion. His eyes held hers, everything he was feeling on full display. She crossed her arms, guarding herself against him.

"When will you stop pushing me away?" he asked, softly.

Carter's pain still burned white hot in her chest.

"When I'm convinced you won't leave on your own!"

Donovan hit the wall with his fist, his patience shattering.

"Damn it, Carter, I love you. When will you get that?!"

Any response she had was stolen away. Her heart beat frantically in her chest as if it was trying to break free and run to him. Part of her still wanted to pull it back, to hide it behind a wall where it could never be broken again, where she could never feel pain again.

But the full truth of his words was hidden in his eyes, his heart laid bare for her, knowing she would see it. The vulnerability there cracked the hard shell she had constructed around her heart.

"Carter, I don't know what else I can say to convince-"

Like a wave, she was hit with a new fear, a fear that she might lose him because of what she was doing.

Terrified, she closed the distance between them and kissed him.

Every thought, feeling, and emotion she had for him was poured into the kiss. Feeling it, Donovan wrapped his arms around her, pulling her against him. They lost themselves in each other, raw with emotions that were too hard to voice.

When they broke apart, Carter rested her forehead against his.

"I hate you," she whispered. "I didn't have a heart before you and now I hate the fact that I have one. And that you hold it."

Donovan let out a deep sigh.

"Can we please stop fighting now?" he asked.

She dug her fingers into his hair.

"As long as you promise to always fight with me."

Donovan responded by kissing her again, his arms gripping her waist like he was afraid she would slip away. Carter reacted, holding onto his with the same fear, needing to know he was still there.

As she kissed him, she felt the full weight of her relief consuming her. He was alive. He was there. He was still hers. Tears of exhaustion and relief rolled down her cheeks. Donovan broke away, worry clouding his eyes.

"Hey, hey, hey," he said, holding her face, his thumbs brushing away the tears. "What's wrong?"

Trembling, Carter rested her head against his chest.

"You were gone. I hadn't heard from you and... It was like with Captain all over again."

Donovan cradled her to his chest, kissing the side of her head.

"I'm sorry, Carter. I'm so sorry. We were tossed into a situation where we were given nothing but a water canteen. I'm sorry. We just got back today. I should have called. I figured I'd come to see you instead. That girl you saw has a boyfriend who goes here and was giving me a ride, she wanted to meet you cause I told her so much about you. Carter, I'm so sorry."

Donovan kept talking and all the while Carter let him hold her, his voice reassuring her again that he was there, that he wasn't leaving her. He held her from him, and for the first time, he really studied her, taking in the dark circles under her eyes and the weariness in her body.

"When did you last get a good night's sleep?" he asked.

Her shoulder's sagged. "I don't remember."

"When did you sleep for longer than three hours?"

She shook her head, the action taking more work than she ever expected.

"I don't know."

"Okay."

Donovan scooped her up in his arms and laid down on her bed. Instantly, Carter curled into him, resting her head on his chest. Her whole body seemed to sink into his, her exhaustion taking over. Donovan tucked a strand of hair behind her ear and planted a light kiss on her head.

"You can sleep now," he said. "I'm right here."

With every rise and fall of his chest, Carter felt herself relaxing. As her thoughts began to slip away, she realized there was one last thing she needed to say.

So with her last bit of strength, she whispered, "I...love...you."

Donovan's reply seemed to come from a great distance.

"I love you more than life, Carter."

She fell asleep in his arms, listening to the sound of his heart as it beat in time with hers.

The story continues in

Case Reopened (Book 2)

followed by

Case Closed (Book 3)

Joy came late to the reading game, due to vision problems. She holds a strong love for Young Adult since it's where her love of reading began.

Now she writes Young Adult hoping to inspire the next generation. When she isn't creating in her little writing studio outside of Boston, Joy can be found buried in a book or discussing literature and drinking tea with her family of artists.

Instagram@joymoment

Twitter@_joymoment_

Support the author, leave a review on Amazon and Goodreads

Made in the USA
Las Vegas, NV
06 December 2023

82216308R00215